The Urbana Free Library

To renew materials call
217-367-4057

PLUMAGE
FROM PEGASUS

PLUMAGE
FROM PEGASUS

PAUL DI FILIPPO

COSMOS BOOKS

12 - 06

33 ⸗

To the woman who always laughs at my jokes, Deborah Newton.

.

TABLE

OF CONTENTS

FOREWORD

Seen in just the right light, at just the right angle, I am first and foremost a satirist, a comic, a humorist, a parodist. The Class Clown of science fiction.

My very first writings—aside from three laboriously typed pages of a *Man from U.N.C.L.E.* pastiche composed circa 1966—were comic inventions for my highschool newspaper. Parodies of SAT tests and official bulletins alternated with mock-anthropological dissections of the curious customs of my peers, from most of whom, of course, I felt vastly estranged. (In what I thought was a brilliant brainstorm, I reversed the name of the town where I lived, Lincoln, to form the name of an imaginary land, Nlocnil, from whence these reports theoretically originated.) When, shortly after graduation, I discovered fandom, I began contributing silly stuff under the heading of "Arrant Nonsense" to Don D'Ammassa's fanzine, *Mythologies*. When I began my own fanzine, *Astral Avenue* (later a department in the semiprozine *New Pathways*), I had a new venue for my cruel distortions, pointed exaggerations and sardonic observations.

None of these earliest efforts will be found, however, in this volume. (The earliest are, in fact, utterly lost, my collection of clippings chucked out circa 1979 in a purge meant to signal to myself some kind of new beginning. So much for my ambitions to be the next William Faulkner.) But the earliest entry here, my pastiche of the fiction of Barry Malzberg, marks my first professional sale and as such seems to deserve republication for the first time in twenty-five years. Not to mention that it's still pretty funny, I think.

My earliest influences were old-time humorists such as Twain, Benchley, Leacock and Thurber, as well as *Mad* magazine. The biting work of Paul Krassner, the Firesign Theater and the writers at *The National Lampoon* (during that magazine's early, funny years) soon lent contemporary flavoring to my japes. But it was only about a decade ago, when I discovered and devoured the rococo and majestically hilarious work of S. J. Perelman, that I really felt equipped to do what I wanted to do in this vein. Most recently, I've enjoyed Mark Leyner's stuff too, and I think this influence shows as well.

I suppose I'll keep writing and selling these pieces—most of which find their targets in the literary world—so long as people keep doing foolish things.

Now, *that's* job security!

INTRODUCTION
BY BARRY N. MALZBERG

ARLECCHINO

Here, a collection of Paul di Filippo's satires on the hardly resistible subject of science fiction. "Satire," George S. Kaufman is reputed to have said in the 1930s, "Is what closes on Saturday night." (This from the co-author of *Can't Take It With You* and *The Man Who Came To Dinner*. All of which closed on Saturday night but only after many Saturday nights. Consistency is for the proles, as O'Brien said. But then again *Merrily We Roll Along* didn't do so terrific.) But these little essays, most of them written under the title *Plumage From Pegasus* for *The Magazine of Fantasy & Science Fiction*, seem to have opened again. So Mr. Kaufman's generalization, questioned by his own biography, comes into question again.

My theory: we are all realists and we are all satirists. Satire, as Brecht wrote, comes only after one has eaten. "First fill the belly, then the principles" is the way Brecht put it in *Mother Courage*. But once that belly is filled, once one can rise from the issue of sheer sustenance and self-preservation to a somewhat wider perspective, then comes that more distanced view, that comic tilt,

11

that sheer rampant desire to overturn which becomes codified into the satirical. First E. Hyatt Verrill and Doc Smith, then Henry Kuttner and A.E. Van Vogt, then Phil Dick and, inevitably, Di Filippo, who is having none of it. Or, putting it another way, is having all of it but only after it has been parsed by a savage and severe intelligence. Of course satire—like parody—is founded upon love, is triggered by the need to celebrate, if only in reverse, and it is love which informs these essays. Do not think otherwise. I will not let you.

Di Filippo, who has been around a long time, reminds me of how long it has been when he notes that the earliest piece here—and his first published work, appearing in that noble, doomed, silly enterprise *Unearth Magazine*—was a merciless parody of your oversigned in his crazed-astronauts, sexually-darkened-rocketships mode. He sent it to me in manuscript before publication, begging my pardon, asking if it was acceptable to me. I wrote him that even if my First Amendment absolutism made his question moot, I would have no quarrel with the work: it manages like successful parody to demonstrate a complete understanding of the author, right through to the last tic and narrative compulsion. Reveals (in the target) the self to the self. I was never quite the same, at least in relation to Falling Astronauts, after I read this one.

Fortunately—or perhaps unfortunately—a good majority of the targets here are hors concours, which may have saved them more than a soupcon of embarrassment. Also fortunately, many of the targets here are not parodied but satirized; the modes are oft allied—like Fantasy & Science Fiction, say—but they are distinct: the satire seeks its effects through mockery or reductio ad absurdum, the parody its effects through the imitative exacerbation of weakness. The author handles both modes with casual, even contemptuous virtuosity.

In so doing Di Filippo may be the great poet of decadence which the modern genre of the imaginative has needed (if not sought) for so many decades. Decadence is that state of the art or politics in which form has superseded function, and no one has a more penetrating insight than this writer into the consequent embarrassing cleavage between form and function. These essays are not only amusing; they manage—through the engine of their terrible wit—to be instructive.

Nice rounding effect: Di Filippo enters print parodying the introductionist; the introductionist in his waning, ever more wistful autumnal period comes to praise not bury. Life, that recalcitrant animal, is Arlecchino himself.

Barry N. Malzberg
New Jersey: April 2004

FALLING EXPECTATIONS

A Malzbergean Tragedy

I

Heller summons up his departing energies, marshals the pitiful forces at his command, and rises above his wife like a small nocturnal apparition, coming to rest on his forearms where he pauses a moment, unsure of his exact intentions towards this vacant-eyed woman. What sort of connection is he trying to make here, he wonders with a weak cupidity, what old pains and still-festering wounds is he trying to reopen? He waits for an answer, but none comes. Fuck it, he decides, entering her mechanically, harshly, pumping away like the automaton he has become, like the machines we all are. The surface of his mind is blank, the primal level is barely stirred.

Curiously tonight the responses he has come to expect from his wife are totally absent; usually, stereotyped as they are, meek as they might be, her small whinings and archings serve to remind him of his purpose, inform him, in mid-course, of his goal, supply him with some outside referents. Tonight, this is not the case. It is almost, he fantasizes, as if she were not under him, as if she had vanished into the vacuum of his past.

Suddenly, dusty traps open within him and memory seeps in like bilge water. His wife is *not* below him, plastically receptive, he has, in point of fact never been married, never (if gratuitous truth be told) even made it with a woman. All this time he has been banging his mild erection against the starchy white sheets, lost in some institutional delusion, suffering from a vocational psychosis. Disgusted, he rolls over, to sink into a fitful sleep.

NASA does strange things to a man.

II

Dull morning finds Heller in the office of Captain Caligula, his immediate superior at NASA, source of his anxieties and fits, by whom he has been called, to whom he has no choice but to go. Heller hates and fears the Captain, while the Captain finds Heller hard to understand, a situation both of them are uncomfortable with. Often, in the stainless corridors of the administrative building, the Captain will meet Heller and stupidly extend his tongue, simultaneously emitting a loud *whuffling* sound, then hurry away like a retreating roach. Later, Heller will contrive to tie together the Captain's shoelaces, all the while lusting for a grosser revenge totally beyond his grasp. Today, such a venomous interchange seems to be building.

The Captain walks wildly around the seated figure of Heller, maniacal eyes popping, labored lungs racing, working himself into the frenzy he finds so necessary to deal with Heller. Occasionally he will stop in his random course and fire off imaginary rounds from his cocked fingers; at other times he will apparently attempt to throttle someone. Heller suspects he is agitated.

Finally, after some minutes of this behavior, he sees fit to address Heller. "I dislike to use you, you know," the Captain says, ropes of saliva webbing his lower lip as he obviously strives for understatement and control. "As an astronaut, you are incomparably bad—we have no other like you—and as a writer, I believe, you stink—yes, I'm sure of it, you stink as a writer." The Captain plainly sees this as a fine statement, almost a revelation, in fact, and an aberrant smile twitches his lips for a moment before he continues. "And besides, I dislike you personally. But we have lost five men on Mars, we have grown slightly piqued at this, our interest, you might say, has been aroused, and you are our only uncommitted man at present. Yes, I think I might put it that way—our only uncommitted *man* at present," (this, reader, being a snide cut at Heller's rather pathetic sexual life, a life whose pale shadows we have just witnessed). "We are sending you there alone, to find out what happened, irrespective of your total lack of talent, overlooking, I might add, your whole grim and blunder-filled record. I only hope you succeed, because if you don't, you may as well not return." He motions to Heller to rise; "Any questions?" The Captain neither expects nor wants there to be any questions as Heller well knows, so he replies with a negative shake of his head. "Fine, fine. Say,"—the Captain extends his hand—"no hard feelings?"

III

Heller suiting up for Mars: the man is outlined against the white walls of the room like an insect on cotton, oblivious to the ministrations of the acolytes attending on him, intent only on a distasteful repast served up by a mind all too apt to annoy him with such courses at the most inopportune times: Heller is resavoring his last time in space.

Heller looks out the capsule window at the leprous moon and knows that he does not belong in space, knows, more to the point, that Man does not belong in space, mainly because of the national deficit and because he is vulnerable to explosive decompression. Heller would have been quite happy (or, at least, less distraught) to remain behind on Earth, where he was a science fiction hack of long standing (or sitting) until he was recruited by NASA in an insane attempt to bolster the flagging public interest in their then-current Moon missions. Heller's job, minimal as it is, consists of tending the orbiting half of the space vehicle while his two companions disport themselves on the lunar surface, and sending back stirring and concise reports on the developing mission which will be released to the press and which, hopefully, will reflect his stature as a professional purveyor of wonder. Heller has his doubts about how well he will be able to achieve this.

The Men In Charge have, Heller now belatedly realizes, unfortunately but quite expectedly neglected to supply him with any of the tools of his trade, not paper, pen, typewriter or even cassette recorder, and Heller, proficient hack though he is, finds it impossible to compose anything of worth off the top of his helmeted head without even seeing or hearing the words take shape for that small amount of time needful to correct the most blatant grammatical and syntactical errors. Even Heller, after all, has his limits, even Heller has never tried simultaneously composing and delivering a story over the phone which is the equivalent of what these nameless technicians below would have him do, a task he doubts even the notorious C. C. Capaladi capable of (take that! you rotten pulp merchant!). No, Heller realizes that he must exercise all his small talents to the utmost on this assignment, must plunge on regardless of accidental or contrived difficulties, if he wishes to improve his lot in the future, if he ever wishes to advance from the lowly position he now occupies, and it is at this juncture that he notices the computer teletype that juts from the wall of the capsule like a paunchy abdomen. Here, gentlemen, we pass a pivotal point in Heller's languishing career and the plot advances (in increments, it must be admitted, smaller than the monetary rewards garnered by superfluous wordage) another notch as Heller floats to the keyboard and with the easy fluency and slick effortlessness, fluent easiness and effortless slickness of the accomplished penny-a-worder begins to type. Unfortunately, predictably, Heller has, however, neglected to switch the device from its on-line status and his sturdy, boring prose is fed directly into the machine where it is interpreted as an order to ignite the rockets of the Lunar Excursion Module, an act which promptly takes place, thereby incinerating Heller's two comrades who happen to be standing underneath the Module at the time, converting them to wandering ashes on the callous surface of the Moon.

Later, Heller will perceive this as a bad omen.

IV

Not, of course, that Heller's life does not already abound in bad omens, is not a life whose very seams are strained to the bursting point with more ugly nuances and direly foreshadowed events than a more perceptive audience would find credible. Life for Heller is a continual expectation of disaster, a never-ceasing search, if you will, for the tag-end of meaning that will enable him to skirt the pitfalls of existence. Examine, for the moment, Heller at large, Heller in public.

The hard back of the folding chair presses on Heller's spine like an admonishing hand as he sits in the audience of an open symposium staged by the American Science Fiction Writers, a group which can and must, however shamefacedly, claim Heller as a member, as one of its own. Heller is glancing warily around the room, anxious to avoid those he has commitments to, even more eager to dispose of those who would seek favors of him, when a small, noisy cluster of fans approaches. What is going on here? Heller asks himself, revealing a bad habit many of his fictional characters share. Exactly where in hell do these people get the idea that I am the focus of their bitterness and disgust and petty squabbles? How am I supposed to deal with this? The fans have drawn up close to Heller now, ringing him menacingly, seemingly intent on doing him actual, physical harm and the pulse in Heller's neck is threatening to unknot his tie when the largest of the fans comes to Heller with grim determination in his ungrateful eyes and begins to speak, saying, "We want—" But Heller, for once, has made up his mind not to take any abuse, verbal or otherwise, and he bursts into a crazed series of imprecations, twirling violently around in a circle to confront each of his tormentors, scattering folding chairs to all sides, screaming and gesturing with earnest frenzy, all the while trying to be fair about the whole matter. Years later, he will note his resemblance now to Captain Caligula in his less sane moments.

The fans are all staring at him with blank incomprehension as he gradually abates his spewing rage, the ongoing panel discussion is completely disrupted, the audience watching Heller guardedly, and Heller marvels at the success of his tactics, wonders if he should from the very first day of his life have adopted just such a strategy, dealt with all intruders so forcefully and with such a clear sense of purpose. The seconds of silence drag on until, finally, the original spokesman for the group, at an obvious loss for what to do, completes his sentence with a tired shrug: "—your autograph."

Heller sighs and takes out his pen.

V

Heading out to long-dead Mars, Heller passes the orbit of the moon quite early in his slow journey and its pocked face reminds him of the face of his adolescent son, whom he has neglected brutally—until he remembers that he has no son. He makes a resolve to stop reading so many absurdist plays.

VI

The landing on Mars is bad, very bad, possibly even worse than that, and Heller is somewhat shaken, indisposed to a certain extent, reduced, in fact, to crawling across the cold, abrasive surface of the planet in painful surges, hoping, as he has hoped all his life, for he knows not what. His mind begins, I say, his mind begins to wander, all the thoughts he would rather not face, all the faces he would rather not think of, begin to besiege his attention, to clamor and jostle for a space in his skull and steamy, obscuring gases fog his vision until he believes that he sees a small alien standing near him.

"Another one." This is all the alien says, evincing no reaction other than a muted boredom, a laconic indifference, a fatalistic predisposition. "Another one."

"Help," Heller asks, without stopping to question how he and the alien can be communicating, if this is indeed what they are doing, "Help me, bring me to your city, your people. Help—" This last plea made with tapering forces. Heller is reaching into an outside pocket for the glass beads NASA has supplied him with when the alien speaks again: "There are no others, just you and I, the others all died when the flatulence from our aerosol cans stripped the ozone layer from our atmosphere like a dirty rag. Nothing grew except cancers, civilization crumbled, I am the only one left." The alien spreads his hands in an endearing gesture and Heller realizes how much he likes the little fellow; how wise and beneficent he is, how truly unlike the Earthmen. Heller scrabbles his hand in the dust and the alien takes his meaning, bends down to him in benediction, as if to shrive Heller, and Heller says with his throat on fire, "Tell me, tell me, the meaning, advice—" In contemplation the alien rests a moment, sits on his heels meditatively before he replies, "Never sell your reprint rights."

Heller dies happy.

MY ALPHABET STARTS WHERE YOUR
ALPHABET ENDS

WORKS DISCUSSED IN THIS ESSAY
And to Think That I Saw It on Mulberry Street
Bartholomew and the Oobleck
The Butter Battle Book
The Cat in the Hat
The Cat in the Hat Comes Back
Dr. Seuss's Sleep Book
The 500 Hats of Bartholomew Cubbins
Fox in Socks
Green Eggs and Ham
Hop on Pop
Horton Hatches the Egg
Horton Hears a Who
How the Grinch Stole Christmas
I Can Lick 30 Tigers Today!
If I Ran the Circus
If I Ran the Zoo
King Looie Katz
The King's Stilts

The Lorax
Oh Say Can You Say?
Oh, the Thinks You Can Think
On Beyond Zebra
One Fish Two Fish Red Fish Blue Fish
Scrambled Eggs Super
There's a Wocket in My Pocket
Yertle the Turtle and Other Stories

In 1989, the year the awards in *Nebula Awards 24* were given, amid the pomp and splendor of the annual Nebula Banquet, attended by tuxedoed and begowned authors, agents, and publishers, the greatest author of SF and fantasy that the twentieth century has yet produced turned eighty-five years old—alone, without fanfare, neglected by his "peers."

Chances are, most SF fans and writers haven't even thought of this author in twenty years. Chances are, most SF fans and writers, even after examining the evidence assembled in this essay, will still try to deny him his accomplishments. Chances are, most SF fans and writers are dead wrong.

We are going to discuss now—belatedly, but perhaps in time to do him justice—a man who has covered more territory more thoroughly and brilliantly; who has influenced more people in their formative years and so throughout their adult lives; who has been truest to his vision of the world, never varying it to suit marketplace forces, than any other author one can point to.

The man's name?

Theodor Geisel.

Who?

Dr. Seuss.

In the limited space available in this volume, any examination of the Good Doctor's fifty-year career, which has resulted in an equal number of books, must perforce be perfunctory. Yet even such an overview will, I believe, establish the man at the pinnacle of SF writers, where he belongs.

Barry Malzberg has a theory that the totality of an SF writer's themes and gifts is present in embryo in his or her first published work. Malzberg's theory is borne out in Dr. Seuss's debut *And to Think That I Saw It on Mulberry Street*, published in 1937.

Like many authors, Seuss, as he has recounted in his few interviews, had to struggle to get published at all. And when one reads this first subversive text of his, the reason is evident. A publishing milieu that considered *The Little Engine That Could* and Campbell's *The Black Star Passes* to be state-of-the-art SF would hardly have been ready for Seuss's book.

And to Think That I Saw It on Mulberry Street asserts the supremacy of the human imagination over mere physical and social constraints. The child's mental transformation of mundane early-twentieth-century reality (symbolized by horse and cart) into an extravagant, otherworldly procession is as clear a statement of Seuss's recurring main theme as one could want: the unfettered human mind is the final frontier, the source of ultimate reality, and it must always be in opposition to society (as symbolized by the boy's obtuse father). (Seuss's vision has remained remarkably consistent over the years. Compare his much later, *Oh, the Thinks You Can Think*.) In this work, Seuss not only echoes the Surrealists and Dadaists who preceded him, but clearly presages Ballard and the New Wave SF of the 1960s, not to mention foreshadowing the generation-gap tumult taking place in the streets at that time.

The fact that *And to Think That I Saw It on Mulberry Street* remains in print, along with all the Doctor's other books, is further testament to its relevance to today and its place in the continuing dialogue about the role of the individual in an increasingly constricted and totalitarian social matrix.

After this initial hurdle, Seuss's career soared from one conquest to another, as his powers matured and flourished. He quickly found his audience, which proved itself loyal and appreciative. Seuss's readers love him. He speaks directly to their unconscious fears, desires and dreams. Once someone discovers Seuss, he never really lets him go, and his life is never thereafter the same.

But, of course, reader affection and social impact, while somewhat valid, are not true measures of literary merit. Let us continue to examine how the Doctor meets the conventional criteria of fictional excellence.

After his first book, Seuss went on to invent the modern fantasy trilogy, years before Tolkien, proving himself an innovator in form as well as content. The three books in this groundbreaking series are *The 500 Hats of Bartholomew Cubbins*, *Bartholomew and the Oobleck*, and the tangential, yet clearly linked third volume, *The King's Stilts*.

The first volume is notable for its foreshadowing of such Borgesian concerns as infinity and regression, which would recur in later Seuss works. (Seuss has much in common with Borges.) The latter two books deal with Seuss's vision of biological forces. For while Seuss's work features many examples of the strange machines, gadgets, and technology typifying SF, it is primarily for his bizarre organic conceptions that he is known, his living creatures and landscapes. The cosmic, Lovecraftian horror of a rain of oobleck shows up again as the sea of "blue goo" in *Fox in Socks* and the "blue goo" weapon in *The Butter Battle Book*. Seuss was decades ahead of his time in dealing with this deadly protoplasm, which Eric Drexler, in his book *The Engines of Creation*, calls "grey goo," and which figures in such SF works as Ellison and Sheckley's "I See a Man Sitting on a Chair, and the Chair Is Biting

His Leg" and Bear's *Blood Music*. The last book in the trilogy marks the initial appearance of another perennial Seuss topic (again, decades ahead of his "peers") that would crop up later in *The Lorax*: ecology. The ring of Dike Trees holding back the sea from the Land of Didd—menaced by Nizzards, protected by Patrol Cats with clearly augmented intelligence, the whole supervised by the all-seeing King on Stilts—well, this is a forceful vision of man working in harmony with nature, and what goes wrong when society is literally deracinated.

These books, however successful, mark a detour into prose for Seuss, a detour that thankfully was only temporary. Seuss's linguistic skills and his desire for verbal experimentation strain at the fetters of this limited medium, as such failed experiments as Joyce's *Finnegans Wake* did too. (Seuss can, indeed, be seen to have triumphed where Joyce failed: he is a genius who has followed his vision to its ultimate limits without losing his audience. Such books as *There's a Wocket in My Pocket* and *Oh Say Can You Say?* have no plot per se, but exist instead for their linguistic puzzles.) Only poetry offered Seuss the means to continue his daring verbal forays, his innovations in language, and he was not to abandon it again.

Neologisms abound in Seuss's work, along with dazzling reworking of conventional words. He truly exemplifies Pound's dictum, "Make it new." Poetry's appeal to the hardwiring in the human brain explains Seuss's incredible staying power in the reader's mind. "Red fish, blue fish." "Hop on pop." "I do not like green eggs and ham/I do not like them, Sam I Am." It brings to mind that other poet of SF, Cordwainer Smith, author of "Think Blue, Count Two" and "Mother Hitton's Littul Kittens." (In fact, there are many intriguing similarities between these two authors. Could it possibly be that the unseen "Paul Linebarger" was really . . . ? But no, it would be too much . . . .)

In short, the man is a supreme stylist. No sentence of his could ever be mistaken for someone else's. There are few other SF authors about whom one could make this claim.

In the 1940s and 1950s, Seuss's work took on a more political stance, as he sought to remake society (*If I Ran the Cirrus* and *If I Ran the Zoo*), and as he dabbled in social issues, especially in the two *Horton* books, and in *Yertle the Turtle*. In *Horton Hatches the Egg*, he cleverly explores the issue of child care, as well as demonstrating more of his patented biological polymorphous perversity (the "elephant-bird"). But *Horton Hears a Who* and *Yertle the Turtle* are Seuss's most *engagé* works.

Horton Hears a Who, published in 1954, is nothing less than a clever parable about Joe McCarthy and HUAC. Horton claims to hear the inhabitants of "another world" (Russia) shouting from a speck of dust. His persecution by the beasts of the jungle—especially by the cretinous tribe of monkeys—is repulsive, but its presentation constitutes one of the finest examples of satiric allegory in 1950s SF. By all rights, Horton's slogan—"A person's a person, no matter how small"—should have branded Seuss a one-worlder and a fellow-traveler. That it did not is a testimony to the ignorance of tyrants.

Yertle the Turtle—written in 1950, a mere year or two after Orwell's *1984*—is clearly a response to that book. It remains one of the century's most poignant, yet hopeful, dystopias. Once again, Seuss chose a biological image to anchor his text: the living throne formed by the stack of turtle subjects, atop which King Yertle perches. The upsetting of this cruel chair by the simple actions of the bottom turtle, Mack, offers hope that the common man will triumph, through the simple quirks of his nature.

(Yertle's significance has been recognized in recent years, notably in a song by the Red Hot Chili Peppers. Moreover, it was cited in a recent brouhaha involving Mayor Koch of New York.)

These works represent the high-water mark of Seuss's political involvement. Never one for joining mass movements, he advanced in the 1960s into a kind of poetic anarchy best exemplified by *The Cat in the Hat* books, which assert as subtext that the sole measure of social justice is the unqualified freedom of the individual. (However, Seuss did later rewrite Yertle in a less powerful version, *King Looie Katz*, in which a kingdom of cats is locked in a ring of protocol, each subject carrying another's tail, until the lowest cat refuses.)

What can we say about Seuss's power of invention, his creation of new plots and incidents, alien societies and cultures? No one can fault Seuss here. As already noted, his diverse universes and swift-moving stories possess all the nightmare logic and fecundity of the best Surrealists, placing him squarely in the mainstream of twentieth-century thought. He leaves clear descendants in such SF figures as Jack Vance, with whom he shares a love of music, language, and biological profligacy.

Seuss also exhibits links to the existentialists and such writers as Beckett and Sartre. His oeuvre features more long-suffering, undeservedly tormented characters than all of Kafka. Why does the Fox in Socks torment Knox? Why do children hop on Pop? Why does Sam I Am (with a name like that could he be . . . God?) insist on force-feeding his dish of green eggs and ham? And we have already mentioned Horton's Christ-like woes. Paranoia also figures extensively in Seuss's work. (See *There's a Wocket in My Pocket.*)

Seuss's work, like much SF, derives additional power from the explicit and implicit interrelatedness of the various books. It means so much more, after reading *Horton Hears a Who*, to realize that *How the Grinch Stole Christmas*, set in Whoville, must take place entirely on a speck of dust resting on a stalk of clover! Seuss's work gains even deeper resonances from the fact that his odd lands are directly linked to the fields we know. It is always only a short step from Weehawken to the edge of the universe in the cosmos of Seuss. (See *Scrambled Eggs Super.*)

Nor does Seuss fail in that area traditionally reserved to SF: the dramatic embodiment of exciting ideas. The infinite regression of that which is contained within the hat of that ultimate anarchist, the Cat in the Hat. (Note also the recurring hat theme in *The Five Hundred Hats of Bartholomew Cubbins.*) The Chippendale Mupp, (from *Dr. Seuss's Sleep Book*), a creature with a long, slow tail (shades of Bob Shaw's slow glass!), where a bite at the tip serves as a wake-up signal eight hours later. Having barely scratched the surface here, we could go on and on. But perhaps most astonishing and deserving of mention is the notion developed in *On Beyond Zebra* that supplies this essay's title: that there could be letters beyond the end of the mundane alphabet. Here is another metaphysical conceit worthy of Borges. Who else in the literature of SF has dared to dream so boldly?

We cannot finish with Seuss without mentioning two recent works. Produced when the artist was in his late sixties and late seventies, these books, by any rational measure, should have each won him Nebula Awards in their respective years of eligibility.

In 1971 (Nebula winner for best novel: Robert Silverberg's *A Time of Changes*), Seuss published *The Lorax*. This tale of ecological devastation concerns the extinction of the Truffala trees and their dependent ecosystem by a family of greedy industrialists (the Once-lers), despite the best efforts of the Lorax, a nature deity, to prevent the destruction. The bleak landscapes are heartbreaking; the portrayal of the Once-ler clan as mere hands connected to never-seen individuals is brilliant; the sweeping indictment of industrialism and its useless products (Thneeds) is stunning. Today, in light of recent assaults on the biosphere, the book is a more powerful experience than ever.

In 1984 (Nebula winner for best novel: William Gibson's

Neuromancer), at the age of eighty, Seuss published *The Butter Battle Book*. Like Wells's *Mind at the End of Its Tether*, this story is clearly a product of the elderly artist in a moment of despair. The insane arms buildup conducted between the Butter-Up and Butter-Down camps echoes the tale of Swift's Big-Endians and Little-Endians. Only by leaving the ending in doubt does Seuss spare the reader the emotional trauma of mass carnage; simultaneously, he poses a moral dilemma and calls us to worldly action.

Needless to say, these two scathing books did not even make the preliminary Nebula ballot.

In closing—and it's almost unfair to cite this, for it is a skill that none of his "peers" possesses—there's Seuss's visual art. His poetry stands by itself, of course, but the drawings elevate his work beyond emulation. The alien physiology of even his ostensibly human characters, the feathery toes and fingers, the plumed appendages, the hidden sexual organs that must be there . . . or must they? (Seuss, by the way, is never shy about sex. Consider how much of his action occurs in beds or bedrooms.) In Seuss, then, is a re-creation of our familiar world in the transfiguring terms of a true artist's unique vision. His transcendent stories and satires, adventures and allegories color the reader's perceptions indelibly.

Dr. Seuss.

Where is thy Nebula, thy Grandmaster, thy Hugo, thy Howard, thy British Fantasy Award, thy Prix Apollo, thy Balrog?

He needs them not. He has our hearts.

THE GREAT NEBULA SWEEP

A review of **Mega-Awesome SF: The True Story Behind *Forever Plus!*** by Amber Max (Serconia Press, 1994, 334 pages, $29.95, ISBN 0-14-009692-2).

We all hoped that we had heard the last about the Great Nebula Sweep scandal. But now we must contend with this book.

The first notice anyone received of the existence of *Mega-Awesome SF* was through the *Today* show. In her interview with Deborah Norville, Amber Max, archetypical Valley Girl, seemed more intent on promoting herself than disclosing any new information. Her mantra—"I rilly, rilly wrote all these pages myself!"—did little to inspire confidence that her book would be of any value.

Opening the book to the first chapter certainly did not dispel my worst fears. Entitled "Amber's Totally Fabulous Guide to Life," this preface is all gossip and beauty tips. I was almost tempted to toss the book without reading further.

I'm glad, however, that I persisted, for in the next chapter—"Riding My Harley"—we begin to reap fresh, hitherto unavailable insights into the actors in the Great Nebula Sweep.

At their first encounter—a literal collision in the local

Waldenbooks, midway between the SF and aerobic-video sections, during February 1990, a collision which developed improbably into a romantic engagement—Amber Max was nineteen, and Harley Prout was twenty-five. Employed by Chipco, the enormous computer conglomerate, Harley was also a lifelong reader of SF. He had for many years harbored secret hopes of becoming a published writer himself. But a decade of unanimous and unmitigated rejection had finally convinced him that he was an utter literary incompetent.

Making up his mind at last to succeed by computer trickery where he had failed with talent, and urged on by the mischievous and adoring Amber Max, Harley sought a cybernetic solution.

Harley was currently working on neural networks for his employer. These computer constructs were intended to mimic the functioning of the human brain more closely than conventional programs. Capable of heuristic fuzzy logic and parallel processing, neural networks offered the promise of replicating human mental abilities more closely than mere serial machines.

Using advanced Chipco hardware and unlimited company time, Harley set out to teach a neural network of unprecedented complexity the rules for producing an SF masterpiece.

In a process known as "training up the system," he started out by feeding the neural net—which had English-parsing abilities—the raw texts of all Nebula and Hugo winners, as well as the texts of all other ballot entries. He followed this up by giving it the voting statistics that had produced the winners. Learning of a poll Ben Bova had conducted among SFWA members to learn what selection criteria they employed in selecting award-winners, Harley obtained, through judicious bribes, the poll results from Galileo Marketing Systems, along with their secret multidimensional scaling techniques. These too were fed to the network.

It was now early spring 1991, and the current Nebulas were

about to be awarded. Harley let his system peruse the contestants and make its choices. The network replicated the exact vote distribution which the members of SFWA later produced.

Amber reports that Harley was overjoyed. "'This is the key,' he told me. 'On the lowest level, writing is just the random generation of words. The secret lies in discriminating which words are the best. And I've got that power of discrimination now.'"

Securing an ultrasophisticated, text-generating program analogous to the famous RACTER, Harley wired it in a feedback loop with his neural network. He set the parameters of the network to maximum and turned the whole thing loose. The network inspected the text produced by the generator and passed only that which met its Nebula standards. The approved text was fed back to influence subsequent choices.

Amazingly, a coherent short story began to emerge. Reading it, Harley wept, and Amber exclaimed, "Holy shit, Harley, this is better'n *Star Wars!*"

Harley knew that his story was guaranteed to sell. He was reluctant to submit it under his own name, however, convinced that because of his reputation it would languish unread in the slushpile. That was when the crucial decision was made to use Amber's name on the byline.

All the story lacked was a title. Harley ran a simple subroutine that permuted all previous Nebula titles, and passed the choices on to the judgment of the network.

Doors of Repentance, Blind Conciliator, Enemy Claw, Slow Passengers, A Letter from the King of Sand, Dancing Chickens and Ugly Deers, God Song, Born with the Shadows, The Quickening Flute, Catch that Hangman!, Childmancer, Mother to Dragons, The Fountains of Saliva, Dream of the Left-Handed Snake, Hard Blood, The Vision Solution, The Planners of Time, The Girl Who Fell into the Unicorn Tapestry, A Helix of Mist, A Dog's Opinion,

Press Love or Death, Revolution Man, Ender is Five, A Time of Worlds, Ringway . . . . All these and more met the thumbs-down from the network. Then came the winner: *Forever Plus!*

As Amber records: "Harley said anyone could see it was a natural. 'The all-purpose ambiguity, the notion of one step beyond eternity, appealing to the immature desire for immortality, the exclamation point—it's perfect!' I just said, 'It's short and rad and real nineties, dude. I like it!'"

It was now the end of August 1991. Harley mailed the story out (under Amber's name) to the highest-paying market, where its publication would be sure to attract the most attention: *Omni* magazine. The story was purchased immediately. Further, it was slated to appear as soon as possible, in the first issue of 1992. This initial sale, however, was merely the first step in Harley's master plan to conquer the SF field. The next stage involved setting the network to churning out two longer versions of the syncretic masterpiece: a novelette and a novella.

Like the Kennedy assassination or the first moon landing, the publication of "Forever Plus!" in the January 1992 issue of *Omni* is an event emblazoned on the memories of all who read it. Entire issues of fanzines were devoted to heaping laurels on this one story. Professional reviewers everywhere climaxed in fits of critical ecstasy. Editors begged the unknown Amber Max for more of her work. Looking back on the short-story version of *Forever Plus!* now, even after the secret of its origin has been exposed, one is still hard put to dislike or resist it. Scientific tests have revealed that, like the "fatal joke" of the Monty Python skit, the text is so constructed as to have actual neurological impact on the mind of anyone conditioned by years of reading SF.

In Chapter Five, "Way Off the Applause Meter," we finally learn what it felt like to be on the receiving end of all this adulation. "It was rilly, rilly super. We were like, 'Hey, more champagne, waiter!'" But as Amber details, their enjoyable buzz did not last long. Almost immediately, Harley had to buckle down to implementing his plan of conquest. "He was mega-anal, like. I just couldn't get him to kick back."

The novelette version of the story was dispatched to Axolotl Press, which of course immediately snatched it up. The limited signed chapbook was released by early March. The reaction to this version was even stronger, if possible. As "Forever Plus!" grew and grew in length, it promoted heavier and heavier semiotic meltdown in the brains of its readers.

By May a Tor SF Double featuring the brand new novella version of "Forever Plus!" on one side was available. For the companion work, Tor editors, knowing it would make little difference what they bundled with Amber's masterpiece, had hurriedly grabbed the first submission moldering in the slushpile, a novella by the legendary eccentric Gerry Saint-Armand, Providence recluse in the Lovecraft tradition. The Double went through six printings before the official publication date, incidentally making Saint-Armand more money than had all of his previous sales combined.

By the time the novella saw print, the network had produced a 500,000-word definitive version of *Forever Plus!* Amber was represented now by the new firm of Meredith-Macauley-Heifetz. They auctioned off the manuscript to Bantam/Foundation for ten million dollars. Bantam had the book in print by August, a simultaneous release in hardcover, trade, and mass-market paperback. It was the first SF novel in a single volume to top a thousand pages.

To recount the long and intricate plot of *Forever Plus!* for an audience already intimately familiar with it would be pointless. Suffice it to note that by choosing an immortal protagonist, particularly one whose immortality resulted from jumping into a new body upon the expiration of each old one, Harley was able to move through an enormous range of times, milieux, and view-points. Opening with the protagonist yet an infant, the novel manages to traverse all the usual Misunderstood Child Prodigy terrain so beloved by SF readers. After this archetypal prologue comes the Awakening Adolescent, the Sensitive Youth, the Competent Man, the Wise Elder, the Disembodied Psyche, and, in a daring shift of viewpoint, the Oppressed Female. Afterward, the cycle repeats with variations extending into the nonhuman. Meanwhile, we have passed through Comet Strike, Realpolitik Scenario, Nuclear War, Nuclear Winter, Psychic Mutants, Eco-catastrophe, New Dark Ages, Gradual Renaissanee, Expansion into the Solar System, Generation Ships, Discovery of FTL, the Backwards Colony, First Contact, Interspecies War, Galactic Empire, Collapse of Empire, Stagnation, and End of Time. Indeed, the protagonist survives the Big Crunch of an entropic universe to preside godlike over the birth of a new plenum!

By now, *Forever Plus!* was the literary equivalent of Beatlemania or *Thriller*-era Michael Jackson fever. The blurbs on later editions reveal a kind of shared madness.

"I am caught like a fly in Amber's prose. This is Pure Story."—Orson Scott Card.

"John Campbell would have kissed her, then married her!"—Algis Budrys.

"This is not a novel, it's Life itself! *Forever Plus!* forever more!"—Faren Miller.

"Scientifically impeccable. Can Amber Max be housing the souls of Heinlein, Herbert, and Hawking?"—Tom Easton.

"Signifier and signified are unified in a deconstructed hyperreality."—Samuel Delany.

"I have ceased working on *The Pressure of Time*. Amber Max has said it all."—Thomas Disch.

"Amber Max is not an absolute Goddess of Literature. But in this age of clones and computer simulations, she ineluctably approaches that state, arguably."—John Clute.

This last quote, as Amber reports in Chapter Eight, "Cut Me Some Slack, Dude!" caused quite a bit of trouble between her and Harley. "He like totally freaked out. 'Simulations,' he kept muttering over and over. 'Simulations. The synchronicity is too weird. He must know . . . . And Jesus, I'm sick of reading your name! I can't stand being unknown. We've got it all, but it's all different than I thought it would be. I wanted to be famous, but instead everybody thinks it's you.' Then he got like totally paranoid and started raving. 'Clute must know the secret. That phrase must be a hidden message to me. He's gonna spill the secret and screw us out of the awards. I'll kill him, I swear it. Gimme that phone!' I had to wrestle it away from him and he only calmed down after playing six hours of Nintendo."

The publication of each new version of *Forever Plus!* was immediately followed by a flood of Nebula recommendations from the members of SFWA. By late summer of 1992, it was clear that all versions would easily make the final Nebula ballot.

At the Worldcon in Orlando that Labor Day, *Forever Plus!* fever was at an incredible pitch. Amber Max, discreetly accompanied by the seemingly insignificant Harley Prout, made her first public appearance. Mobs swarmed around her.

When, on the final day of the convention, a representative from the Lucas-Spielberg studio made the announcement that the film of *Forever Plus!* was already in production, the crowd erupted and trashed the entire hotel in its exuberance. The movie was released in time for Christmas, making it eligible for the freshly reinstated Dramatic Production Nebula.

Nineteen-ninety-three broke with *Forever Plus!* mania unabated. The Nebula voting was a mere formality. *Forever Plus!* won in every category, sweeping the board.

At the Nebula Banquet—well, here's Amber:

"I was wearing like this ultra-chic dress from Azzedine AlaVa with my Manolo Blahnik heels. I got up to make my fifth acceptance speech when Harley went apeshit. 'Don't listen to her! I wrote it, me, Harley Prout! Or my program did, which is the same thing!' He tried to rush the stage, but security got to him first. All I could think was, God, my feet are so-o-o-o sore in these shoes! It's like, why now, Harley?"

After the banquet Harley was not to be found. Amber went back home to wait for his return. Now things began to go sour.

The people assigned to translate *Forever Plus!* for foreign editions found that it was impossible to capture the magic that had made it work in English. The neurological effect proved to be language-specific. The whole pretense shattered when, in December of 1993, Harley himself released the machine-code for his neural network to every BBS and publication from *Byte* to *Popular Computing*. Amber's tearful confession on *Entertainment Tonight* finally disillusioned the last of her fans.

The controversy that ensued was enormous. Amber was stripped of all her awards. Publishers tried to reclaim their monies, but Amber was smart enough to hire the law firm of Holland, Dozier, and Holland to represent her, and managed to hold on to it all (minus legal fees, of course).

In her final chapter, "Harley, Come Home," we are presented

with a portrait of a repentant, faithful, wiser Amber, longing patiently and publicly for the return of "my Silicon Valley squeeze, my gnarly circuit-bender, my rad lad, the one and only Harley Prout—before the money's all gone."

YOURMONEY™

Secretary of the Treasury, Washington, DC

Dear Friend of the Dollar:

If you're anything like me, you have a soft spot in your heart for cash. The convenience, the tangibility, the glorious tradition of this wonderful medium of exchange.

Dad handing you your allowance money. Taping the first dollar your very own business ever earned to the wall above the cash register. Grandma tucking a set of Lincolns into her card to you at Christmas.

And there's no exaggerating the fuss-free, feel-good, sheer spendability of plain old folding money. Even in today's up-to-the-minute world of commerce and high finance, you won't find anyone turning up their nose at a bag or two of neatly banded tender.

These are important qualities that credit cards, debit cards or electronic funds transfers—of any magnetic stripe—just can't deliver. Sure, like all of us, I rely on plastic for transactions I don't really care about. Renting a car. Paying taxes. Buying insurance. But I just don't feel right without some of the old "cabbage" bulking out my wallet.

Buying your child an ice-cream cone from a smiling Good Humor™ vendor. Impulsively purchasing a dozen TeleFlora™ roses for your spouse. Tipping your bellhop at one of the fine Disney™ resorts. Try doing that with plastic, and you'll quickly see just how much satisfaction you're missing. Call me nostalgic or sentimental, but I'll bet you feel exactly as I do. And; believe me, we're not alone.

Still, let me be the first to admit that America's cash has lately fallen a little behind the times, style-wise. Sexy, it's not! Although honored and esteemed worldwide, its image isn't what it once was. The Mighty Dollar looks just a wee bit drab these days. Memories of Hoover, Pearl Harbor, Eisenhower and all that. After all, there have been no major design changes in our money for decades! It's as if Detroit were still producing Packards and Edsels. They might get us where we want to go, but it wouldn't be very stylish or up-to-date, or even much fun.

Well, YourGovernment™ has listened to your complaints and suggestions regarding United States currency. And we've taken action. Assembling some of the nation's finest minds from the fields of advertising, industrial design, law enforcement and fashion, the Treasury Department has completely reworked the whole concept of how the nation's money should function, and what it should deliver to the consumer. We feel it's the most exciting idea since the invention of wampum.

We call it YourMoney™.

RENDER UNTO CAESAR

Our first move was to "free up the canvas" represented by each bill. After careful consideration, it was determined that YourGovernment™ actually needs very little space to validate each bill as official issue of the Mint and to prevent counterfeiting.

Gone are all the old, outdated, confusing symbols and scrollwork which no one ever noticed anymore anyway. Each YourMoney™ note now restricts visible government information to the upper righthand corner of the obverse side. There, an embedded, non-duplicatable hologram of the proud American Eagle sits above a unique serial number. Intelligent threading and the fine-quality linen paper you've always enjoyed—as well as a few unobtrusive secret features—complete the common hallmarks of YourMoney™ shared by each user, insuring the currency's integrity.[1]

And the rest of each bill?

It's yours to design!

Front, back, color, and much, much more!

YOUR LIFE, YOUR WORLD, YOURMONEY™

Just imagine.

You're in a store or at your favorite restaurant, when the time comes to pay. Proudly opening your purse or taking out your wallet, you remove not the same anonymous tattered musty money that anyone else—from homeless bum to CEO—might once have carried, but a gorgeous assortment of unique YourMoney™ bills which bear images selected specifically by you! Images which convey your personality, your taste, your history!

Everything else that really matters to you—from your clothes to your car, your home to your favorite recreations, your checks to your credit cards, your choice of beer or lipstick—reflects your individual style. Up till now, only your money has failed to keep in step with your desire for personal expression.

But now there's YourMoney™!

THE SKY'S THE LIMIT

Here's how YourMoney™ begins.

Start to think about what images you'd like YourMoney™ to have on it. Your pets, your loved ones, your diplomas. Perhaps a statement of principle, a motto, a creed. The ancestral homestead, the summer cottage, the weekend yacht. Reproduce (within copyright limitations) a favorite work of art. Go abstract! Anything. After all, it's YourMoney™.

When you have a good idea of what you want YourMoney™ to look like, collect text, photos or even physical memorabilia. Sketch out your notions, if you're artistically inclined. Hire a professional artist or graphics studio to design something. Get your kids involved! Only your own imagination limits what you can do.2

Finally, visit any local participating bank. They'll be happy to get your designs into machine-readable form, if they're not already.3 Then, the glorious full-color images which will adorn the front and back of Your Money™ will be transmitted to the nearest Federal Mint.

There, the latest model of computer-driven dye-sublimation printing presses, which easily accommodate short or long runs of any quantity (unlike our balky old mechanical presses), will churn out YourMoney™.

And you'll be spending it within seven business days!4

Guaranteed!

IMAGINE THE POSSIBILITIES

YourMoney™ is a lot more than simple legal tender.

It's advertising. As YourMoney™ circulates throughout the economy, it carries your message with it. The ultimate in hassle-free networking!

It's friendly. Who knows what new acquaintances you'll make, as YourMoney™ passes from hand to hand? Could it lead to sharing a Budweiser™ with a new pal—or even to love?5 YourGovernment™ can't guarantee it—but we wouldn't bet against it!

It's character-building. Children and adolescents learn through the use of their own YourMoney™ the intrinsic link between them and their cash.

It's socially responsible. If you want to exclude certain ethically or aesthetically objectionable institutions or individuals from handling YourMoney™, you can do it! We also know that you wouldn't want YourMoney™ to fall into the hands of any illegal or illicit enterprise or individual. That's why we give you the option of blocking or tracking YourMoney™ through every transaction.6

WHO CAN PURCHASE YOURMONEY™?

YourMoney™ is not limited merely to any US citizen never convicted of a major felony. YourMoney™ is also available to:

Civic organizations, clubs, casinos, or businesses large and small.

State, county and city governments.

Foreign governments with Most Favored Nation trading status.

IN fact, practically anybody!

And the cost is quite reasonable. Every dollar of YourMoney™ costs merely $1.25. And the shipping's on us!7

You simply won't find a better return for your money than YourMoney™.

So order today! Before it's too late!8

NOTES AND DISCLAIMERS

1) Sensors incorporating a modified Clipper™ chip which will validate all YourMoney™ notes are available to merchants, wholesalers, retailers, healthcare providers, local police departments, licensed financial institutions and others for a reasonable fee.

2) NEA guidelines apply.

3) Additional charges will be made for on-site digitization and/or format conversion.

4) Overnite delivery available from Federal Express™ at a modest additional cost.

5) YourGovernment™ not legally responsible for the untoward effects of any unsolicited advances, business, personal or otherwise.

6) See 1.

7) See 4.

8) While all old-style currency will of course remain redeemable for the indefinite future, a ten-percent surcharge to be collected by the receiving party and transmitted quarterly to Your Government™ will be assessed on all such transactions.

IT WAS THE BLESSED OF TIMES,
IT WAS THE CURSED OF TIMES

Splatterclassics, Inc.
Hell House
666 Gore Lane
Amityville, NY 10666

Dear Secondary School Educator:

Are you tired of fighting a losing battle to get your students to read the Great Works of Literature?

Do you despair of ever hearing your students exclaim, "Yo, Milton rules!"

Have you exhausted all the conventional tricks intended to stimulate their interest?

• Emphasizing the "relevance" of the work (*Romeo and Juliet* and teen pregnancy; *Moby Dick* and Japanese whaling violations).

• Staging dramatizations of certain fictional scenes calculated to appeal to modern youngsters (the suicide by sled in *Ethan Frome*, the guillotining of Sydney Carton from *A Tale of Two Cities*).

• In-school motivational appearances by local authors (usually, to be charitable, second-rate writers and unappetizing personalities).

Well, fret no longer! Splatterclassics, Inc., has the solution to your problem!

Simply put, we have made the classics appealing by inserting the exact element which countless surveys of high-school students have revealed makes the subjects actually want to read!

In a word, horror.

Nothing attracts today's jaded students like horror. (Many of them of course are living it!) From the suburbs to the inner cities, horror draws young readers. No one has to force a youngster to pick up the latest Stephen King, Dean Koontz or Anne Rice book. They do so eagerly and without prompting, devouring them by the dozen! (And that's just Mister King's monthly output!) Our scientific studies have demonstrated that horror has the ability to lure and impress budding minds more than any other type of writing, including such once-popular genres as fantasy and science fiction, and even series books like *The Babysitters' Club*, *The Hardy Boys*, and *Dink Stover at Yale*.

Accordingly, we have enlisted dozens of brand-name horror writers to rework the classics in your curriculum. All of our offerings are guaranteed to contain at least fifty percent of the original author's words, cleverly retrofitted into a spine-tingling, gut-churning, edge-of-the-dunking-stool modern horror novel.

Please send for free desk copies of our sample titles listed below.

We think you'll be so impressed that you'll soon convince your local school board to make Splatterclassics, Inc., your sole supplier of quality literature for today's teens!

The Scarlet Letter
Nathaniel Hawthorne and Ira Levin

Hester Prynne, impregnated by Satan in the form of a randy televangelist named Arthur Dimmesdale, gives birth to an unnatural daughter portended to usher in Armageddon on her sixteenth birthday. Dismayed by the monster she has brought into the world, Hester commits suicide by carving the letter A (for Armageddon) deep into her chest. Hester's grieving husband, disguised as a plastic surgeon named Roger Chillingsworth, later gains access to the child (who has been adopted by Dimmesdale and his coven after Hester's suicide) through promising to repair the young Antichrist's cloven hooves. In a *Gotterdammerung* finish, Dimmesdale is forced to confess from his telepulpit, and his whole Crystal Cathedral is brought down around him by the psychic storm unleashed when Chillingsworth manages to apply a mixture of holy-water and Desitin to the Satanic child.

The Adventures of Huckleberry Finn
Mark Twain and Stephen King

Huck and Jim set out on their raft, little knowing that an interdimensional flaw has opened up beneath the mighty Mississippi, filling its waters with nightmarish creatures. Their voyage downriver is one long battle against the warty, tentacled horde. The combat makes Huck and Jim good friends, overcoming their racism and ageism, and their prolonged and agonizing deaths during the destruction of New Orleans will leave the reader in tears.

Remembrance of Things Past
Marcel Proust and Anne Rice

Marcel, an ageless vampire, inspired by his first nostalgia-provoking taste of blood after a long hibernation, narrates the whole complicated history of his relations with the Guermantes, Swanns and Verdurins, families on whom he has long preyed, both arterially and sexually. Joined by his undead fiancee, Albertine, Marcel wreaks havoc on Paris and the French countryside.

Great Expectations
Charles Dickens and Robert Bloch

Orphan Pip, enduring an abusive childhood, grows up to be a serial killer, his mentor the career criminal Magwitch. Tracked down by detective Bentley Drummel, Pip is eventually revealed to be a split personality and a transvestite, his other persona the reclusive Miss Havisham.

The Old Man and the Sea
Ernest Hemingway and Peter Benchley

An old fisherman, his gorgeous daughter, and a bachelor millionaire, accompanied only by a crew of documentary makers, set out to capture a Great White Shark that is terrorizing their home port.

As I Lay Dying
William Faulkner and Kathe Koja

The unburied corpse of Momma Bundren, harboring a malign spirit, draws the rest of the family down in a spiral of chaos, torture and mental instability.

Mrs. Dalloway

Virginia Woolf and Tanith Lee

Clarissa Dalloway, an English society woman, exists on another plane as an archetypical figure known as the Mistress of Boredom. Or so she believes. Gradually this persona—hallucinated or objectively real—comes to dominate Clarissa's earthly life, infecting all of those around her with terminal ennui. Will all of England succumb? Woolf and Lee keep the reader guessing till the very last minute!

Ivanhoe

Sir Walter Scott and Robert McCammon

Wilfred, son of Cedric, falls in love with Rowena, his father's maid, little wotting that she is a werewolf! Only the Talmudic spells of Rebecca the Jewess stand between Wilfred and a savage lycanthropic honeymoon!

Babbitt

Sinclair Lewis and Dean Koontz

George Babbitt, a prosperous real estate broker, foolishly breaks ground for a new housing plat on the site of Zenith's old Indian graveyard.

The Ambassadors

Henry James and Dan Simmons

Lambert Strether, sent to Paris to rescue Chad Newscome from the clutches of the Countess de Vionnet, discovers that the Countess is in reality an ancient succubus who has Chad in her erotic thrall. Reinforcements arrive in the form of Chad's sister, but she too proves to be a lamia! Upon Chad's exsanguination, Lambert arrives back at Woollett, Mass., a drained husk of his former self.

But wait, educators—there's more! Coming soon are *The Last of the Mohicans*, by James Fenimore Cooper and Clive Barker; *Madame Bovary*, by Gustave Flaubert and Poppy Z. Brite; and *Robinson Crusoe* by Daniel Defoe and Peter Straub. In addition, noted horror anthologist Ellen Datlow is now compiling the *Norton Book of Splatterclassic Hybrids*, available Fall 1996.

So, as Joseph Conrad might have said, "Dial 1-800-THE HROR now!"

Sincerely yours,
Asmodeus Murdoch

MANUSCRIPT FOUND IN A PIPEDREAM

Knowledgeable readers know that one of the most famous unwritten stories in SF is "The Stone Pillow." Part of Robert Heinlein's Future History series, this story was to have told how America fell under the sway of the infamous evangelist, Nehemiah Scudder, the First Prophet, and became a dictatorial Theocracy. Scudder, as Heinlein describes him in an afterword to *Revolt in 2100*, was "a backwoods evangelist who combined some of the features of John Calvin, Savonarola, Judge Rutherford and Huey Long." (The forgotten Judge Rutherford, my encyclopedia informs me, was an early pamphleteer for the Jehovah's Witnesses.) Teaming up with an ex-senator, Scudder and his associates "placed their affairs in the hands of a major advertising agency and were on their way to fame and fortune. Presently they needed stormtroopers; they revived the Ku Klux Klan in everything but name . . . . Blood at the polls and blood in the streets, but Scudder won the election. The next election was never held."

So repugnant was this vision to Heinlein that he declared, "I probably never will write the story of Nehemiah Scudder; I dislike him too thoroughly."

It comes as a major surprise then to learn that even a snippet of "The Stone Pillow" does exist. Found recently amongst the files of

Analog magazine (formerly *Astounding*, of course, which had published the other portions of the Future History) during their recent move from Lexington Avenue to their new Broadway offices, this fragment is now reprinted for the first time. Although the title page and many others are missing, close textual analysis and typewriter-font matching make it almost certain that this work derives from Heinlein's pen, circa 1939. We think this fragment alone will make obvious the terror and disgust felt by both Heinlein and his editor, John Campbell, which led to the suppression of the work in question.

The Stone Pillow
attributed to
Robert A. Heinlein

"—quiet, Lennie! Here he comes!"

The paired Angels of the Lord flanking the doors to the House of Representatives snapped to attention, butting their ceremonial spears into the thick carpet. At their waists hung both daggers and blasters, ready for either close combat or mass annihilation. But chances were neither weapon would come into play; the First Prophet's victory was too complete. The whole country—that portion that had not heartily endorsed Scudder, but had dared to oppose the man's rampant jingoism, right down to its formerly independent and cantankerous elected representatives—was too cowed and beaten to utter a whimper of protest, much less stage an uprising. That day, if it ever came, still lay far in the future.

"Gee, Zack," whispered the younger of the two Angels, "he's mighty impressive, ain't he?"

Gruffer and more worldly, his companion replied, "Yeah, I guess—if you're at all inclined to fall for that silver-haired, pudgy, sanctimonious type."

Shocked, the young Angel said, "How can you speak of the First Prophet that way? Ain't you scared such talk will get back to him? You'd be in for a heck of a disciplining then. Why, it might even result in a court-martial. Or worse!"

"Yeah," said Zack sardonically. "They might force me to watch that damn loony televisor course he teaches!"

All talk between the comrades ceased then, as Nehemiah Scudder, formerly a poor Georgia farm boy, now ruler of the mightiest nation on the globe, First Prophet, All Holiness Incarnate, came within earshot.

Scudder was a roly-poly figure with a double-chin indicative of easy and over-indulgent living. His most striking feature was his massive silver pompadour, much beloved by the frightened and repressed elderly women, gullible lackwits and similarly coiffed arrogant male peers who had helped propel him to power. His expensive suit spoke persuasive volumes, all its accents calculated by the advertising agency of Blankley and Bane, who had groomed the backwoods preacher into the very model of a serpent-tongued snake-oil salesman.

Scudder, trailed by his entourage of lickspittle lackeys and strongarm goons, brushed imperiously past the Angels and entered the chamber where the assembled Representatives nervously awaited the arrival of the nation's new leader.

It was the first time Scudder had visited them. And although no one then knew it, it was also to be the last.

Once on the dais and behind the podium (which no longer bore the familiar seal of the United States of America, but instead the sigil of the Theocracy: a mailed fist athwart a cross), Scudder waited for silence to descend. Then he spoke.

"Friends and fellow sinners under the Lord," Scudder unctuously began, "the stern yet loving transformation of our beloved country, demanded by the perilous times in which we live, is now well under way. Irreversible and unstoppable, the remaking of America into a God-fearing fortress of strength is now as solidly established as any free-market contract between seller and buyer. Let me summarize just a few of the new measures we have rammed through in our first hundred days.

"Thousands of orphanages have been opened to hold the children of those security risks whom we have been forced to arrest. In these establishments, these wards of the Theocracy will receive the correct education, becoming the first generation properly raised on the principles of Scudderism, ensuring a long and bright future for the Theocracy.

"Two-way, perpetually open televisors have been installed in nearly forty percent of the nation's homes. We estimate one-hundred percent coverage by the end of next year. These televisors allow us to monitor the needs and desires of the people continuously and so effectively that voting is no longer a necessity. Knowing the will of the people intimately, we can respond in their best interests immediately, dealing with every threat to stability.

"All forms of individual and family public assistance have been terminated, freeing up funds for increased armed defense against our numerous enemies internally and abroad. All able-bodied citizens, whatever their personal circumstances, will now be encouraged to become fully self-supporting. Whatever labor cannot find a home in the marketplace will be welcome on the government pressgangs. These parasites and drones who used to ride the government gravy-train will become productive members of society at last, aiding in the building of various Theocratic institutions, such as palaces and churches.

"Likewise, all government assistance to public transportation has been abolished. Travel permits will now be issued upon examination by the proper authorities. Additionally, tax breaks given to publishers, museums and concert halls are a thing of the past.

The Board of Censors will now administer these areas in the public interest.

"As I'm sure you will all agree, these measures and the dozens of others of like nature which we have established have put the country on a self-sustaining course under my firm control. A strong hand which no longer needs the assistance of an antiquated body such as this one I am now addressing. It is therefore my solemn pleasure to announce the dissolution of the House of Representatives. If you'll excuse me now, I have to go address the Senate."

Under a pall of silence, Scudder turned to leave. Suddenly, a figure in the audience shot to his feet. Everyone recognized Representative Francis Barnacle of Massachusetts, birthplace of the First American Revolution.

"You're on mighty chummy terms with the Almighty," Barnacle shouted, "and that lets you lay down the law to us mere mortals! But I say you're just a knothead with a loud voice, an IQ around 90, hair in your ears, dirty underwear, and a lot of ambition. You're too lazy to be a farmer, too stupid to be an engineer, and too unreliable to be a banker. But brother, can you pray! And now that you've gathered enough other knotheads around you who don't have your vivid imagination and self-assurance, you're no longer plain old Nehemiah Scudder, but the First Prophet!"

Angels rushed to restrain Barnacle, but he proudly shook them off. Everyone waited for Scudder to respond. When he did, his voice was mild.

"I'm glad to see that Mr. Barnacle wishes to be the first among you to volunteer for one of the roadgangs. May he wear his chains lightly. Any others wish to step forward? No, I thought not . . . ." With that, Scudder made his exit.

Later that same evening, Scudder and his cronies sat in the Oval Office, congratulating themselves and drinking. A timorous knock signaled a visitor. "Come in!" roared Scudder.

A young aide entered, bearing a Western Union telegram. "Prophet, I—I hate to disturb you, but it's about your wife."

Scudder laughed and swilled some raw bourbon. "Ain't she dead yet?"

Some of the Prophet's compatriots seemed inclined to wince, but repressed the unhealthy urge.

"No, sir, I'm afraid not. And the doctors wired to say she's calling for you."

"Well, hell, boy, you don't expect me to leave these here well-deserved celebrations and travel halfway across this goddamn city to see some goddamn weak bitch who can't even kick the bucket without me holding her hand, do you? Besides, now that my Mother has established the order of Sacred Virgins, I don't rightly need ol' Mrs Scudder anymore, do I?"

"Uh, no, Your Holiness, I guess not . . . ."

"Then why are you still standing there like a frog-faced idiot!" bellowed Scudder.

The aide gulped and turned tail. After he had gone, the room burst out into crude laughter. When the cackling had ceased, Scudder summed up the prevailing sentiment.

"That used-up old nag of mine has her head on a stone pillow now!"

One of the lackeys chimed in. "Just like the rest of the nation, Chief!"

HAVE GUN, WILL EDIT

"He writes like I used to . . . . I should have him assassinated before it's too late."

—Larry Niven, blurbing Stephen Baxter's *Raft*.

"Do I sound a little envious? Well, let's say that if I was 50 years younger I might have considered terminating Mr. Savage with extreme prejudice."

—Arthur C. Clarke,
introducing Marshall Savage's *The Millennial Project*.

I studied the address on the business card once again, then compared it with the polished brass numbers and letters on the heavy oak door. They matched. I was impressed. The door belonged to a mansion worth at least a cool three million, or my name wasn't—well, you don't really need to know my name. Anonymity is a survival trait in my line of work.

The mansion was surrounded by two acres of manicured lawn and gardens straight out of *Architectural Digest*. A circular gravel drive carved out a grassy island, where a chrome fountain in the shape of a retro 'Forties rocket burbled gently. The whole estate was set in a fenced neighborhood where the security guards earned more than your average Silicon Valley programmer, and made the agents of Mossad look like Greenpeace wimps. After I had flashed my guy's business card back at the gates and claimed an appointment, I had been expertly frisked. I wasn't carrying a piece, since I didn't need one—yet. But a call to my prospective client had still been necessary to let me pass. (And you don't need to know his name either.)

But he had done all right for himself, my client-to-be. Not a bad place to end up in his senior years, especially for a guy who had started out writing for the pulps at a penny a word fifty years ago. He was the biggest customer I had landed so far, after two years in this new racket. I guessed maybe my reputation for delivering the goods was really starting to spread. The fact that my handiwork had indirectly garnered two Hugos, six Nebulas, a Tiptree, a Sturgeon and a Campbell award for my various clients didn't hurt either.

Hell, maybe if this kept up, I'd spend my own retirement days in a place like this.

I had a better chance at it than my victims anyhow. Their estates measured six feet by two by one, and were deep underground, with grass doormats and granite nameplates.

Now I rang the bell. It took only ten seconds for the door to be opened by the maid.

"Your boss is expecting me . . . ."

She nodded and led me through the antique-laden house.

My client's study was paneled in lumber that had once sprouted out of the soil of the rainforest. Now the shelves of exotic woods that had formerly supported monkeys and macaws held arrays of the writer's awards and published volumes. It looked like a comfortable bulwark against death and eternity, and would have fooled anyone but me. I knew how easy it was to render such shoddy defenses meaningless.

The writer himself was nothing much to look at: a scrawny,

self-important, balding schlump dressed in a Hermes-patterned silk robe—at two o'clock in the afternoon, for Christ's sake! He sat behind a big desk whose top bore a neat stack of papers and a lot of computer hardware. A single unmarked manila envelope caught my eye.

I figured the setup was supposed to make me go all wiggly and deferential, like. But any respect and awe I had once held for writers had been wiped out by my very first client. At our first meeting, I had caught the jerk unawares while he was masturbating as he re-read his best reviews. Then it turned out he wanted me to frag some pitiful *fan* who was bugging him.

This one must have picked up my cynical vibes, because he got real nervous. He tried to cover it up by turning his back to me, moving to a wet bar and offering me a drink.

"What will you have, Mister, uh—"

"Just some Perrier with lime," I said coolly. "I don't drink hard stuff while I'm working. Unlike some types I could name."

He decided to take offense at this, focusing a weak glare on me. "Listen here, Mister, what do you know about the stresses and rigors of a writing lifestyle? So what if I keep a bar in my study? I still turn out the pages. Two solo novels and a collaboration last year alone."

I took my drink from him and sipped it before replying, to keep him nervous. "I know plenty. Believe me, I've seen it all. And as for turning out the pages—well, it doesn't seem to be quite enough nowadays, does it? Otherwise, you wouldn't have called on me."

He sank despondently into an overstuffed leather chair next to his desk and wiped a clammy hand across his brow. "It's true. The competition is too fierce these days. I just can't come up with ideas fast enough. Not like I used to in my prime. It's bad enough worrying about the other survivors of my generation pushing me aside. But now there's all these young kids moving up through the ranks, nipping at my heels, invading my niche. I can't take anything for granted anymore. Why, even the critics are against me! I used to have them all on my side. But now some of them are even calling me a die—die—die—"

He couldn't say the D-word, but I could. "Dinosaur?"

He collapsed like a neophyte's shoddy plot. "Yes. That's it."

Now that I had put him in his place, I felt a little sorry for the poor little guy. It wasn't easy living past your prime, no matter what your line of work. How would I feel when I was finally outgunned? And he *was* the client, after all, the one footing the bill. So I decided to toss him a bone.

"Well, you shouldn't feel so bad, you know. It's not just you old guys who employ me. A lot of the young turks have hired me too. At least the ones who've gotten big enough advances to afford me. Usually they've got to sell at least a trilogy before I'll consider them. But it's even more savage down on their level. They're just getting started, right, and they don't care what it takes. They'd knife their own grannies just for a short-story slot in one of the prozines. Anyhow, I'm sorry if I was a little rough on you. But you can't go treating me like your agent or editor. I'm an independent contractor, a freelancer. Just like you." .

In a pig's eye, I thought to myself. But what the hell, a little flattery never hurt.

Hearing this, he perked up a little. "A freelancer. Why, of course. Quite understandable. Why, I suppose you people even have your own trade organization, something like the Ess-Eff-Double-You-Ay?"

"Not quite so vicious. But yes, we do."

Now he was positively beaming, as if we were peers. "Very good. Let's discuss terms then. Here's the, ah, competition I would like to see, ah, removed from the marketplace."

He handed me a glossy black-and-white publicity photo.

It showed a woman.

I recognized her face from last month's *Locus*. Seven-figure advance for her next two books. Twenty-city tour for her current novel, which sat smack dab in the middle of all the bestseller lists. A lot of hype about Spielberg being interested in the movie rights, with Schwarzenegger to star.

A little butterfly of queasiness fluttered in my gut. I hadn't known the victim was going to be a woman. If I accepted this assignment, she'd be the first female writer I had taken out.

But then the butterfly drowned in my stomach acids. A job was a job. I couldn't afford to have any scruples in this line of work. It was a mean, nasty arena, and I had chosen it. If only the Feds hadn't legalized drug sales, I'd still be shaking down cheating pushers for the Mob. That was sweet and easy, compared to this writing business.

I felt cold and disgusted and rotten all at once. The least I could do to make myself feel better was to force my client to share it, rub his nose in reality a little, rattle his cage and shake his comfortable tree.

"So," I pretended to misunderstand, "you figure breaking her hands will take her out of action long enough for you to catch up?"

He squirmed. "Well, I had something more permanent in mind . . . ."

"Oh, I get it. You want me to whack her, ice her, cut her off at the knees. A little simple wetwork. No problem. You want it to look like an accident, a suicide, or random violence? For a little extra, I can even burn her house down after I do it, or make her suffer a little beforehand."

He tossed up his hands in a warding-off motion. I think it was the part about burning the house down that got to him more than the torture stuff.

"No details!" he shouted. "No details! I just want it done!"

"Funny. I thought details were kinda your stock in trade . . . ."

He didn't reply, but just grabbed the envelope off the desk and shoved it at me. I could tell by the thickness that it was something a lot more valuable than a manuscript inside. I didn't bother to count it. If it wasn't the amount I had stipulated, the job just wouldn't get done.

I turned to leave, but couldn't resist one more parting dig.

"Hey, you know what the Golden Age of Ess Eff is nowadays, right?"

The writer's face was the color of acid-free bond. I foresaw some heavy drinking after I left. He forced his attention away from his thoughts and back to me.

"No. What?"

"Dead."

NATURE, WINEBERRY IN TOOTH AND CLAW, WITH A HINT OF CLARET

A Letter From Martha

Don't we all love Nature? Of course we do!!! The delightful babbling Teal-tinted brook that enters each and every one of Martha's Secure Living Estates through its Kiwi-mossy, Slate-colored, mock-rock culvert (with electrified anti-intruder grating tastefully camouflaged as a beaver dam). The rolling, dotted-with-clover-in-shades-of-Ecru, Light Loden lawns (distribution of clover flowers guaranteed to be not fewer than five per square inch), where happy children frolic (hourly rental rates for pseudo-progeny vary depending on prevalent socioeconomic circumstances in the neighborhood of your Estate). The fragrant breezes that gently stir the hand-crocheted Driftwood-hued curtains in all the identically busy kitchens (breezes by Vornado and scheduled every quarter hour, with rotation of scents varying according to minute and season—let Martha choose for you!). What a marvelous assortment of carefully packaged wonders Nature offers the individuals lucky enough to inhabit one of Martha's exclusive Residence Enclaves!

Yet don't we all long to get away from home once in a while, however perfect our little faux-marbleized, sponge-painted, bent-twig-furniture castles might be? (And rest assured that if you've qualified to live in one of Martha's Estates, you and your home *will* be perfect!) It's that longing civilized people feel to escape to some exotic location for a change of scenery. To experience all the globe's natural wonders in their unmatched (as in "clashing") magnificence. Yes, even Martha herself gets a ladylike itch now and then to take off my neatly pressed hand-embroidered Loganberry apron, indulge in a long, elaborate manicure (my current favorite polish is Sunwashed Seashell) to get the old cuticles clean of gardening grime and stenciling splatters, tousle my girlish bangs, assemble my extensive set of matching luggage (in Heather, Flax, and Garnet), and jet off to faraway places!

But up till this very moment, if truth be told, there's been an eensy-weensy problem with traveling to the foreign places that by virtue of historic accident happen to host many of the world's natural wonders. Even the most cultivated globe-trotter often found herself hard-pressed to maintain her *sang-froid* in the face of conditions in these so-called "underdeveloped" countries. (Personally, I think it's not so much underdevelopment as plain old laziness!)

What am I referring to? I think we all know! Uncouth, non-English-speaking natives, many with visible medical problems. Dirty, disgusting WCs lacking not only monogrammed towels but even the heated racks to hold them! Acres of tiny hovels with no sense of proportion and truly dreadful color schemes (although frequently, I must admit, looking expertly "distressed"). And arrogant Customs Officials who insist on pawing through Martha's most intimate apparel and asking boorish questions about Martha's crates of simple souvenirs (such as delightful real ivory knicknacks and archaeologically irrelevant coins, vases and statues).

If you're like me (and if you're reading this, you must be!), you've often wished aloud, "If only someone would smooth out all the little annoying difficulties associated with reaching these natural marvels and make the whole travel experience as soothing and untroubling as life on one of Martha's Secure Living Estates!"

Well, fellow creative crafters and canny connoisseurs—your wishes have been heard!

Martha is proud to announce the debut of her—of my!—Designer Nature Tour Packages!!!

Thanks to the overwhelming success of Martha's various one-gal, homey, amateur enterprises (for your copy of our most recent annual report—this year a whopping 547 pages!—please send $59.95 to this magazine), Martha has found herself in a financial position to secure absolute sovereignty over many of the world's natural treasures. And as you might have guessed, Martha was not content to leave them unimproved!

First off, Martha has erected the very same reliable, feel-safe, hi-tech fencing around each and every one of her Designer Natural Wonders that you enjoy in her Residence Enclaves. No natives (except for workers and decorative units personally vetted by Martha—and you know my standards!) or uninvited, lower class daytrippers will appear to disturb your peaceful meditations on all the natural beauty surrounding you. Entrance to Martha's "preserves" (quite a change from the usual jams and jellies, ha-ha!) is made directly by chartered international flights landing on Martha's private airstrips, eliminating those tiresome brushes with Customs.

Once arrived, Martha's guests will stay in the most luxurious surroundings, furnished from the choicest little country antique stores Martha could discover. (Martha has personally troweled the nubby ceiling plaster in each room and hand-painted each floor, first applying glaze to a base of color, then removing part of the glaze with a comblike tool in alternating directions). Guests, of course, will be continuously attended by a gracious staff (gratuities and cost of staff ankle-monitors included in the total package price). Then begins the appreciation of what Martha has wrought, starting with the rather unimaginative materials Nature has provided and using the most advanced biotechnology (a big hello to all those drab geniuses at Genentech!), software (love ya, Billy G.!), and construction tools (Martha's thanks to the staff of *Victory Garden* and those brawny roughnecks at Bechtel!).

Here are just a few examples:

Martha's Serengeti

Over a million hand-preened acres where each blade of grass, waterhole, tree and animal has been coordinated to provide the most serene esthetic thrills. Wildebeests now come in a handsome mix of Umber and Fawn; lions really shine in shades of Khaki and Golden Sand; cheetahs are adorably zippy in Espresso and Salmon; and the giraffes seem to love their Pale Chamois and Cocoa patterning. The elephants presented a big challenge to Martha—so much hide, and that ghastly unkempt hair! But she thinks they look just splendid now in Tapestry Blue with accents of Indigo. Perfect sunsets were another problem, but a set of orbital filters in Russet, Hot Azalea, Waterlily and Fuschia did the trick!

Martha's Everglades

A flat watery plain of marshgrass, a few submerged reptiles, some Spanish Moss, and flocks of monotone birds. What could be more boring and less promising material to work with? Yet Martha was up to the challenge! Now lush groundcovers such as bunchberry and pachysandra alternate with elaborate topiary displays. Herons in Coral and Electric Pink share the scene with kingfishers clad in Emerald, and storks sporting their Copenhage Blue with pride. And those pesky gators? Hunter Green slashed with Cypress, of course!

Martha's Grand Canyon

While not technically a foreign site, the old Grand Canyon might very well have been, what with its hordes of Winnebago, grimy unshaven hikers (girls—those furry legs just have to go!) and flabby, Wal-Mart-outfitted families. But under Martha's supervision, the majestic grandeur of one of America's natural treasures has been restored and enhanced. Martha was holding her breath until the scaffolding came down and the painters put away their Number Zero Windsor & Newton camelhair brushes, but now I'm so happy with the results. Great swaths of Eggshell, Pueblo Brick, Vintage Rose, Maize, Olive Gray, Sea Mist, and Purple Quartz invoke dreamy afternoons spent lying in a hammock listening to the Dow Jones rise. The rental mules look charming in their Stars and Stripes motif. And the Colorado River has never worn its Classic Navy so well!

Martha's Antarctica

Let it never be said that Martha doesn't appreciate the subtlety of a basic white color scheme. (Why, in some important matters, white is my absolute *favorite* color!) But lack of imagination can masquerade as good taste, and Martha is nothing if not daringly imaginative. So that's why guests at Martha's Antarctica will discover that her little bit of the Pole has been laboriously hand-batiked! That's right: wax resists in traditional Indonesian patterns have been laid down by crawling laborers supervised by aerial spotters; then an Indigo dye was applied by specially modified crop-dusters. When the wax was removed—presto! A charmingly decorated landscape resembling the finest fabric. (Upkeep after storms necessitates a slight surcharge on this package.)

And that dour Mt. Erebus? Stripes of Mandarin Orange, Inca Jade, and Deep Lake are such fun!

Sound like your kind of vacation experience? I hope so! Remember, Martha's counting on you to buy what she's selling. And if your past behavior is any indication, you will!

And watch for Martha's Hawaii, Martha's Nova Scotia, Martha's Paris, Martha's Outback, Martha's Sahara, Martha's Siberia, and—my biggest challenge!—Martha's Mars!

NARRATIVE CONTENTS MAY HAVE
SETTLED DURING SHIPMENT

"In September, [they] will launch a line of children's books, with titles like *Bernie Drives a Tractor*, available only through Shaw's supermarkets. 'We don't pretend we're Doubleday,' said Shaw's spokesman Bernard Rogin, 'but we're serious about our private label. As good as the national brand is our mantra.'"

—Paul Davis,
"Food for Thought,"
The Providence Journal-Bulletin.

A History of Supermarket Fiction: How SF Swept the World, by Roger Barnard, Procter and Gamble, available in Mini, Personal, Regular, Large, or Jumbo Economy packages, priced variously from $0.99 upwards, depending on contents, with applicable coupons (no doubling, please), sales, promotions or discounts. Consult label directory for list of narrators. Running time approximately one oil-change, ten breakfasts, twelve showers, or one hundred applications of deodorant. Free samples in Aisle Twenty-one of most P&G-affiliated stores. External use only.

To fully appreciate this new monumental history of a phenomenon now taken utterly for granted, it is necessary to travel back in time to the period when SF was born. Deeply cognizant of this necessity, author Barnard devotes *the entire first fifteen minutes* of his long-running package to a synopsis of the historical condition of literature several decades ago. I'm sure most consumers will find it as fascinating as I did.

At that time, many seemingly independent factors were conspiring to spell the death of literature in book form as it had existed for previous centuries. None were insurmountable or had primacy, yet together they spelled doom for the printed word.

The populace at large, thanks to failed schooling, was becoming less capable of reading. Shortened attention spans, fostered by various twentieth-century stimuli, disinclined people to sit quietly for long stretches with a book.

Dinosaur-sized book-retailers squashed their small, individualistic competitors, inadvertently breeding a uniformity of product and atmosphere repellant to all but the most dim-witted customer, who lacked true allegiance to reading, being attracted to these outlets mostly by hype.

The bottom-line, blockbuster mentality of the megacorporations which controlled publishers created a geriatric cadre of "proven" yet rapidly staling brand-name writers, supplemented by the occasional market-tested "fresh voice."

The environmental impact of old-fashioned book production—with its insatiable demand for paper and its freight costs—could no longer be ignored.

Finally, glossy new computer technologies—the Worldwide Web, CD-ROM multimedia, hypertext—began to lure the more adventurous readers and writers away from ink on paper.

Unseen by most people at the time, as Barnard deftly illustrates, was another whole set of factors which would lead to the invention of SF.

One of the few growth areas in publishing at the time was that of audio books. It was obvious that an increasingly busy citizenry preferred to read to while on the go. A diminishing resistance to corporate sponsorship of recreational events—rock concerts, sporting events, celebrity trials—was a second converging trend. One subtle version of this was "product placement," a tactic which inserted brand-name icons into prominent roles in movies and books, stadiums and courtrooms. Lastly, the marketing of books in odd and unexpected places—supermarkets, airports, discount chains, salvage stores—began to accustom people to impulse purchases of reading material in unfamiliar settings.

But the final catalyst for the formation of SF was—inevitably, as with so many other modern advances—a new technology. As miniaturization crossed the barrier into nano-structures, it became possible to create what came to be known as CDM: Cheap Dimensionless Memory, a spray-application, self-patterning circuitry.

The uses for CDM were manifold and practically inexhaustible. But the one that concerns Barnard here was CDM's use in packaging.

Every product under the sun became encased in interactive, audio-visual spray-on labeling. So great was the capacity of CDM for information that manufacturers soon ran out of advertising content! It was only natural, then, for them to begin to attempt to lure consumers to their products by including samples of interesting material drawn from other sources. Arrangements with cash-hungry book publishers, record companies and movie studios were soon cemented.

These latter two groups never really moved beyond their initial relationship of providing snippets of their licensed entertainment content for use by novelty-seeking manufacturers striving to catch the eyes of consumers by standing out on the crowded, noisy, flashy shelves. The distribution channels and usage-patterns for music and cinema were already digital, efficient, and well-established. But with book-publishers, it was a different matter entirely. This new medium offered everything they had previously been lacking.

To fill the intelligent label of every box, can, dispenser, jar, carton, tray, bag, tin, sack, cellopack, pump and aerosol with an entire novel, collection of short stories, or non-fiction work (all of them abridged for modern tastes, of course) was only a small jump in both cost and intention.

Within two years of the release of CDM, books were dead, except as a rare handicraft.

But Supermarket Fiction had been born in their place.

Now, for the first time, instead of the consumer reading the cereal box at breakfast, the box could read to the consumer!

Although much continued as before (authors still received their advances from the combined operating capital of the victuallers and retailers, charged against their penny-per-unit-sold royalties; *Consumer Reports* simply added literary critics to their staff), the whole world of literature was changed. A congruence between certain types of literature and the products which they adorned led to the creation of entirely new forms of story-telling.

Cereal serials became the prime vehicle for juvenile literature, ensuring the rapt attention of formerly rambunctious youngsters in the morning and after school. Romances on shampoo bottles became truly steamy, with their climaxes hosted separately—and appropriately—on either kleenex boxes or champagne bottles. (Pornography, of course, eagerly made the transition to the new era, sprayed onto a host of obscenely crafted or pervertedly misused innocent objects.) Diet guides were incorporated into healthy products—a case of preaching to the converted, as Barnard notes. Minimalist novels were popular on springwater bottles, while the maximalists occupied extra-thick, extra-rich comestibles. Mysteries found a home on any poisonous cleaning product, and science fiction eked out a niche on candybars and soda bottles, of all places.

Perhaps the most curious incident which Barnard cleverly recounts is the shortlived fad of "sixpack sensationalism." Featured exclusively on malt liquor cans, these fictions were formulaic in the extreme. Starting out on the can numbered "one," they were intended to be consumed by lonely individuals at a single boozy sitting. The generic plot—such as it was—usually involved elaborate revenges enacted upon all those (boss, girlfriend, politician) who had slighted or offended the protagonist.

But all these later moments of Barnard's opus—the names of best-selling writers and forgotten cult authors and the products they were inextricably associated with; the trends and scandals (who can forget the botulism incident that ruined many a career?); the legislation that finally put an expiration date on SF, so that landfills were not full of ghostly voices—will be mostly familiar to the modern consumer, and I must confess that I found my attention wandering, despite a profusion of soundbites and filmclips. Ultimately, it is in its presentation of historical context that this product will most appeal to the consumer.

I myself consumed Barnard's book in its drain-cleaner package, and it performed quite efficiently in unclogging my plumbing.

Be a responsible consumer: please dispose of this used review properly.

THE ONLY THING WORSE THAN YET ONE MORE BAD TRILOGY

Reprinted with permission from *The Journal of Popular Culture*, Vol. XXXI No. 9, September 1998.

"What Killed Science Fiction?"

by

Dr. Josiah Carberry, Professor of English,

Brown University at San Diego

ABSTRACT: The nearly extinct publishing and cinematic genre once known as "science fiction" was born in 1926 and reached its pinnacle in the year 1966, after which a series of unforeseeable catastrophes, both literary and extra-literary, led to its steep decline and virtual disappearance.

Hard as it is to believe today, in our current media landscape devoid of works of fantastic speculation, the worlds of literature and cinema once bade fair to be dominated by a now-forgotten yet once flourishing brand of entertainment called "science fiction." A few surviving aficionados may very well fondly recall favorite works of "SF," as it was familiarly called, while hoarding their disintegrating first editions, flaking pulp magazines and deteriorating film prints, but recent surveys reveal that—far from recognizing the peculiar reading protocols and out-of-print landmarks of the genre—those born since 1966 are mainly ignorant of the very notion of SF. This severing of a generational link, in fact, represents one of the main hurdles to the resurrection of the genre.

Perhaps a very brief survey of SF's glory days is in order first, before examining the factors in its quick and infamous expungement.

When a Welsh immigrant entrepreneur named Hugh Gormsbeck launched his magazine *Amazing Stories* in April of 1926, he gathered a disparate body of stories and variety of writers under the rubric "scientifiction," a term later modified to "science fiction." Codifying the rules and playing field of the SF game, so to speak, Gormsbeck paved the way for sustained growth, popularity and reader-writer camaraderie. For the next forty years, in various venues, the genre acquired an increasing complexity and sophistication, laying down benchmarks of excellence. Moving out of the magazines and into hardcover and paperback format (circa 1950-1960), SF began to produce genuine mature masterpieces, such as Theodore Sturgeon's *Other Than Human* (1953), Alfred Bester's *The Galaxy My Destination* (1957), and Henry Kuttner's *The Nova Mob* (1961).

Concurrently, SF began to infiltrate other media. Radio dramas like *The Shadow Lady* and *Dimension X Squared* thrilled millions. Daily newspaper strips such as *Flashman Gordon*, *Buckminster Rogers* and *The Black Flame* vied with bound monthly comics such as *Captain Marvelous*, *Kimball Kinnison*, *Galactic Lensman* and *Superiorman* for the attention of the average, slightly less literate reader. Hollywood weighed in with a variety of entries, ranging from the wonderful—*Things that*

Might Come (1936) and *Destination Orbit* (1950)—to the execrable: *I Married a Martian* (1949) and the anticipated but disappointing *Eye in the Sky* (1958).

The end half of the 1950s was a particularly exciting time for SF, as the Red Chinese launch of the first artificial satellite birthed a wider interest in the genre, reflected in dozens of new magazines, paperback publishers and television dramas (eg., *Orson Welles's The Twilight Zone*).

With the dawn of the 1960s, SF appeared primed to explode as a true mass pop phenomenon. "Cult" classics such as Robert Heinlein's *Drifter in a Strange Land* (1961), Thomas Pynchon's *Vril Revival* (1963) and Frank Herbert's *Dunebuggy* (1965) were wholeheartedly embraced by both older and younger readers, flirting with the lower ranks of best-seller lists. (The same happy fate was predicted by knowledgeable insiders for a triumvirate-in-progress of British fantasy novels—fantasy having been long allied with its more scientifically respectable cousin—tentatively called *The Lord of the Rings*. But the untimely death of author J. R. R. Tolkien in 1955, after the publication of only a single volume, precluded such a fulfillment.) Additionally, a vigorous new generation of writers employing sophisticated literary approaches (cf., H. Ellison, S. Delany, R. Zelazny, B. Malzberg, U. Le Guin), had begun to make themselves known.

All looked bright then for SF as the decade reached its midway point. But unbeknownst to all, doom for the field in all its manifestations was just around the corner.

And the name of SF's Nemesis was *Star Trek*.

September 8, 1966, 8:30 PM EDT. Seldom before has it been possible to nail down so exactly a historical turning point. But in retrospect it was certainly this moment that marked the beginning of the end for SF.

A Hollywood stalwart best known for his aforementioned

respectable *Destination Orbit*, George Pal had moved to the medium of television after the large-scale failure of his final theatrical release, the unintentionally hilarious *A Clockwork Orange* in 1965. Conceiving of the imaginary voyage of a 23rd century interstellar cruiser named *The Ambition* as a clever device for using up a quantity of pre-existing stagesets, Pal proceeded to exercise complete (un)creative control over every element of the new show.

Pal's first and biggest mistake was in the casting of his starship crew. Nick Adams played the histrionic Captain Tim Dirk as a third-rate James Dean. The alien officer named Strock was woodenly embodied by a narcotic-addled Bela Lugosi. Ship's Doctor "Bones" LeRoi was laughably portrayed by Larry Storch. Engineer "Spotty" (so named for his freckles) found an aging Mickey Rooney far from his prime. And as for the female element—well, an emaciated young model named Twiggy (as Yeoman Sand) and a seedily voluptuous Jayne Mansfield (as Communications Lieutenant Impura) eye-poppingly contrasted each other like the ship's ludicrous "neutron-antineutron" drive. Lesser parts were filled with similar wince-provoking choices.

Pal's next major mistake was to insist on writing all the first season's scripts himself, as a money-saving measure. Ransacking every cliché of SF, as well as plenty from Westerns, WWII films and a dozen other genres, Pal's scripts have to qualify in this critic's opinion as some of the worst writing ever to appear on television.

Given these two major strikes against it, the other factors militating against *Star Trek* 's success—primitive special effects, ridiculous villains, costumes more attuned to Oz than outer space, a theme song at once maddening and inexpellable from the mind—were mere icing on the cake of disaster.

Nearly every TV viewer of the requisite age can recall where he or she was when that infamous first episode of *Star Trek* (an ultra-confusing time-travel farrago entitled "When Did We Go From Then?") aired. Jumping the gun on the Fall season, insuring that its only competition was reruns, the opening minutes of the deadly drama-bomb found millions tuned in. As jaws dropped across the nation and viewers phoned others, the attention-wave surged. By the time the West Coast was treated to the debut of the new series, it had attained the highest ratings of any television show ever presented. This was not, however, a positive sign.

The next day found ridicule unanimous and at a high scathing pitch. Newspaper columnists and editorialists had a heyday with the spectacular failure, as did stage and TV comedians. (Johnny Carson, for instance, devoted his entire opening monologue of September 9 to the episode.) The following week, a special edition of *TV Guide* was given over to an abrasive assessment of *Star Trek* and televised SF in general.

Unwisely, NBC, wowed by Pal's lingering prestige, had already contracted for a full 39 episodes of the new series. And rather than back out or seek help, Pal held the network to the letter of the agreement and bulled ahead in the face of ignominy.

Week after week, the viewing public was treated to one stinker of an episode after another. Numerous tag-lines from the series ("He's—he's deceased, Tim!"; "I'm a twenty-third-century physician, dammit, not a Christian Scientist!"; "Bleep me up, Spotty."; "Highly non-axiomatic, Captain.") became the ironic stuff of everyday conversation. And then the inevitable happened.

Written SF became tarred with the same brush.

Latent prejudice against "all that *Buckminster Rogers* stuff," never far from the surface of public consciousness, resurged. To be seen reading an SF book in public became tantamount to wearing a "kick-me" sign on one's back. Whatever literary cachet SF had laboriously earned evaporated overnight.

As sales of book and magazine SF plummeted, fair-weather

readers and writers began to desert SF in droves. Bankrupt-
cies—both personal and corporate—proliferated. Movies in
mid-production were written off. The field was caught in a down-
ward spiral wherein failure begat further failure.

Finally, by 1968, long after *Star Trek*'s demise—brought on by
a determined letter-writing campaign organized by true SF
fans—yet while memory of its awfulness was still fresh, only a
hard core of readers and authors remained, a shabby remnant of a
once vital legacy.

There is little doubt that SF had the capacity, literarily, to
recover from even a tragedy of this dimension. The field had
always been prey to boom-and-bust cycles, and had always
bounced back before. It took a set of truly unique, large magnitude, extra-literary cataclysms to finally kill the whole genre,
testament to its strength and its inherent appeal to human nature.

First and foremost came the Apollo 11 disaster in 1969. When
the Lunar Excursion Module failed to depart the Moon's surface,
the whole world was treated to a protracted tragedy that soured
any technological optimism left intact by the Vietnam War and
the growing awareness of mankind's pollution of his environment
(cf., The Earth Day Riots, 1972-75). The perversion of computer
technology for the maintenance of "Big Nurse" domestic
counterintelligence databases by the FBI under the third Nixon
Administration, and the subsequent passage of laws limiting the
manufacture of computers to low-capability machines, further
diminished the allure of a future dependent on sophisticated
machines. A final nail in the coffin of SF was the uncontrolled
meltdown at Three Mile Island in 1979. Rightly or wrongly, SF
had long been equated with nuclear power in the public's percep-
tion, and this seaboard-contaminating catastrophe made SF
synonymous with mass carnage.

One final stroke of bad luck appeared in the shape of an underground sixteen-millimeter film that had the misfortune to gain notoriety shortly after TMI. Arising out of the San Francisco pornography scene, *Close Encounters of the Star Wars Kind* was an XXX-rated venture by the then-unknown directing duo of Lucas and Spielberg, starring equally unknown actors and actresses (Charlie Sheen, Rob Lowe, Hugh Grant, Louise Ciccone, Janet Jackson, Hilary Rodham, Sly Stallone, Arnie Schwarzenegger, et al). In this repugnant farce, representatives of a decadent interstellar empire made Earth their sex playground, only to meet with resistance from naked rebels who turned out to be more lickerish and reprehensible than the tyrants. After the Supreme Court finished with Lucas and Spielberg, no sane person would approach SF with a ten-light-year pole.

Nearly two decades after these various debacles, SF remains a form practiced only by a handful of eccentric amateurs, appearing in mimeographed samizdat publications limited to a circulation of a few hundred maximum (at least in the U.S.; the situation in the U.K. has a complex history of its own. See this author's previously published "The Media Empire of Moorcock and Ballard, Ltd.: Can Murdoch Offer Any Competition?"). That a once-proud literary tradition should have ended up in this state seems inevitable, given the chain of circumstances herein adduced. Yet just for a moment, we might ponder—if it is not venturing too far into a heretical old SF trope known as "the alternate world"—how things might have been different.

YOU WON'T TAKE ME ALIVE!

(WITHOUT AT LEAST TEN PERCENT OF THE BOX OFFICE GROSS)

"A romance writer's two-year flight from justice ended in a style befitting one of her novels this week, when law enforcement agents knocked on her door at a low-budget motel just outside Los Angeles. Rather than surrender without a struggle, Barbara Joslyn stabbed herself in the chest.

"As Federal agents closed in on her . . . Ms. Joslyn barricaded herself in her cramped motel room and shouted that she 'would not be taken alive.'"

—*The New York Times*, May 5, 1997.

"Let me through, I'm from the SFWA."

As soon as the hard-eyed, big-shouldered young cop—standing intimidatingly with folded arms on the crowd side of the yellow police tape—heard those words, he gave me a deferential nod, lifted up the plastic ribbon, and ushered me under. Even this rookie plainly knew who had saved the asses of his buddies in countless similar situations across the country. I was hoping his superiors did too.

Once on the far side of the barrier, walkie-talkies crackling practically in my ears, I found myself in the middle of a barely controlled mob. Plainclothes detectives, armored SWAT snipers, squat HAZMAT robots, reporters, priests, psychologists, editors, agents, publicists, film directors—the usual mix of do-gooders and vultures you always find at this kind of tragic scene. Using perceptions and intuitions honed from dozens of equally chaotic past confrontations, I zeroed in on the guy most likely in charge: a smartly coiffed City Hall type wearing a suit that probably cost as much as I made in a month.

I waved my open wallet, credentials showing, under his nose. "Dorsey Kazin, SFWA Griefcom. Whadda we got here?"

Maybe it was the sight of the understatedly famous silver rocket next to my name in gold-leaf, maybe it was the calm assurance in my voice. Maybe it was the chance to dump this whole mess in somebody else's lap. Whatever the case, the guy's stern but nervous exterior collapsed faster than the Wizards of the Coast publishing program, and he spilled his fears into my tender ear like a kid telling his mother what he did that day in second grade.

"Am I glad to see *you*, Mr. Kazin! Ruben Spinelost here, assistant to Mayor Whiffle." I tendered the guy a perfunctory shake. "Afraid I'm in a little over my head in this dustup. Never dealt with one of these new-fangled hostage-based contract negotiations before."

I cut him off. "Get used to it, Rube, this new tactic's all the rage—and I do mean rage. Brief me quick now, before our gun-toting Gernsbackian decides to lay a few of his more violent cards on the table—or maybe his hostage's ear."

Spinelost consulted a paper. "Well, the writer involved is someone named Theodolite Sangborn. He's published—"

"Not necessary. I got everything I need to know about him along those lines out of his SFWA file. I'm an instant Sangborn expert on his whole life, from his formative childhood traumas down to how he deducted his mistress's hotel room as a convention expense on his last 1040. Not to mention his entire miserable midlist genre career. What I need from you is some idea of the kinds of demands he's making, and who he's got in there."

Spinelost used his cheat notes to answer the last question first. "He's holding his editor, a woman named Sherri Drysack. Ex-editor, I should say. Apparently she made the mistake of deciding to pay him a visit in person to offer her condolences—"

"On Bollix Books dropping Sangborn like a squirming roach when his last novel stiffed. What a damn fool! Didn't she know her presence would be like holding a lit match to a powder-keg?"

"Obviously not. I believe she's, um, fresh out of Bennington. Fine school, of course, but . . . . Anyway, now Sangborn is using the leverage represented by her peril to demand a new three-book, seven-figure contract, with twenty percent royalties and assured softcover editions. Oh yes, he also wants Leapsgerb Studios to option his last book for a cool million."

I cursed eloquently. "These Heinlein wannabes with their delusions of canonical stature make me sick. They should consider themselves lucky to get a Whelan cover, like Sangborn did on his *Interstellar UPS*, never mind options and kick-in clauses. And it always falls to Griefcom to hand them a reality check."

Spinelost coughed politely. "Speaking of checks . . . ."

"Don't get your boxers in a twist over nothing, Rube. Assuming I can bring this whole debacle to a safe conclusion mutually agreeable to all parties, the city will be fully compensated for any extraordinary expenses—as long as no charges are pressed against our author, of course. Whichever publisher picks up Sangborn will cut a check to the municipality tomorrow—and probably make a nice little donation to the FOP. It's standard industry practice now. They just write it off as a line item on the author's royalty statement."

"Very good. Still, I rather miss the old days—"

Just then a bullet zipped by over our heads like something out of Harrison's *Deathworld*. Spinelost and the other suits fell to the ground, while the rest of us hardened campaigners just groaned cynically at the requisite touch of melodrama. From the innocent looking suburban house where Sangborn was holed up came a shouted threat.

"Hey, people! I want to see some goddamn action here, maybe a cover proof or a multi-city book-tour itinerary, and fast! Or Little Miss Blue Pencil is going to have a new buttonhole in her Donna Karan jacket!"

I patted my coat pocket to make sure my cell-phone and palmtop with speed-dialer attachment were there, then grabbed a loud-hailer from a gape-mouthed social-worker.

"Sangborn! It's Dorsey Kazin! I'm coming in for some face time. Don't shoot anymore, or these guys will put you on the remainder table faster than you can say Robert James Waller!"

Silence for a moment, before Sangborn answered. "Okay, Kazin, I trust you. But no one else!"

Handing back the hailer, I marched forward, the mob of officials falling aside respectfully to let me through.

The time spent crossing that inevitable empty and unnaturally silent street to the writer's house is always unnerving, no matter how often you've done it before. Sure, you figure they're not gonna do anything crazy at this point, with a solution to their problems so close, but you never know for certain. I still broke out into a sweat when I remembered how my onetime partner, Alyx Jorus, had gone permanently out of print, drilled through the heart as she approached a writer involved in that hellacious work-for-hire *Star Wars* novelizations snafu. There are some cases I wouldn't touch with a ten-light-year pole.

As I crossed to Sangborn's bungalow, I tried to reassure myself by thinking of all my peers who were even now successfully and routinely doing my same job across this nation of mad-dog, Cagney-imitating writers. Those various Griefcom professionals from all the sister and brother organizations to SFWA—the guilds of the mystery writers, the romance writers, the western writers, the horror writers, the screen- and teleplay writers, even PEN—they all stood invisibly shoulder-to-shoulder with me as I strode up to Sangborn's door. So bolstering was my ghostly crew that when I got there I was able to knock with confidence, call my name, then enter.

A disheveled Sangborn sat on the couch in the darkened living-room, semi-automatic rifle loosely gripped. (SFWA sold armaments through the *Forum* now, and had coffers overflowing with cash.) His hair was as messy as a sheaf of manuscript pages dropped in a wastebasket, his face was stubbled, and he was sweating like one of Fabio's fans getting an autograph. Perched insouciantly on the edge of a coffee-table, Sherri Drysack was, by contrast, cool as one of Anne Rice's vampires. Tucking long hair behind one perfect ear, she said, "It's about time you got here, Kazin. My Dayrunner's showing two appointments and a meeting later this afternoon, and I'm like, *hello*, can we get these negotiations moving, or are we still in like the *Stone Age?*"

"Sangborn didn't kidnap you, did he? You're in collusion with him."

"Duh, Earth to Kazin, Earth to Kazin: wake up and smell your double-latte! Of course I'm in this with him. I was planning to jump ship at Bollix all the while, and Sangborn is my meal-ticket out."

I looked at the pitiful hulk on the couch. Shoeless, his hands shaking, his eyes redder than Mars before Robinson got his mitts on it, he looked the most unlikely prospect for success I had ever seen.

"You must have an ace in the hole. What is it?"

Drysack whipped a manuscript out of her briefcase. "Thought

you'd never ask, Kazin. Here's three chapters and an outline for an open-ended series that's going to take the SF world by storm. Sangborn's going to make Niven and Pournelle look like Hall and Flint after this."

I took the handful of papers from her and started reading. After a while, I let out a genuine whistle of astonishment.

"Looks like the real thing. A postmodern space opera based on an amalgam of *Wuthering Heights* and *Jane Eyre*. Didn't think the old hack had it in him."

Drysack moved to sit beside her property, draping a possessive arm around his shoulder. She slitheringly crossed one Victoria's Secret-sheathed leg over the other. Sangborn let out a plaintive mew like a Hurkle. "Oh, Theo's far from washed up. He has a lot of good years left in him. All he needs is some tender loving care from the right editor—and of course some fat residuals on any TV series based on the Bronteverse."

I dug out my cell phone and palmtop and summoned up a list of publishers in a screen window. Having picked a likely candidate, I mated the speed-dialer and phone. While the connection was being made, I moved to one of the windows, pulled the drapes aside, and gave the all-clear sign to the cops. As they began to move in, I saw one of the figures in the crowd answer his own ringing cell-phone.

"Loomis Harmonica here. Is that you, Kazin?"

"Damn right. And I'm sitting on the hottest concept to hit SF since Asimov read Gibbon. Is the publisher of Mary Kay Books interested?"

"You bet your bottom Imperial credit we are. Put Drysack right on."

I passed the phone to the eager lady editor, then walked across the room to a shelf of liquor bottles. I poured myself an undiluted vodka, and knocked half of it back.

Hell of a way to earn a paycheck. But when the Muse calls, you gotta answer.

Especially if she's packing heat.

NEXT BIG THING

Imaginary Realist: The Life of Timothy Eugene *The Birth of Fabulaic Surmimesis.* Written by Milton Sharp, uploaded by HarperOptics, 2025. Download price: E$35.00. Size: 2 meg (xvii + 458 pages, plus AV attachments). Download time: approximately two minutes through most ISPs.

The story of *sui generis* author Timothy Eugene and of the strange cult of readers and writers his short life and four novels inspired continues to fascinate. Although Eugene's work, subject of extensive criticism, has been continuously available ever since he first leapt into the world's literary consciousness, the author himself has been a figure shrouded in shadows and rumors. Not so any longer. Milton Sharp's superb biography of Eugene—based on five years of ground-breaking research and indefatigable interviews with the few people ever to meet the hermit-author—brings the "Psychopomp of Poultney" out from obscurity for all time. Also featuring Sharp's perceptive exegesis of Eugene's fictions, this volume seems destined to drive Eugene's literary cachet higher than ever. And although much of the factual mystery surrounding Eugene is hereby removed, the end result of this biography is paradoxically to foster a deepening of the aura of inscrutability and wonder attending this nonpareil and his novels.

Sharp opens his story in 1985. In this year was born to Eudora and Sinclair Eugene a son they christened Timothy. The elder Eugenes were unlikely candidates to conceive and raise a literary genius. Subsisting on odd jobs and food stamps in Rutland, Vermont, in the northeastern U.S., they exhibited no affinity for literature or learning. In this respect, it was a cruel but necessary act of Fate which removed them from Timothy's life, in a car accident when he was only five years old and safely at home with a babysitter.

Now the scene switches. Eugene's closest surviving relative was a widowed great-aunt, Frances Hooghly, resident of nearby Poultney, Vermont, and proprietor of a struggling turkey farm. She assumed custodianship of toddler Timothy, and full responsibility for his upbringing. Thus was Eugene's future course determined.

The Hooghly turkey farm was a rural enclave that could have survived from a previous century or millennium. Miles from its nearest neighbor or commercial district, lacking a telephone or electricity, heated by wood and lit by kerosene, a battery-powered radio its only media connection, Eugene's new home—in fact, the only residence he would know during his entire lifetime—was to be instrumental in shaping his peculiar perceptions and mind.

Beset by endless grueling work simply to survive, Frances Hooghly—not unkind or unaffectionate, but supremely practical—quickly determined that little Timothy would have to assume his share of the endless chores. As for his education, it would have to be on a home-tutoring basis, as the overlong bus ride to and from the far away school could not be accommodated.

This prospect accorded well, it eventuated, with Eugene's natural bent. For the boy proved, from an early age, to be utterly agoraphobic, gripped by a neurosis that only worsened with age.

During his teens for instance, on his worst days, even the usual trip from the security of his bedroom to the turkey sheds would prove impossible. Leashed to the farmhouse and immediate yards by his mental disability, Timothy Eugene lived an isolated life practically unimaginable by the wired and networked citizens of the late twentieth and early twenty-first century.

Luckily for Timothy Eugene and for his future readers, the Hooghly homestead offered one major educational resource—and one further connection with the world. Years before Eugene's birth, in a barter transaction, Frances Hooghly had accepted a small library of old fiction consisting of moldering uniform editions of several Victorian novelists. Lining the farmhouse walls were the complete Dickens, the complete Trollope, the complete Thackeray, the complete Balzac (in translation), and several others. These giants of realism were to be Eugene's tutors. He read and re-read them endlessly from approximately age ten until the end of his short life. They inspired him to believe that one career choice—other than turkey-raising—remained open to him: that of author.

At age nineteen, in the year 2004 when his beloved great-aunt died of untreated pneumonia (contracted while trying to rescue a pair of prize turkeys from drowning), Eugene availed himself of his one link to the outside world: a bent-armed antique Underwood typewriter, and the weekly arrival of the RFD postman.

At this point in his study, Sharp takes a small detour to survey other famous reclusive artists, and to illustrate what made Timothy Eugene so unique. Giving precise thumbnail sketches of such figures as H. P. Lovecraft, Thomas Pynchon, Robert E. Howard, Marcel Proust, Henry Darger and Joseph Cornell, Sharp illustrates one salient fact about all such creators: no matter how eccentric and sequestered they became in later life, they all had fairly normal childhoods marked by extensive immersion in and acclimation to society. Such was not the case with Eugene. Seeing only a few tradesmen as they delivered necessities, never venturing from the farm property, Eugene was a modern "boy raised by wolves." Or in this case, "raised by dead authors." Sharp compares him to the perhaps apocryphal tradition found in some South American tribes: deliberate isolation of a child in a cave from birth, to foster an otherworldly connection that would turn the subject into a shaman.

Timothy Eugene became a modern version of that shaman.

Now bereft of kin, possessing a sharp and active mind, desirous of bettering his lot and expressing himself, young Eugene sat down at his typewriter and composed his first story. Like James Joyce's early, comparatively staid short fiction, it was only partially indicative of what was to come.

"Hope Wears Feathers" (there was of course a volume of Emily Dickinson in the Hooghly cache) was a novella told from the point of view of an aspiring and bright thirteen-year-old boy who resided on an isolated turkey farm with a single adult guardian. The farm's daily routines, the rich essence of such an archaic rural life, as well as the boy's dreams and ambitions, were rendered with heartbreaking vividness—as how could they not be? Upon completion, Timothy Eugene sent the piece out to *Green Mountains Review* in Rutland, where it was promptly snapped up.

Against all odds, publication instantly brought Eugene many things: comparisons to Faulkner and Steinbeck, fan mail, and a number of solicitations from Manhattan publishers. If he could conceive of a novel, it seemed, he could easily sell it.

But there was the rub. What was Eugene to write about? He had exhausted his stock of first-hand experience with the one novella. At the same time, his worship of the great Victorian realists dictated that he should embark upon a major project of large scope, a vast and intricate tale that would attempt to encompass truthfully all of modern society, and range across all socioeconomic scales.

But what did he know of the modern world? Only what he could filter from the few radio programs and occasional fish-smelling newspapers that entered his house. For instance: he knew from observing their passage overhead that airplanes existed; but he had never seen one up close, nor any supporting infrastructure like airports. "Computers" he had heard of, some sort of mechanical brains; but how a person interacted with one was blank to him. Cars he had seen also, but never a "gas station." Likewise, the most common customs and manners and recreations were utterly alien to him; what, for example, was "dancing" or "a basketball playoff" or "a press conference" or "a Chief Executive Officer"? And so on and so on, through the catalog of early twenty-first-century existence.

Yet Eugene had held for a long time now—in his active imagination—nascent pictures of all these myriad objects and activities. His confidence and enthusiasm led him to believe that he had a firmer grasp of things than he actually did. And the more he contemplated life outside the Hooghly turkey farm, the more he convinced himself that he had some real conception of what it entailed.

Here in his narrative, Sharp pauses for a bit of amateur psychoanalysis. Bravely, he tackles the essential question any reader of Timothy Eugene's four astonishing novels must ask: did Eugene really believe he was depicting reality, or was he simply constructing what he knew to be castles in the air, semi-standard "fantasy" or "magical realist" novels? After much weighing of each view, Sharp descends firmly on the side of the first proposal. Maintaining that Eugene worshipped his Victorian role-models to such a degree that he could never betray them by "falsifying reality," Sharp insists that the young writer was scrupulous in depicting only what he honestly believed to be the "real world." A further proof is the internal consistency among the four books. Once having established a "fact," Eugene never retreated from it or contradicted it.

In a fever of creativity, Eugene quickly drafted a proposal for a novel. He accepted the first offer for it (from a perhaps overeager publisher, St. Merton's, who soon had cause to regret their haste), although he could have held out for more. Ordering a bottle of ink to replenish his obsolete ribbon, along with reams of paper, the Psychopomp of Poultney fell to writing. Thus was born fabulaic surmimesis: the unwavering depiction of a reality inhabited by only a single citizen.

Anyone who has ever stumbled upon *The Casserole of the Line-backer* (2007) without forewarning of its unique nature can surely recall the heady sense of disorientation and cognitive estrangement the book engenders. Here is a tale that plainly fancies itself to be the apex of realism, yet which depicts a world as strange as, say, Peake's *Gormenghast* (1950) or Ishmael Reed's *The Free-Lance Pallbearers* (1967). Yet nowhere is there a lick of irony or deliberate straining for effect to be found.

The main thread of the novel concerns the story of Lyle Rosebower, restaurateur and professional athlete for the Chicago Cowslips, his wife, Becky, a Greyhound Bus Lines stewardess, and their quest for happiness in the face of the machinations of the villainous radio-talkshow host, Sternman Partch. Secondary characters number in the dozens, and the subplots are manifold, as with Dickens. Particularly engrossing is the plight of young Goodly Ament, a teenage cheerleader who falls under the sway of a travelling Satanist preacher and clove-cigarette smuggler, Lance Allson.

On the simple level of story-telling, Eugene proved that he had a decent grasp of cause and effect, and of such common emotions as love, hate, and avarice, much like any other competent writer. But in the staging of action and in the details of "everyday" life provided, such an abundance of oddness exists as to render the novel utterly otherworldly. Even those aspects of reality which Eugene intuited almost correctly are off by a disturbing hair. Just the costumes of the characters—Lyle's ruffled collars and velvet jodphurs when hosting at his dining establishment, and his spike-topped playing helmet; Becky's harem pants and Partch's swallowtail coat—are enough to conjure a scene out of, say, Jack Vance. Add to this elaborate word-pictures of the absurdly designed appliances and vehicles, buildings and possessions populating Eugene's world, and the final effect is one of opening a window onto a universe that is simultaneously ours and not ours. Yet it must be stressed that not one event incompatible with scientific fact or the tenets of realism is ever introduced.

The reaction to Eugene's first book ranged from utter bewilderment and castigation to indifference to enthusiastic adoption by the avant-garde, who viewed Eugene with complete misunderstanding as a fellow literary transgressor. His publishers—who had almost balked when they received the manuscript—decided to take another chance on Eugene. Thus in 2011 was released *Monster of Wall Street*.

Buoyed by what he chose to interpret as his total success, Eugene had resolved to make his next book even more dramatic and encompassing. It is certainly all of that. The "exposure" of the decadent lifestyle and unethical business practices of financier Scaramouche Spitnail—a man whose every whim affects millions, and whose fortune was rooted in speculating on turkey futures—resulted in a work most closely approximated by a fusion of Philip K. Dick and David Lindsay.

Widespread hostility greeted this sophomore effort, causing St. Merton's to drop Eugene. Undaunted, he began his next book, casting about for a smaller press to print it. *Explosion at the Fireworks Factory* (2014) eventually found a home with Four

Wallabys Press. This tale of a small town—seen through the eyes of the Pickwickian Wittold family, whose lives centered around the titular factory—earned Eugene his most famous critical quote, from *The New York Times* critic Mistakeo Kakophany: "Reads like a mix of Robert Coover and Doctor Seuss."

Eugene's growing bafflement and hurt at the incomprehension of readers and reviewers was evident in his fourth and final novel, *Starmaker Machinery* (2020), a bildungsroman about a novelist named Muchly Small. (The only music station available on Eugene's receiver was devoted to oldies, and Eugene was particularly fond of Joni Mitchell, a kindred soul.) Despite—or perhaps because of—this new wounding, Eugene produced what many have come to regard as his masterpiece. An aging yet perceptive John Crowley, just finishing up his own quartet begun with *Aegypt* (1987), lamented that his book had the misfortune to be released in the same year as Eugene's. The critical consensus, however, was much less kind.

At age 35, Eugene paused to reconsider his whole esthetic goal and method. Fancying himself the reincarnation of George Eliot or Wilkie Collins, he instead found himself reviled as that most detestable thing, a "fantasist." As Sharp speculates, he must have finally experienced a critical mass of doubts about his self-developed *weltanschauung*. And so he made his fatal mistake. He decided to broaden his intimacy with the world. Purchasing a computer, subscribing to a dozen online newspapers, bringing a surround-sound HDTV monitor and a satellite dish into his newly electrified hovel, Eugene made contact at last with the world around him.

A Good Samaritan postman found Eugene shortly thereafter, empty of life in front of his new audiovideo digital connections. Cause of death was indeterminate. Like one of his feathered charges, Eugene had simply "drowned" in the flood of distasteful information so at odds with his own precious mental constructs.

As Sharp wistfully concludes: "We may only hope that the afterlife includes the whimsical unborn world Timothy Eugene believed in, and that even now he rides those famous caterpillar-jointed trolley cars to the crest of his lurid San Francisco, there to gaze upon Eskimotown and a Golden Gate Bridge that connects the city directly to Seattle, where all the coffee-shops feature miniature braziers on each table, and the women are all beautiful in their dirndls and wimples."

ESCAPIST VELOCITY

Reprinted from *Cahiers du Multimedia*, published in the colony of Nouveau Marais on Baudrillard IV, from the issue dated (local system calendar) 15/63/2159, by kind permission of the publishers, Vian & Ubu.

ESCAPIST ENTERTAINMENTS
THE WHORES OF FANTASY VERSUS
THE VIRGIN OF REALISM
by
Didier Bonlatté

Never in the glorious history of narratological mankind has the art of storytelling through moving pictures and sound—2D or 3D pictures, simple external stereo or full cerebro-stim sound, these combinations captured on any substrate from optical-weaves to quantum-freckles—exhibited a more dire and parlous disease! I am referring, of course, to the unavoidable clichéd fantasy content of nearly ninety percent of the professionally released entertainments loosed on the tasteless, gawping public in recent months.

In these objectionable, pandering extravaganzas, all sensation and no thought, directors turn their backs on the admittedly grim and unexciting realities of today, instead substituting meretricious and gaudy fantasies dredged from the warped imaginations of money-hungry scriptwriters mining outdated works from the scrapheap of history. (Never have pointless remakes been so prevalent!) AI-generated special effects become the new gods, replacing human finesse with the oldfashioned digital paintbox. Desperate for work, fine actors and actresses—some of them non-virtual!—debase themselves by portraying freakish, outrély costumed characters adrift in various exotic Nevernever-lands, the relevance of which to mankind's current concerns is absolutely zero. Critics cry out stridently to no avail! Profit is the only voice the studios listen to, and as long as the public continues to vote with their chip-purses in favor of these lurid abominations, the current sad state of affairs will never change.

And yet, one has a moral obligation to speak out, to argue unceasingly for a return to realistic chronicles of everyday galactic life. Perhaps this very essay will be the hagthistle that breaks the swampwolf's jaw!

The birth of this vile trend toward unreality is easy enough to date: in the year 2148 appeared *Mr Sammler's Planet*, directed by Giorgio Scula, of California VII. Despite its modern-sounding and realistic title, the work proved to be the most arrant fantasy! Set on a barely technological world ignorant of space-travel, a milieu still subscribing to numerous discarded paradigms, this film featured absurdly dressed characters in ridiculous situations no sane contemporary person could imagine! Millions were spent on makeup and sets (a fairytale environment called "New York"), as well as on props and the recreation of extinct animals such as cockroaches and Republicans.

Although this foolish entertainment should have failed miserably, by some caprice it did not! Apparently, the viewing public had been sated with too many by-the-numbers realistic works.

Like suicidal cliff-leaping yellowrats, across a thousand thousand worlds they swarmed to every public venue showing Scula's debased yet—even I reluctantly concur—hypnotically weird entertainment.

To the eternal despair of realists everywhere, the floodgates of fantasy were opened wide. Tentatively at first, then with accelerated speed, every studio and director jumped into this polluted river, each vying to outdo the other in the bizarreness of their productions. And even now, eleven years later, the highwater mark of this fetid inundation has not yet been reached.

Quickly following *Mr Sammler's Planet* came *Dos Passo's USA* (2150), directed by Paul Evenhoover; *The Executioner's Song* (2151), by Steffen Talkcity; *Midnight Cowboy* (2151), by Stanley Ickbru; *Easy Rider* (2152), by Clive Rekarb; and *The Ginger Man* (2153), by Robert Kismetkiss. By virtue of their infrequency, these early works of fantasy possessed some small vapid allure. But any storytelling or audiovisual virtues were overwhelmed by nonsensical and counterfactual touches.

The isolated worlds depicted were all ones where humans were the only intelligent species (an arrogancy which by itself has spawned a number of penetrating analyses; see Gabrielle Sansculotte's *Speciesism in the Oeuvre of Terry Lillygam, op. cit.*). With their unaugmented and irreplaceable bodies cloaked in the crudest synthetic fibers or—horrors!—dead and dumb organics, the travesties of humanity in these films offered eager viewers an outlet from the dullness of the present. Flaunting their unrectified emotions and laughable goals, wasting their time in pointless "work" and "play" and "love" situations, the characters in the typical fantasy film inspired the same kind of empathy to be found in a virtuality icon.

Now came the second wave of even less talented directors playing their willfully unreal games: *The Kindness of Women,*

Turtle Moon, The Deep End of the Ocean, Libra, (all 2154), *The Horse Whisperer* and *M.A.S.H.* (both 2156), *Casino* (2157), *Leaving Las Vegas* (2158)—the tiresome list of wild and pointless dreams could be extended for pages. And in each of these fantasies, new attempts were made to impose on the audience's credulity. Could any balanced sapient today actually believe the interpersonal or political relations depicted in, say, Ray Hairyhouse's *Primary Colors* (2155)?

Meanwhile, what of the poor realists? Either their projects were denied funding upfront by short-sighted and trendy executives, or, if made, their meticulously realistic entertainments were dumped into a few minor sensoriums without publicity. And what is the result of this ignorant policy? Only that the most significant events of the current era—sometimes boring, sometimes trivial, perhaps, yet still near and dear to our modern hearts—are left unchronicled, deprived of art's transmuting and enlightening touch. We are now a culture that refuses to deal artistically with its own present, for fear of being seen as tedious and "unimaginative."

The wealth of unused contemporary material is astonishing. The interstellar battle between the Aldebaran and Ophiuchian polities, in which ten thousand Limbaugh Class war vessels were annihilated, has found no historical director willing to stage even a small-budget re-enactment. The invasion of Webb IX by the Gaseous Horde has no interpreters. The burgeoning symbiosis between humans and the Earwig culture of Edelman V goes begging for a journalistically minded artist who could capture its complexities. The settlement of Shepard's Dyson Sphere finds no one to give it voice. And the simple yet affecting tale of the supernova that wiped out the Hundred Habitats of the Laidlaw Nebula seems not to merit even the assignment of a lesser director such as Ron Wardhow.

If there is any comfort to be taken, it is in the fact that no trend, however brainless and mercenary, lasts forever. Soon, if there is any justice in the world, the public will tire of the colorful exotica summarized by one critic as "the extramarital affairs of dentists," and reawaken to the simple, homey, mundane attractions of death-rays and bug-eyed monsters, rogue planets and unstoppable hiveminds, imperial princesses and jaunty starship captains.

NEVER LET THEM SEE YOU NOVA

As I sat in the posh anteroom at Dreamworks SKG, waiting for the most important appointment of my entire professional life, one obsessive thought kept running through my mind like a warfarin-maddened rat: *The first thing they'll hit me with is* The Foundation Trilogy . . . .

I knew there was absolutely no way I could skip dealing with that fiasco, the stench of which still ascended heavenward two years after the release of that mega-expensive dog. My best bet, I figured, was to get the goddamn corpse out of the way as quickly as possible. Blame the studio, the director, the cast, the special effects crew—hell, blame the grips and the gophers, if it came to that. Anyone, in short, except the infamous pariah of a scriptwriter.

Because that pariah was me, Curt Boardmender.

I had penned the scripts for a dozen fantasy classics, a handful of genuine hits, a couple of lower echelon box-office record-holders, and all anyone could remember was the one bomb. Where was the justice in that? I asked whatever Hollywood gods were listening. Since that debacle, I hadn't been able to sell so much as a lousy treatment. Two years of living off my bank account, trying to keep up the necessary face-saving facade of success, had left me utterly tapped. The vultures at the repo agency were one step behind me and my unmufflered Jag, and the bank was ready to kick my ass out of my former dreamhouse. I almost felt like letting the weasels take the dump. The bone-dry pool had a crack in it like the combined cleavage of the Arquette sisters, the lawn was a jungle since I had been forced to let the landscapers go, and the remains of the most recent mudslide were still banked against the uphill picture window. But the sheer smarmy vindictiveness of all the bastards ranked against me roused my fighting spirits. There was still plenty of piss and ingenuity left in ol' Curt Boardmender! With one little break, I'd finally show them all. The pitch I was going to make today was inspired. It couldn't fail. It *couldn't*.

"Mr Boardmender?" The sleek receptionist's sexy voice interrupted my sour memories. "The Triumvirate will see you now."

I stood up and polished my once handsome, now shabby Italian shoes on the back of my pants legs. I slicked back my self-administered haircut and tugged at the lapels of my silk jacket. That latter move was a mistake, as I heard a seam in the shoulders pop open. Oh well, onward and upward. With confident stride and beaming tanned face (at least sunshine was still free), I marched in to meet my fate.

Behind a massive table sat three of the most powerful men in Hollywood: Steven Spielberg, Jeffrey Katzenberg and David Geffen. Their familiar faces were expected, but not that of the fourth man with them. To my immense dismay, I saw the smirking puss of one of my peers, J. J. Martin Michaelgeorge. Creator of such television hits as *Tigris 7* and *Bimbo and the Bugbear*, Michaelgeorge had always been a rival, and represented nothing but bad news for me. Plainly, he had been drafted today for his expertise in science-fictional matters. His presence would make my pitch that much harder.

As I stepped forward and shook hands all around, a sudden

surge of confidence boiled through me. Despite all the odds against me, I was back in the gaudy, brutal arena I knew and loved. And I was armed with an idea no one else had ever dared to conceive. That alone might be enough to guarantee my success.

After the hellos and how-are-yous—pleasant and businesslike enough—once we were all seated, the sucker-punch came. Beaming nastily through his speckled beard, Spielberg said, "Before we hear your new proposal, Curt, I just want to ask about some dialogue from your last script. I believe it came out of the mouth of Woody Harrelson as Hari Seldon. Let's see . . . if my memory is accurate, the line went something like, 'That fucking Mule, I'll blow his telepathic brains out his ass.' Did that come straight from Asimov's text, or was it your invention?"

Figuring I had nothing to lose, I countered with a sly offensive. "Neither, Steve. That was Woody's ad-lib. You know how these headstrong stars are with their lines. Why, I imagine something similar could have happened with Robin Williams in *Hook*, or John Belushi in *1941*."

Reference to those two turkeys settled Spielberg's hash mighty fast, and his colleagues quickly stifled their own jibes, not anxious for me to bring up any of *their* ancient duds.

"Well," the solemn Spielberg said, "maybe we should leave the past alone for now. Tell us about your new idea, Curt."

I had honed and rehearsed this high-concept soundbite for so long, it practically leaped from my lips. "One hundred billion years of a Julia Roberts universe."

They jerked to attention like puppets, and I made haste to capitalize on their greedy attention. "Two highly respected and classic science fiction novels have just entered the public domain, providing this project with an instant savings. No payment to the writer's estate is needed to secure the properties. And the first person to film these linked classics is guaranteed an instant audience—and critical esteem. I've known and loved these books for years, and have already worked up a treatment. To the best of my knowledge, no one else has any plans to make these books into a film. If we move fast, we can foreclose any other studio from so much as winking at this project. I can promise you a script within, oh, four months. Shooting could start before the year is out."

Geffen spoke up. "What are the names of these books, Curt?"

Here came the make-or-break moment. "*Last and First Men* and *Star Maker*, by Olaf Stapledon."

The executives looked blank, but Michaelgeorge brayed like the jackass he was and practically fell out of his seat. Katzenberg snapped his fingers at the scriptwriter and commanded, "Martin, what's so funny?"

Gradually the gloating Michaelgeorge recovered his composure. "Oh, man, I thought I had heard every lamebrained scheme under the sun, but this one takes the cake. The two books he just named were written by this eccentric British philosopher who didn't even know real sci-fi existed! They're totally plotless, without any individual characters as such. They're full of way-out speculation and endless details of physics and biology and even religion! It's as if I proposed filming—"

I cut the moron off. "Filming the *Bible*, maybe? Seemed to work for DeMille and Heston. Or maybe you had in mind Woody Allen's *Everything You Always Wanted to Know About Sex*? It's not that far-fetched, believe me. No plot and no characters in the original are not bad things—it lets us impose our own smarter ideas on Stapledon's skeleton. It's the same recipe as any other movie, really. Big names and a kickass script. And if I provide the latter, you guys can surely attract the heavy hitters."

"Let's hear the man out," said Spielberg, and I wasted no time launching into my rap.

"Okay, first of all we're talking about just a single film. *Last and First Men* is folded into the plot of what I call *Starmaker! The Musical.* This is a story about evolution, from slime to superman, with plenty of catchy tunes. Kinda like that riff in *2001* with the apes, but bigger, bolder and more action-packed. Yet it's not going to annoy the fundamentalists, because it has a theological angle too. Anyway, here's the scenario. We open while the universe is still young, and life is simple. 'Long ago in a galaxy far away,' right? There's a planet with some kind of cutesy alien life on it. And one of those aliens is Julia Roberts."

Michaelgeorge snorted derisively. "Cutesy aliens? Stapledon's books had intelligent herbs and squids, slime molds and insect swarms. Humans the size of Danny DeVito who looked like bats, or big ones ugly as Jon Voigt mated with Andre the Giant."

I bulled past those objections. "We ditch all of that, keep the various makeup jobs simple, of course. Wouldn't do to hide Julia's assets. Maybe give her a sexy tail, or high-heel hooves. You get the idea. Anyway, Julia plays this brainy scientist or philosopher type, very noble. She's lonely, though, because she can't find a mate worthy of her. 'Oh, where is the alien guy worthy of my love? Alas, I fear he doesn't yet exist.' That pitiful lament sets up the whole movie. During the next hundred and fifty minutes, we are going on a dizzying, rollercoaster ride through all of time and space, watching the physical universe and the league of inter-stellar civilizations mature together, until they finally produce a mate worthy of Julia. I see an educational hook, too. Maybe we can get an endorsement from Stephen Hawking even. Anyway, this is going to be the kind of star-turn for Julia that *The Nutty Professor* was for Eddie Murphy. She's in practically every scene, in a hundred different shapes and roles. Fighting barbarians like Xena, discovering radium like Marie Curie, piloting spaceships like Carrie Fisher."

I could sense they were interested, and I didn't let up. "Of course, we need some conflict. So Julia has a rival. I see Madonna here, a bad girl type who wants to pervert the universe to produce the ultimate bad boy type for *her*. Now, these boyfriend roles will be the two male leads. I picture George Clooney as Julia's ideal, and maybe Jeremy Irons as Madonna's mate. They keep popping up in imperfect forms throughout the story. Each time after a steamy sex scene, Julia and Madonna say, 'Sorry, buddy, you're not ready yet. Back to the drawing board.' This is the hook for the ad campaign too. We honor Stapledon by using an actual line from his book: 'In the waste of stars, love is crucified.' Classy, huh?"

Now Geffen interjected, "What about the musical angle?"

"We can go either of two ways. If we want some kind of Broadway sound, we hire Andrew Lloyd Webber. If we want more of a pop thing, we assemble the hottest acts available. Snoop Doggie Dogg, Puff Daddy—hell, I don't need to tell a musical genius like you how to do your job, David."

Geffen beamed, and I plunged on. "The great thing about this concept is that it's totally elastic. Whatever market research and focus groups reveal the audience wants, we dump it in. They want a jungle world, they got it. They want furry teddybears or scary bugs, they got it. All that ultimately matters is bringing Julia and George together at the end."

Katzenberg asked, "And exactly how does that happen?"

"Simple. Julia and George become the entire universe! They make the final leap into sheer godhood. It's right there in Stapledon. I picture the camera pulling back to reveal one galaxy after another, until we realize that the galaxies are forming two luminescent naked bodies! Julia and George in the ultimate clinch!"

My shirt and jacket were soaked with sweat. I sat back in my seat without enough energy to power a pinwheel. I had delivered my best shot. Now it was up to the three movers and shakers. They put their heads together and whispered for a few minutes, while Michaelgeorge and I glared at each other. Then all three of the execs stood up like Siamese triplets and extended their hands.

"Curt," said Spielberg, "we're greenlighting *Starmaker!* to the tune of a quarter-billion. How's ten percent of that sound for your share?"

Only nerves honed by years of experience allowed me to shakily stand. "Sounds like I can afford a new muffler now, Steven."

They laughed, not realizing I was just speaking the truth. Michaelgeorge stalked off like a foiled Snidely Whiplash, and I soon had a drink in my hand and a cigar between my lips. The rest of that day was surely going to be lost in celebration, but when tomorrow dawned, I'd be busily at work, using every iota of my skills to make *Starmaker!* sing.

Hell, maybe I'd even go back and give those Stapledon books more than a quick skim.

SCISSORS CUT PAPER,
PAPER COVERS SCHLOCK

"If Stephen King, John Grisham, and Michael Crichton got together, they'd become one of the top three publishers overnight."

—Morgan Entrekin, publisher for Grove Press,
quoted in *The New Yorker*, 10/6/97.

Sweating despite the cool recirculated air, his nervous stomach spasming, his lanky shock-cushioned body nearly folded in half around various struts and controls, Michael Crichton IV rolled into the luxurious boardroom of KGC Publishing, secure in the cramped interior of his armored trundlebug. This model, equipped with a wide range of sensors, weapons and defenses, was the same one used by the troops of such protectorates as Microsoft-Snapple and Harvard-Sam Adams. Nothing short of an illegal quantum-disruptor could penetrate *this* heavy carapace.

With the announcement Crichton IV intended to make today, he knew he'd need every ounce of shielding.

No one could be counted on to react more fiercely than partners betrayed.

Not that Crichton IV's confederates were especially pleasant even when coddled. Their three-way partnership was riven with strife. Day-to-day management of KGC involved too many violent emotions, too many bruised artistic sensibilities. Literary trespassing and poaching, even if unintentional, on what the partners deemed their personal territories raised hackles and frequently brought down massive internecine firepower. This was the forty-second headquarters they had gone through in the nearly one hundred years of their existence—and it certainly wouldn't be the last.

Assuming KGC even continued to exist after today.

Crichton IV tracked his vehicle around the teak conference table and into a power position from which he could monitor the entrance to the boardroom. Calling this meeting for ten AM, he had deliberately arrived before the others so as to secure the most advantageous spot. One of the building's load-bearing beams ran directly above him, and he hoped it might serve to protect him from the eventual falling debris.

Now on his monitors Crichton IV saw his partners arrive, concealed in their own armored carriers. Deliberately built only wide enough for one vehicle at a time, the boardroom door was the first test of status. Crichton IV watched as Stephen King VI and John Grisham III jostled for precedence, with King VI eventually winning. Crichton IV wasn't surprised: King VI was as daring and impulsive as all of his identical ancestors, taking risks the other partners shied away from. That was why there had been six of him, though, compared with four Crichtons and three Grishams.

Now on two of Crichton IV's screens popped up the images of his partners. Neither of them looked very happy.

"You'd better have a damn good reason for making me haul my ass away from my studio this early in the morning," said King VI. "I barely got fifty pages written since breakfast."

"I concur," said Grisham III. "We might have the basis of a suit or at least an actionable tort here. *Scribendi interruptus.*"

Beating around the bush wouldn't make the fateful words any easier to say. Crichton IV cleared his throat with a rasping sound and uttered the deadly sentence.

"Gentlemen, I want to resign—"

Ravening gouts of belligerent hell-energy erupted from the one-man tanks of his partners, setting off coruscating force-shield reactions amongst all three. Instantly, the walls of the boardroom were reduced to atoms, opening the suite to the cool air two hundred meters above groundlevel. The ceiling was partially evaporated, along with a good-sized chunk of the seven remaining floors above, and a radiant flare shot out from the top of the KGC building, as if signaling construction crews to begin pouring the foundations for HQ number forty-three.

Thank god I gave the publicity department the day off, Crichton IV thought.

Luckily, the floor of the boardroom was reinforced with the same material used in the Quito Beanstalk, so the partners did not plunge to the basement. Instead, they remained in place for the downfall of debris that quickly followed the spectacular attack. And, as Crichton IV had foreseen, King VI and Grisham III were buried, while he was protected by a truncated portion of the building's structural components.

Quickly, before his opponents could extricate themselves, Crichton IV whipped his trundlebug over the junkpiles and extruded two metal tentacles which burrowed down intelligently to the immobilized vehicles, clamped on and administered a paralyzing surge that fried their electronics. Into the defenseless tanks, the tentacles next insinuated audiovideo feeds under the control of an exultant Crichton IV. The shaken but unharmed faces of King VI and Grisham III reappeared on his screens.

"Okay, you two—now you're going to listen to me."

His partners scowled, but acquiesced, having no choice in the matter.

"I said I wanted to resign, and you two immediately assumed I was joining another firm, a rival."

"Well, what else would we think!" King VI shouted. "That *has* to be what you're up to!"

"Who is it?" queried Grisham III in his coolest prosecutorial tones. "Clancy, Koontz and Steel? No? Don't tell me you're still entertaining those laughable literary pretensions you once had. You'd never get an offer from Updike, Mailer and Bellow, not in a million years. Or are you finally affirming your genre roots? Did you cut a deal with Bear, Benford, Brin, Baxter and Egan?"

"None of those. I'm striking out on my own."

King VI laughed harshly. "You fool! You'll lose all the synergy of our partnership, all the economies of scale. Your rackspace in the protectorate retail outlets won't be guaranteed anymore. Your brandname will sink like a stone."

"I'm retiring not just from publishing as we currently practice it, but from writing as well," Crichton IV announced. This unbelievable statement shocked his soon-to-be ex-partners into silence. "I think the Crichton lineage has said all it can say over the past century. I think the same is true for all the rest of us amalgamated, incorporated writers. But of course that's a recognition I leave each individual to reach on his own. No, I plan to embark on a new venture entirely. Gentlemen—I'm going to become an early-twentieth-century-style publisher."

An even deeper stunned silence greeted this announcement, until finally Grisham III found his tongue. "You mean, soliciting manuscripts from non-commodified, even previously unpublished writers and printing small and medium-sized quantities of an extensive number of titles twice a year, risking your own money while trusting the marketplace to discriminate between good books and bad?"

"Precisely."

"You're bughouse!" exclaimed King VI.

"Not at all. It's the only way out of the stagnant, uncreative pool we're drowning in. The only books that see print nowadays are predigested, by-the-numbers, focus-group-approved rehashes of past bestsellers. We've killed the vital kind of fiction that once existed. Face it, gentlemen—we're dinosaurs squashing the life out of the very field we profess to love."

King snorted. "Shoulda known the dinosaurs would come into this somehow."

Grisham III spoke. "How do we know this, ahem, disclosure is not some roundabout way of stabbing us in the back? What guarantees do we have that this is not an underhanded plot?"

"I'm not joining Pynchon, DeLillo and Erickson, believe me."

"It's a sob story," said King VI. "He's just angling for a bigger share of the profits."

"And I'm not joining Krantz, Collins and Pilcher either. No, I'm telling you the simple truth. I'm going to start an old-fashioned publishing firm, one that doesn't even bear my name. I'm thinking of calling it Andromeda Publishing. Our motto will be: 'A new strain of books.'"

"Well, in that case, if you don't need your name, we'll just clone you again. I'm sure Crichton V will see things our way."

Crichton IV smiled. "You forget, gentlemen, the medical training associated with my lineage. I've secured all my cell-samples from the corporate vaults, and incinerated my living quarters. There'll be no more Crichtons after me. That's part of the problem, not the solution."

Finally admitting defeat, the two abandoned partners addressed each other.

"I suppose we'll just have to merge with some other hacks in order to compete."

"The mystery field has been having a good year. Let me initiate negotiations with Leonard, Hiaassen, Burke, Vachss and Westlake."

Satisfied that he could now take his leave safely and embark on realizing his new dreams, Crichton IV began to reel in his audiovideo taps, but was brought up short by a shout from King VI.

"Hey, Mikey!"

"Yes?"

"Uh, would you read something by a friend of mine named Richard Bachman?"

AS THROUGH A PAIR OF
MIRRORSHADES DARKLY

WHERE ARE THEY NOW?

A regular feature of *Rolling Stone Online*, copyright 2021. Click on boldfaced words or phrases for audiovisual attachments or additional reading material (definitions, contemporary equivalents, etc.).

Thirty-five years ago, the cloistered, complacent world of **science fiction** was rocked by the official birth announcement of a courageous, intelligent, angry new movement, the **cyberpunks**, a group of young writers intent on dragging SF kicking and screaming into the **1980s**, that decade which seemed so turbulent at the time, but which now, in the light of our own era, appears so innocent and easy-going. With the publication of the **anthology** *Mirrorshades*, this bubbling-under revolution in the depiction of the future was forever captured in a single literary snapshot. The eleven authors—ten men and one woman—immortalized in that 1986 **book** went on to produce a variety of work. But with the advent of new modes of content-production and transmittal, these writers—as well as many others—disappeared from the literary scene, their archaic skills outmoded, their will to write shattered, transformed or displaced, as they witnessed their visions randomly debunked or confirmed. Not one of them managed to survive (in the old-fashioned sense of the word) into the near-term future about which they so famously speculated. They all ultimately met fates which, taken together, constitute a primer in the extensive global changes we have witnessed over the past three and a half decades.

Here then, in the order in which we encountered these fallible visionaries in *Mirrorshades*, are the follow-up capsule histories of these prescient authors who were all paradoxically blindsided by circumstance.

Cheerleader, strategist, and guiding light of the cyberpunks, **Bruce Sterling** always exhibited an extraliterary side to his activities. Cosmopolitan to a flaw, he frequently extolled the virtues of such author-politicians as **Vaclav Havel**. It came as little surprise to those who truly knew him that in the Russian elections of the year 2000, surprise candidate Sterling, his U.S. citizenship traded for Russian papers, quickly emerged as the front-runner. Elected handily, he soon began to rule the faltering **nation** firmly yet beneficently, pulling his adopted country into the 21st century. Such accomplishments as the Mars mission of 2010 and the Circumarctic Dike System can be laid entirely at his doorstep. But hubris engendered his one fatal misstep: his attempt to change the Russian diet, mandating Texas Bar-B-Q in place of such staples as borscht and potato pancakes. After his assassination by a disgruntled beet farmer, Sterling's preserved body came to lie perpetually in state where Lenin's once reigned.

The sight of **William Gibson** in dreadlocks, his complexion darkened by melanin boosters, a huge spliff in his grip, will instantly be familiar to reggae fans even today. Seduced by the heavy drug scene in his hometown of Vancouver, Canada, Gibson gradually abandoned writing in favor of ardent Rastafarianism and Jamaican music. Going by the nickname "Tuff Deck," Gibson soon had a recording contract with Virgin Records. His subsequent career included such milestones as helping to create the fusion style known as "Nashville-ska" and recording the Number One Single of 2005, "I and I No Idoru, Mon." Unfortunately, on his Virtual Light Tour of 2009, Gibson fell victim to a fatal jolt of electricity when he absentmindedly attempted to insert a jack into his navel rather than into his guitar.

Few people today recall the noble experiment known as "Chemical Schooling." Yet it was in this brave but misguided effort that **Tom Maddox** met his doom. Intent on raising the educational achievements of American youth, Chemical Schooling represented the first crude attempts at today's **brilliant drugs**. Attempting to prep for an upcoming semester, Maddox accidentally ingested an overdose of **semiotics** pills. In itself, this would have been crippling but not necessarily fatal; however, the overdose left Maddox with an overwhelming compulsion to smoke Gitanes and drink espresso, and he quickly succumbed to massive nicotine and caffeine poisoning. A memorial chair at a Paris cafe has been endowed in his name.

Lone anointed female cyberpunk, **Pat Cadigan** had by the 90s expatriated herself to **London**. Initially, this seemed a wise and healthy move. But Cadigan had not reckoned with changing climatic conditions. After the Great Flip of 2009, when London began to be submerged by rising sea levels, Cadigan refused to leave her beloved city. "I'm gonna ride this out like a **Ballard** protagonist," she was quoted as defiantly saying. In the general crazed exodus, the stubborn Cadigan's whereabouts became hazy, even her continued existence in doubt. After a decade, she has been transformed into an iconic, mythic figure, "The Lady of the Thames." Brave souls exploring the aquatic ruins of Mother London claim to have seen her gaunt and shrouded apparition poling a skiff through the urban channels while singing "Cockles and Mussels, Alive, Alive-O."

The first of the governing **City Brains** that enjoyed a brief vogue were all patterned on human intelligences. The AI for the San Francisco-San Jose district had **Rudy Rucker** as its template. (Rucker was chosen for this honor as he lay in the hospital suffering from terminal Mandelbrot's Fever contracted from overexposure to fractals. Only humans soon to die were allowed to become artificial intelligences, thus avoiding legal problems of duplicate identity and ownership, etc.) At first, the Rucker AI proved very moderate and capable in its governance of the metroplex. But then strange orders began to issue forth: memorization of Kerouac's *On the Road* was to be mandatory for high-school graduation; **Frank Zappa's** "Peaches En Regalia" replaced "The Star-Spangled Banner" at official functions; and so on. Only after a tremendous struggle between citizens and the capricious cyberpunk-on-a-chip, with the Rucker AI employing civic robots in its defense, was the rogue silicon freestyler disabled. Videotaped as its boards were pulled, even today the AI can be heard plaintively singing in diminuendo "Oh Lord, would you buy me a Mercedes Benz."

Having moved into the **videogame** industry in the 90s, **Marc Laidlaw** was eager to participate in a revolution in that field that occurred in 2005. Unable ever to achieve satisfying virtual reality, the game industry decided that the problem lay in the human demand for hi-res 3-D input. Various firms began to offer neurosurgical operations that allowed players to see the real world in familiar lo-res pixel form, complete with special effects. Large theme parks that simulated famous videogames were built, and the players turned loose. Naturally, the programmers and writers had to undergo this same operation in order to develop the parks effectively. Laidlaw's demise came when, attempting to "reach a new level," he jumped from his tenth-floor apartment onto a "magic mushroom" below his window that proved to be a passerby's umbrella.

James Patrick Kelly never intended to search for Champie, the legendary atavistic monster of Lake Champlain. But a simple fishing trip in 2003 proved his undoing, as Champie, attracted by Kelly's unusual choice of bait—champagne-marinated caviar—surfaced alongside Kelly's canoe and swallowed both boat and fisherman. This meal brought on Champie's own death, and the recovered corpse was opened to reveal that Kelly had survived for a short time within the monster, just long enough to compose a final story on his durable laptop, "In the Belly of the Beast," which went on to win that year's Nebula, Hugo, and Field and Stream awards.

Accidentally stepping into a pool of "grey goo" during the famous Seattle Scum Splash of 2016 opened up a new way of living for Greg Bear. After absorption, his intelligence now resided in a million tons of aggressive protean undifferentiated protoplasm. Reining in the monstrous formerly nonsentient blob earned Bear the Congressional Medal of Honor as well as exile to the Mojave Desert. Once penned by an acid-filled moat in his sandy Coventry, Bear became a prime tourist attraction and continues right up to the current day to amuse children and adults alike with his various Jello, blancmange, and Rush Limbaugh impressions.

Becoming fascinated with Deep Ecology, Lewis Shiner arrived at a point where he abandoned job and family to become a monkey-wrenching eco-guerilla. His legendary career protecting Mother Gaia reached a climax when he singlehandedly sabotaged further development of the Amazon Rain Forest by introducing a bioengineered defense against human predation: Organic Muzak.

Implanted in vegetation and animals, the virus-borne circuitry that allowed animals and trees to emit Muzak insured that humans would remain far away from the ear-assaulting forest, whereas other forms of life would not be bothered. But Shiner, his GPS unit broken while he sought to leave the Amazon, became lost amid the cacophony and quickly succumbed to his own deadly defense.

How many times before their actual arrival had science fiction predicted the advent of "the feelies," entertainment that offered tactile sensations to the audience? Few people would have guessed that **John Shirley** would be instrumental in helping perfect this medium. As Hollywood ramped up to introduce this entertainment option, the moguls discovered that test subjects were hard to come by. Sure, everybody wanted to test the porno options, but few people were willing to undergo the alpha software for the slasher or combat feelies. Enter Shirley, notoriously open to any and all experiences. By becoming Subject Number One in Hollywood's grand drive to perfect the feelies, Shirley allowed the experts to calibrate their effects. But a few years of this intense nervous-system stimulation proved too much for even the life-hardened Shirley, and he ended his days comatose in a sensory-deprivation tank.

After publishing his final "humor" column, "As Through a Pair of Mirrorshades Darkly," **Paul Di Filippo** vanished without a trace.

AND I THINK TO MYSELF, WHAT A WONDERFUL WORLD

"I believe *The Magazine of Fantasy and Science Fiction* appeals to me because in it one finds refuge and release from everyday life. We are all little children at heart and find comfort in a dream world, and these episodes in the magazine encourage our building castles in space."

—Louis Armstrong,
rear-cover endorsement, *F&SF*, circa 1964.

From backstage at the Newport Jazztopian Festival of 1965, Louis "Satchmo" Armstrong, editor of *The Magazine of Fantasy and Jazztopian Fiction*, heard the ecstatic roar of the crowd and smiled. The band now departing the stage—The *Amazing* Herd, under the charismatic leadership of editor Woody Herman—was going to be a hard act to follow. That little cat on drums, Ray Palmer, was a pint-sized dynamo. But Satchmo continued to grin broadly, confidence flowing almost visibly from his bulky suited form. The lineup he was going to bring onstage was one of the strongest he had ever fronted, even going way back to the early glory days of the Hot Five. Armstrong was certain that his band would wow the crowd today, just as the magazine he headed wowed its readers monthly.

An arm fell around Satchmo's shoulder, and he turned to face the festival's organizer, George Wein.

"Any butterflies, Dippermouth?" joshed Wein, using Armstrong's oldest nickname.

"No, sir," growled Armstrong in his famous rumble. "We're fixin' to turn Newport Harbor into steam. Serve up some fine music and cooked lobster all at once."

Wein released Armstrong and his face grew serious. "Who'd have thought we'd ever find ourselves doing what we love again, huh, Louis? During all those bad years, the whole Noteless Decade, it seemed impossible that our music would ever flourish again."

"Don't forget the fiction, too, George. We can't neglect the other half of the Jazztopian program. Only solidarity got us through the hard times and brought us to where we are today."

"True, true. But you're more heavily into the written stuff than me. The music's always been my first concern."

"You got to keep the lesson of the camps in mind though, George. If we don't hang together, we hang separately."

Wein shook his head ruefully. "The camps. Nothing seems hard after them, does it?"

"No, sir, it sure don't."

And Armstrong cast his mind back some twenty-odd years to that convulsive time—so horrible while ongoing, yet a blessing in retrospect.

In early 1942, during the grimmest days of the Second World War, when the Allied cause looked doomed, the worst possible thing that could have happened to the USA—not excluding the previous year's massacre at Pearl Harbor—had occurred: President Roosevelt was assassinated by a lone gunman. The assassin, who died almost immediately under return fire from the Secret Service, was quickly identified, his prints on file from a series of minor robbery and vagrancy arrests. One William Burroughs, dope fiend, petty thief, wastrel, and, incongruously, black-sheep scion of an industrial dynasty. On the assassin's body and in his tawdry apartment had been found extensive scribblings. Burroughs's writings spoke of a vast conspiracy involving jazz men, hobos, pulp writers, and other mysterious lowlife figures, a conspiracy bent on subverting all authority from the highest levels on down. Some held that these manuscripts were plainly the hallucinatory work of a madman; others that they were a viable blueprint for an actual attempt by anarchists to overthrow the country.

The government of the United States, faced with attack from abroad, could not take a chance on subversion from within. Less than a week after Roosevelt's death, pursuant to special orders from President Garner, the nationwide roundup of all the suspicious types delineated in Burroughs's manuscripts had begun. By the thousands, musicians, writers, artists, and tramps were swiftly corralled and sent to the same detention camps that already held—much to the surprise of the uninformed newcomers—innocent, law-abiding Japanese-Americans.

Armstrong had been in the studio, cutting a record with Bing Crosby, when their arrests came down. He and Bing hadn't been allowed even to pack or call their families before being hustled onto a westbound train. (Apparently, Armstrong's trip to Europe in 1933 rendered him particularly suspect.) Armstrong hadn't felt this crummy since he was sent to the Colored Waif's School at age 12. Arriving at an Arizona camp exploding with construction by WPA crews in order to hold the new influx of prisoners, Satchmo resigned himself to a few weeks of being held hostage to the nation's fears. Surely this whole mess would soon be straightened out.

After the first six months of confinement, he realized his sanguine expectations might be due for revision. But even then no one quite believed that their internment could possibly last some ten years.

Life in the camp sorted itself out after an initial period into something quite different from what the authorities had intended. The prisoners were allowed by a manpower-short Federal government to manage their own affairs with minimal supervision, and soon the camp was humming with organized activities. By cooping up so many creative, talented people, the government had inadvertently created a hothouse environment where ideas and enthusiasms bred like bacteria. "The swing tanks" was what the camps eventually came to be called by their inmates, and by the few citizens on the outside of the fences who heard dribs and drabs of whispered leaked information.

Acquiring musical instruments through bribery or Red Cross charity, the musicians among the prisoners swiftly fell into both new and old groupings prone to jamming nearly all their waking hours. By similar licit or illicit means the writers incarcerated in the swing tanks glommed onto typewriters and mimeographs and continued their interrupted work, mainly in the speculative and noir genres. And painters likewise with their tools.

But neither the musicians nor the writers nor the painters any longer maintained suspicious barriers between their clans. Forced to mingle by proximity, they found stimulation, enlightenment, and inspiration in the media different from their own. Many laid down their pens and took up trumpets, and vice versa. And from the assorted tramps, bums, addicts, and hobos came an underclass perspective on national affairs that many of the middle-class artists might never have otherwise encountered.

Thus, in parallel with their secret Manhattan Project elsewhere, the Feds had accidentally built in the swing tanks a system for high-gear cultural cross-pollination.

As best as Satchmo now recalled, it was during the third year of their imprisonment that someone coined the term "jazztopia" for the ideal state toward which all of the prisoners were striving with their art. Maybe Duke Ellington had come up with the term, maybe Dave Brubeck. It could have fallen from the lips of Woody Guthrie or Cyril Kornbluth. Whoever the originator, the term spread like wildfire. Within weeks, there appeared "The Jazztopian Manifesto," penned by a team consisting of Henry Kuttner, Thelonius Monk, Mezz Mezzrow, Fred Pohl, and Billie Holiday. Signed by nearly every inmate of the swing tanks, the proclamation became the Jazztopian Declaration of Independence.

Outside the swing tanks, the global war had stalemated. Garner was not the strategist Roosevelt had been (although historians later attributed much of the military inertia to a national lassitude stemming from a dearth of entertainers other than a few goodie-goodie quislings such as Kate Smith, Bob Hope and L. Ron Hubbard). In the elections of 1948, the electorate replaced Garner with Eisenhower, popular ex-general invalided out of active service after the failure of D-Day. Eisenhower pressed the scientists of the Manhattan Project for a breakthrough (one of the key figures of the Project, Richard Feynman, had been sent to the swing tanks for his bongo-playing, leaving the Project fumbling), and success finally came in 1951, bringing a decisive end to the war. But at his moment of triumph, Eisenhower was swept up in scandal, caught having an affair with his secretary, Kay Tarrant. Outraged, the voters in 1952 carried Adlai Stevenson into the Oval Office. Liberal Stevenson immediately used his mandate and the new peacetime conditions to dissolve the swing tanks.

Out into the general populace burst the Jazztopians, burning to bring their optimistic, speculative visions in words and music to the rest of the nation. They infected the country like a virus never before encountered by the body politic's immune system.

The 1950s, "The Swinging Fifties," were the biggest renaissance in the nation's history. The domestic economy soared, global reconstruction got underway, and the soundtrack was Jazztopian music. Jazztopian speculative literature, marching forward arm-in-arm with the music, blossomed. Scores of magazines were born or reborn, the masthead of each boasting a musician as the nominal (sometimes actual) editor. There was *Astounding* with Guy Lombardo; *Unknown* with Charlie Parker; *Galaxy* with Sun Ra; *Planet Stories* with Benny Goodman; *Infinity* with Glenn Miller; and of course, *The Magazine of Fantasy and Jazztopian Fiction*, helmed by Louis Armstrong.

Open-air festivals became the favored tribal gatherings of the Jazztopians and their enormous flock of fans, replacing stuffy literary gatherings and smoky non-literate night-clubs. And the Newport gathering was perhaps the most prestigious.

Satchmo's reverie ended as his bandmates surged past him, heading for the stage. Each one, youngster and old friend, gave him a high five as they bustled by him. Armstrong let them take their positions. He made sure he had his big white handkerchief ready. When he heard the band start to vamp to "Jeepers Creepers," he strolled onstage.

The crowd went wild. Satchmo held his hands up for quiet, surveying the spectators, noting the various booths set up to sell Jazztopian literature and art. When the fans finally settled down, Armstrong picked up his trumpet.

"Thank you, ladies and gentlemen. I suspect that the President and Jackie can hear you all the way 'cross the bay at Hammersmith Farm!"

The crowd roared again at the mention of the ever-popular second-term President. When they quieted once more, Satchmo said, "Let me introduce the *F&JF* band first. On drums, Mister Eddie Ferman! On bass, Mister Chip Delany! On sax, Mister Roger Zelazny! On vibes, Mister Gary Burton! On keyboards,

Mister Chick Corea! On clarinet, Mister Barry Malzberg! And for
our first tune, we're gonna hear an old favorite—
   "'Hello, Hugo!'"
   Satchmo put embouchure to lips and began to play.
   For a sixty-five year old editor, he could still blow one mean
horn!

THE HISTORY OF SNIVELIZATION

Ed Ferman
143 Cream Hill Road
West Cornwall, CT 06796

April 1, 1999

Dear Gordon,

Recently I was clearing the detritus of years out of one of my six untenanted stables here, in preparation for receiving my newly purchased herd of Mongolian Steppe Ponies. The musty old building contained a lot of boxed miscellaneous materials connected with The Magazine, and I probably spent as much time rummaging through heaps of correspondence and piles of old contracts (the unique clauses Harlan inserted into several of his were most entertaining, including the codicil that obligated *F&SF* to release a ton of jellybeans at the 1966 Worldcon if "Repent, Harlequin . . . " won the Hugo—even though the story had been published in *Galaxy*!) as I did supervising hordes of forelock-tugging Cornish handymen as they scrubbed stalls and laid in Italian-tile oat-troughs. Only frequent deliveries by

Audrey of champagne and caviar snacks kept my energies up for the task.

Surely the most interesting item I discovered during this nostalgia-provoking chore was "The Smith File," and I've enclosed it with this letter, since traditionally "The Smith File" has become the property of every *F&SF* editor since The Magazine began. (Upon my stepping down from the editorship of The Magazine in June of 1991, I could not at all lay my forgetful hands upon "The Smith File," which is why Kris R. never saw it. Just as well, for its contents might have been too strong for her trusting sensibilities.)

I well recall my own acceptance of "The Smith File" from Avram Davidson when he reluctantly relinquished the editorship. (He in turn had of course received it from Bob Mills, who for his part had taken it from the hands of Tony Boucher. My dad, Joseph, being editor for a year between me and Avram, should have been the custodian for that interval, but because of the circumstances I'm about to relate, Dad never fulfilled that role.)

Avram was living in La Gordita, Belize, at the time of his stepping-down, and I had to make a special trip there in 1965 to retrieve "The Smith File," a trip my father was unwilling to venture on. Wisely so, as events proved. I nearly lost my life several times in the hideous jungle as I made my way (with the help only of several dozen porters and guides equipped with the best Abercrombie & Fitch could provide) to Avram's palm-roofed shack, there to encounter the fever-wracked, hallucinating Davidson, who could not resist muttering, as the folder slipped from his weak fingers, "The horror, the horror . . . ."

In any case, here's a little background on the contents of "The Smith File".

When *F&SF* began publication in the Fall of 1949, The Magazine was of course immediately deluged with submissions from all the famous professionals of the time. One of those would-be contributors was none other than Edward Elmer "Doc" Smith, Ph.D. Of course, Smith's antiquated type of story represented exactly the opposite of what Boucher and Mick McComas intended to publish, and all of Smith's first trunk-cleaning manuscripts sent over the first couple of years were quickly rejected. In no way daunted, Smith began to write fresh stories, all slanted toward this prestigious new market. Every time *F&SF* printed a praise-garnering story, Smith would swiftly attempt to capitalize on the other author's ground-breaking work, with consistently ludicrous results. So wildly awful were these submissions that Boucher took to photostatting and saving them in a special folder. Thus was "The Smith File" born, and all during the fifties it fattened

Then in 1960 came Smith's bitchy, semi-public comment in issue No. 134 of *The Proceedings of the Institute for Twenty-First Century Studies*, Ted Cogswell's famous fanzine aimed at his professional peers: "*F&SF* does not publish what I call science fiction at all." (I don't expect a young gentleman like yourself, Gordon, to be familiar with this ancient history, but you can check page 77 of the Advent reprinting of *PITFCS*.) In reality, Smith's words were the ultimate sour-grapes jab, as he had been trying to place with The Magazine for more than a decade. Bob Mills thought Smith's comment signaled the end of Smith's zany submissions, and closed "The Smith File" with a sigh of relief. But such was not the case; Smith could not control his desire to be a part of The Magazine, and continued to deluge us with his awkward pastiches—many of them under transparent pseudonyms—right up until his death in 1965. Why, once when he heard that The Good Doctor was temporarily incapacitated from a bad case of the flu, he even dared offer us a substitute Science column! That move nearly caused Ike to resign from First Fandom!

Entrusting this folder to you, Gordon, I caution you never to let its contents become public—not so much as excerpts! Even at this late date, if the field learned how one of its most revered writers spent his final fifteen years, it might rock the very foundations of the genre!

Yours in leisure,
(Signed)
Ed Ferman

"The Gnurrs Come from Eddore Out"
by
Reginald "Doc" Bretnor, Ph.D.
(1950)

When Papa Seatonhorn heard about the war with Bobovia, he bought a box-lunch, wrapped his secret weapon in brown paper, and took the first bus straight to Washington. What the old Karfedix carried, straight to the Secret Weapons Bureau, was an Osnomian beam projector powered by the instantaneous release of kilowatt-hours of energy derived from immense copper bars driven nearly to the point of disruption by subatomic force generators . . . .

"Of Time and Tellus, Third Planet of Sol"
by
E. E. Bester, Ph.D.
(1951)

What Macy hated about the man was the fact that he squeaked. With an irresistible and impetuous lunge, Macy ripped the lifelike India rubber mask from the squeaking man's face, revealing—an Overlord from the Hell-Hole of Space!

"Quit Zoomin' Those Mile-long Battlecruisers
Through the Air"
by
Elmer Finney, Ph.D.
(1952)

Hey, quit zoomin' your *hands* through the air, boy—I know you
was a crewmember on the *Skylark of Valeron*! You flew *good*
against Blackie DuQuesne, course you did . . . .

"Three Hearts and Three Arisians"
by
Poul Smith, Ph.D.
(1953)

By chance, I happened to be working for the outfit which hired
Holger Carlsen on his graduation, and got to know him quite well
in the year or two that followed. Right off, I could tell he'd make a
swell Lensman . . .

"My Boyfriend's Name is Boskone"
by
Avram Smith, Ph.D.
(1954)

Fashion, nothing but fashion. Virus X, latest insidious plague
unleashed by the cowardly Boskonians, had not even half-run its
course of ravaging Rigel Four when Virgil Samms arrived . . . .

"Call Me from the Valley of Nucleonics"
by
Manly E. E. Wellman, Ph.D.
(1954)

. . . The storekeeper hung a lantern to the porch rafters as it got
dark . . . "Friend," he said to me, "did I ask your name?"

"Neal Cloud," I named myself, and added, "I'm here to blast your vortex."

"The [Widget], the [Wadget] and Worsel"
by
Edward E. Sturgeon, Ph.D.
(1955)

Throughout the continuum as we know it (and a good deal more, as we don't know it) there are cultures that fly and cultures that swim . . . . And then there are those cultures that breed scaly yet lovable creatures like Worsel the Velantian . . . .

"Second Stage Tweener"
by
Leigh "Doctoress" Brackett, Lady Ph.D.
(1955)

A taxicab turned the corner and came slowly down the street.

"Here he is!" shrieked the Children of the Lens. "Uncle Kimball!"

"Wilderness of Interpenetrating Galaxies"
by
Zenna Smith, Ph.D.
(1957)

. . . "What canyon?" I asked.

"The canyon where The People live now—my People. The canyon where they located after the shields of their starship, the Z9M9Z, were overwhelmed in incandescent coruscating waves of offensive power and their multi-million-plugged boards were blown!"

"MS. Found in a Nth-Space Fortune Cookie"
by
E. E. Kornbluth, Ph.D.
(1957)

They say I am mad, but I am not mad—angry, sure, but not mad! Damn it, I've written and sold two million words of fiction, and not a single one has placed at this big-headed, fancy-pants, not-even-a-real-pulp, New-York-literary-type digest! And it's dollars to doughnuts (and I know my doughnuts!) that they won't take this one either, even though I've tarted it up like an Aldebaranian hell-cat!

"Flowers for Lensmen"
by
"Doc" Edward Daniel Elmer Keyes, Ph.D.
(1959)

progris report 1 martch 3

Doctor Smith says I should rite down what I think and remembir and evrey thing that happens to me from now on while I am still suffrin from the stuperfying ray of the Fenachrone . . . .

"The Quest for Saint Kinnison"
by
E. Elmer Boucher, Ph.D.
(1959)

The Bishop of Rome, the head of the Holy, Catholic and Apostolic Church, the Vicar of Christ on Earth—in short, the Pope—brushed a cockroach from the filth-encrusted wooden table, took another sip of the raw red wine, and resumed his discourse.

Every word the Pope uttered was picked up by Eddorian spy rays from light-years away . . . .

"Rogue Moon of Radelix"
by
Algis Smith, Ph.D.
(1960)

Late on a day in 1959, Edward Hawks, Doctor of Science, cradled his long jaw in his outsized hands and hunched forward with his sharp elbows on his desk.

His own wife, a thionite-sniffer! And all because of him! What a zwilnik he was!

"Science: Secrets of the Kettle"
by
Isaac Smithimov, Ph.D.
(1963)

In 1915, when I was working for the Bureau of Standards, helping to establish tolerance standards for the weight of commercially sold butter, I often pondered the mysteries of efficient packing moduli. But the mathematical rigors of this field were beyond me until I obtained my doctorate. Then, in 1936, while employed by Dawn Doughnuts in Jackson, Michigan, I was splattered by some hot oil from a sizzling batch of Boston Kremes. The ensuing hospital stay allowed me to focus my mind on this never-forgotten riddle, and I soon was the proud papa of Patent No. 17349128, which detailed the famous "Thirteenth Doughnut in a Dozen Box" algorithm . . . .

"Cantata 140 to the Tenth Power"
by
E. E. K. Dick, Ph.D.
(1964)

The young couple, black-haired, dark-skinned, probably Mexican or Puerto Rican, stood nervously in front of the Arisians, and the boy, the husband, said in a low voice, "Sir, we want to become Lensmen."

"The Lonely Overworld"
by
E. E. Vance, Ph.D
(1965)

On the heights above the river Xzan, at the site of certain ancient ruins, Smithcounu the Beloved Pulpster had built a manse stocked with fiction to his private taste: an eccentric structure housing gee-whiz heroics, interstellar battles, instant paradigm-shattering inventions, and sensawunda. But lately, despite all his spells, he could never entice anyone to visit . . . .

MISSED CONNECTIONS

Missed Connections
by
Jaime "Zero Degrees of Separation" Birch
[Reprinted by kind permission of *Scienterrific American*]

I was pedaling my training-wheel-equipped unicycle—a device whose inventor remains stubbornly anonymous—across London Bridge—the old structure, now transplanted into the desert wastes of the Colonies—when the effects of the unmediated solar photons landing on my fuzz-fringed bald pate and thus raising my cranial temperatures triggered one of my typical elaborate insights into just what a wild and woolly world of might-have-been "missed connections" we inhabit. My Amtrak Metroliner of thoughts (Philadelphia to Boston in only fifteen hours!; what would our ancestors have thought of that!) went something like this, as best as I can reconstruct the mental chain from engine to caboose as I lie here in my hospital bed.

One of the engineers (from the Greek, "en-gynos," or "watcher of women") responsible for reconstructing the London Bridge in the USA was named Gib Prinker. A graduate of MIT, Prinker had of course lived in Boston while attending that school (which never matriculated anyone from my family), since he found the daily commute from his native Moosescat, Wisconsin beyond his capacities. While resident in "Beantown," Prinker began to wonder about his adopted home's nickname. A little research at various libraries (an institution developed during proto-Classical times, at an unknown location somewhere between Mohenjo-Daro and Brooklyn) soon revealed to Prinker that he had no idea how to discover this bit of trivia, and he quickly gave up and returned to his now much-quoted study, "Mozzarella As High-tensile Denture Adhesive."

Had Prinker persisted in his quest, however, he would have discovered that the cognomen "Beantown" derived from the exploits of one Abraham Bean, early Massachusetts colonist. Bean (whose family in England hailed from Lower Twaddle, only a dozen counties away from my own birthplace) had nearly founded Boston, overshooting that city's current location by mere scores of leagues to plant King George's flag right where the construction of the Quabbin Reservoir would one day expunge all traces of his endeavor from the face of the globe. In honor of this, the capitol of the state was named after a common foodstuff which half the colonists couldn't tolerate.

The main ingredient of this delightful dish, the humble legume, *should* be our focus. Instead, we look to the familiar crockery in which baked beans are, well, baked. This type of pot owes its existence to German ingenuity. Hermann Schlegelmilch was a minor chemist in the town of Krebs-Rhenghune during the pre-heyday of the post-halcyon German dominance of the non-southern-hemispheric industrial establishment (circa 1650 AD or 329 BC). One day while testing various lacquers which he hoped would render the splintery seats of outhouses smooth to the touch, Schlegelmilch concocted a type of glaze with an incidental property that allowed ceramics not to interact atomically with the potent mustard most often used in baked-bean recipes. Dimwit-tedly, yet with high hopes, Schlegelmilch applied this fixative to a three-holer owned by Nasty Prince Ruprecht, causing a Royal Arse Rash and earning his subsequent beheading. (Only centuries later did some other German whose name escapes me rediscover this commercially valuable glaze.)

Mustard, of course, was first cultivated by the Hindu culture in the district of Kapok. Legend has it that the god Chakramulabonda first introduced mustard seeds to mankind. Because mankind had prayed, however, for potato chips, Chakramulabonda is little worshipped today.

Another deity little worshipped today started life as a histori-cally verifiable mortal. Pompilius Rhinelander first appeared in the historical record in the year 1849, when he made a huge strike during the California Gold Rush. What Rhinelander struck was oil off the California coast. Building the world's first floating oil recovery platform (assembled out of milkweed pods collected by an army of women named, not as one might expect, "Rhinelander's Rhinemaidens," but "those unlucky harlots grown too old for turning tricks"), Rhinelander soon became the richest man east of the Yangtze. Taking his vast fortune, he retired to a mansion in San Francisco, where he talked about funding a laboratory for the investigation of the potential uses of what he referred to as "an undervalued commodity," H_2O. (Apparently, Rhinelander had no idea what compound two atoms of hydrogen and one atom of oxygen actually constituted! Answer to be revealed in next month's column!) Anyway, nothing ever came of all this boastful hot air, and Rhinelander soon wasted his wealth in a series of wild parties, which earned him the aforementioned short-term worship from many sycophants and hangers-on.

Hot air today, of course, has numerous applications, not the least of which is drying hair. The first practical hair dryer—a behemoth weighing nearly six stones and standing ten hands high—was the lifework of Rapunzel Shoat of Bleeding Oaks, California. (Shoat was not one of the first female pioneers of technology, but merely a cruelly misnamed male.) In 1926, Shoat—through a company he had funded with his life-savings and misleadingly named John Held's Flapper Girl Products—offered his patented invention to the marketplace, expecting many units to be eagerly snapped up. Not one was sold, however, and Shoat committed suicide by filling his lungs with hot air, not from his own machine but from the exhaust of a Model T.

Henry Ford never knew Shoat, nor did Thomas Edison. Other figures of that critically fertile period whom Shoat avoided meeting were Elinor Glyn, Charlie Chaplin, Albert Einstein (not the physicist, of whose existence Shoat was actually unaware, but the same-named sole barber in Shoat's hometown!), and a thirteen-year-old Richard Nixon.

Today, the President of the United States has many science advisors to help him guide the nation's policy toward research and development. One of the largest projects ever recommended by several administrations (both Democratic and Republican, but never third-party because no such candidate has ever been elected) was the Superconducting Super Collider, which, as some of us in the know recall, was never built.

And that big expensive worthless hole in Texas is as close as we're going to get to my inexplicable and ill-fated pointless crossing of that little bit of Old Blighty far to the north. Except that both this mental hegira and my pedal-driven transit of London Bridge have left me with a splitting headache!

IN THE AIR

I don't get into New York City that often these days. Consequently, I'm always overwhelmed during my visits not only by the vivid stimuli attendant on that unique urban milieu but also by the effort of maintaining a mental appointment book that includes as many visits to contacts in the publishing business—editors, agents and fellow writers—as can possibly be crammed into my unavoidably brief stay.

These distractions were my only excuse for telling the Port Authority-trolling cab driver who picked me up my real line of work when he asked.

"Science fiction writer, huh?" Contrary to expectations, the cabbie was not a foreign-born low-rung struggler but a young white goateed guy, some member of the Tamagochi generation earning a few bucks between Phish concerts.

It was too late now to deny my foolish admission, so, bracing myself for the flood of snide derision that so often followed such a revelation, I replied, "Yes. Just had a new novel out last year." I didn't offer my byline or the title, hoping to avoid the obligatory, "I never heard of you or your book" response. But the cabbie's next words shocked me completely.

"Let me ask your expert opinion then. Don't you think the

old-fashioned plot potential of an integral Dyson Sphere has been completely superseded by the pointillistic Dyson Cloud concept?"

I couldn't find my tongue for about thirty seconds. When I managed to reply, I stammered, "Wuh-well, not entirely. There's still a lot of mileage left in the older version that even Bob Shaw didn't extract."

"Who?"

"Bob Shaw? The British writer who died not long ago—"

"Never heard of him."

"But I assumed you were a fan . . . ."

The driver took a hand off the wheel to make a dismissive gesture, and we nearly ran up the business end of a garbage truck bearing the colorful urban motto, "Open wide, West Virginia!".

"Nah! I can't remember the last time I read a *book.*"

"Movies then?"

"Old media, dude."

"You surf the e-zines?"

"Not the fiction ones. I really like the WWF site though."

My face must have registered my utter confusion. "How did you get interested in the fictional use of Dyson Spheres then?"

The insouciant driver shrugged, and we elegantly sideswiped a bike messenger. "I can't really say. It's just, like, something in the air, you know. People are always talking about some topic or other. I must have overheard a conversation and started wondering."

The rest of our intermittent dialogue was unmemorable, and by the time the cabbie deposited me outside my hotel, I had managed to put aside the conundrum. Having my first-offered credit card embarrassingly declined at the check-in desk helped concentrate my mind on the grim realities of maneuvering through the unforgiving city in pursuit of my livelihood. So when the bellhop, tip in hand, hesitated on the threshold of my room, watching as I unpacked a stack of my latest paperback, and then asked me, "Sir, exactly how do you portray a working nanotechnology so as to avoid rendering it indistinguishable from magic?", I was completely flummoxed.

I focused on the bellhop for the first time and saw a wizened oldster, one of those New York working stiffs who seemed to have survived from a prehistoric era. I decided to adopt a friendly manner.

"Ah, my friend, you must be an old pulps fan! Do you know I've actually shaken Jack Williamson's hand?"

"Who?"

"Aren't you perhaps a member of First Fandom, conversant with science fiction from its earliest days?"

"That Buck Rogers stuff? Never touch it!"

"Why are you quizzing me about Clarke's Law then?"

"I don't know what the hell you're talking about, mister! I ask you a simple question and you fancy it all up! Thanks for the one-dollar tip, big guy!"

With the noise of the slamming door filling my ears, I sat on the bed and tried to make sense of what had just happened. Ten minutes later, acknowledging my utter failure to comprehend anything, I got up and had a shower. Then I went to my noontime appointment.

Gardner Dozois sat in his office at *Asimov's* with a strange expression on his normally jolly hirsute face. Gazing abstractedly out the window, he fondled an expensive-looking chrome gadget which I mistook at first for a *Star Wars* prop. I clapped the editor heartily on his shoulder and made what I thought was a decent joke.

"Shouldn't you leave those toys to Scott Edelman's *Sci-Fi Entertainment* magazine, Gardner? After all, you're running a *literary* SF magazine here!"

My editor swiveled around to regard me with utter solemnity. "This isn't a toy. It's a professional-grade chef's mandoline. It slices vegetables in a special way. Watch."

From a desk drawer he took a large Bermuda onion, which he proceeded to turn into a heap of redolent slivers while I watched in total astonishment.

"That—that's wonderful, Gardner. But I wanted to talk to you about my novella . . . ."

From beneath the pile of traumatized onion shreds, Gardner withdrew a soggy manuscript. "Is this it? You'd better take it back. I haven't read it yet, and I doubt I ever will."

"But I submitted it six months ago! It can't be *that* bad!"

"It's not, it's not. But I'm out of this whole stale business now. I'm going to open a restaurant in Philadelphia. *Chez Dozois.*"

"You're abandoning your whole career, a lifetime spent in the field? I can't believe what I'm hearing! Why not at least wait until retirement age? Why now?"

"I can't explain. It's just something in the air."

"I—I'd better leave now."

"One minute." The ex-editor reached into the drawer that had supplied the onion and took out a fluffy chef's toque. He donned it, smiled, and asked, "What do you think?"

"Beautiful. Now if I can have my story back, please—"

Storming out, I passed Stan Schmidt. The Burl-Ives-like editor of *Analog* was standing by the water cooler, strumming an acoustic guitar while the vivacious Sheila Williams sang a Peter, Paul and Mary song for an audience of coworkers.

Out on the sidewalk, the smell of onions from my briefcase made me start to salivate, and I zeroed in on a souvlaki vendor, resigned to forgoing my editor-sponsored lunch (unless of course I was content to wait for the imminent opening of *Chez Dozois*). Assembling my sandwich, the vendor caught a glimpse of my Nebula nominee lapel pin.

"Maybe you can help settle an argument 'tween me and the wife, buddy. Do androids and other human simulacra question the epistemological basis of reality, or are they just displaced ethnic stereotypes?"

I dropped the sandwich and fled.

My next appointment wasn't until two. I killed time on a bench in Washington Square. During that interval, I overhead average children, teens and adults discussing, among other topics, the practicality of governing interstellar empires, whether artificial intelligence would be achieved through top-down or bottom-up architecture, in what ways the term "water-margins" differed from "borderlands," and whether the Wellsian dictum warning against "one oddness too many" in fantastic stories was still applicable in postmodern fabulations.

Dazed and bewildered, I staggered over to the Flatiron Building to meet with Gordon van Gelder.

For one brief moment I could pretend that the strange mental virus "in the air" had failed to infect the youthful editor of *F&SF*, for he sat calmly, reading a magazine. But then I noticed that the stubble-cheeked boyish blue-penciller was examining not his usual copy of *Publisher's Weekly*, but rather a glossy museum catalog. Spying me, he set the catalog aside and extended his hand.

"How are you doing?" Gordon graciously asked me.

"I've felt better. And you?"

"Just wonderful! I have a new job now. Director of the Curt Teich Postcard Archives out in Wauconda, Illinois. I curate my first show next month. You'll be getting an invitation of course."

I edged carefully toward the exit. "And my column?"

"Oh, naturally you'll have to take that up with the new editor, whoever that might be. There's a wealth of applicants—folks you've never heard of have come out of the woodwork—but Ed's too busy earning his Florida real-estate broker's license to interview them yet. However, if you can write entertainingly about postcards—"

I knocked down a Chinese restaurant delivery-boy in my haste to clear Gordon's offices. Helping the lad up, I was somehow not surprised to hear him exclaim, "TANSTAAFL!"

The downgoing elevator opened its doors to pick up passengers, and I was startled to spot Tom Doherty, Tor's own dapper publisher. Dressed as if he had stepped out of Tom Wolfe's sartorial dreams, the grinning Nebula Banquet sponsor wore a pair of binoculars around his neck.

"Can't talk now," Doherty blithely informed me. "I'm off to Saratoga for the opening day of Race Week. I've invested all of Tor's working capital in a stable of Kentucky thoroughbreds. Bye!"

In the Tor offices, pandemonium reined, as workers hurriedly cleaned their desks and conducted phone interviews with potential new employers. I stopped Patrick Nielsen Hayden and asked despondently if perhaps he planned on remaining behind to salvage this mess.

"*Moi? Au contraire.* Theresa and I have been tapped as hosts for a new network morning show. Regis and Kathie Lee, watch your ratings!"

My last hope was a certain silver-haired science-fictional patriarch. I stumbled into David Hartwell's office. He was busy on the phone, but waved me to a chair.

"What do you mean they can't get the fabric to us? Damn it, we placed the order weeks ago! Well, hold their feet to the fire on it!"

He slammed the phone down and turned to me. "Sorry about that. But my new line of Hawaiian shirts is slated to debut in Milan next week, and I need to make sure we can fill all the anticipated orders. As soon as the buzz starts in *Women's Wear Daily*, I'm outta this sinking ship!"

Well, I beat Hartwell out the Tor offices by a week or so. But unlike him, I had no destination other than a dark bar. After six drinks—and a desultory discussion with the bartender about first-contact protocols—that was where the ghost found me.

He looked a lot like Heinlein and a little like Asimov, but there were elements of Frank Herbert in the beard, and a little Simak around the eyes.

The wavery ghost said, "Don't worry, son. It's just our field's version of the Negroponte Flip."

"The what?"

"Nicholas Negroponte, bigwig at MIT. He noticed that media that were once delivered by wire had gone wireless, and vice versa. He called it the Negroponte Flip."

"And you're claiming—?"

"That all the common people, the mundanes—the mob who once knew nothing about science fiction—have become saturated with it, thanks to seventy years of exposure. Especially lately, with the new high profile of the field. The tropes are all in the air now. No one even has to read or watch the stuff anymore. It just drifts out of the noosphere straight into their heads."

"What about the professionals?"

"The high priests have burnt out. Their mental circuits are overexposed. They're the only ones in the world now who are immune to a sense of wonder."

"Well, at least we oldtimers will be famous and revered for our literary inventions."

"Not really. It's all too generic. Can you name the guy who invented the cinematic car chase?"

I pushed away woozily from the bar. "There's only one thing left for me to do then."

The ghost looked nervous. "You can't kill yourself over this."

"Who's going to kill himself? There's a Starbucks franchise for sale back home that I've had my eye on for some time now!"

WHEN YOU MIDLIST UPON A STAR

"Oprah Winfrey may have her reading club, but other celebrities are joining efforts to persuade more Americans to pick up a book. In a campaign designed to make reading cool to young people—and by extension, to sell more books—the actress Whoopi Goldberg and the talk show host Rosie O'Donnell are being featured in ads promoting reading as hip."

—Dana Canedy, *The New York Times*, April 20, 1999.

My books weren't selling well, not well at all. So my publisher called me into his office, handed me a business card, and said, "These people are your last hope. Go see them right now."

Out on the cold street, I consulted the card:

CELEBRIBLURBS
"You hack 'em, we flack 'em!"
Ogilvy Hozzana, President

I reached the address given on the card and was ushered into the office of Hozzana himself. A fat, buoyant fellow with a greasy comb-over, an expensive suit that had certainly originated in Hong Kong but had apparently traveled to these shores on the back of a stowaway in a dirty cargo hold, and an unlit cigar clenched between his tombstone teeth, the genius behind Celebriblurbs kindly bade me sit.

"Your publisher has already called me, kid. You sound like just the kind of client whose career we can turn around. Apparently, you write swell stuff—for them what likes it—but you come off as a little highbrow, and your books don't move out of the stores any faster than a salted slug."

"Well, I suppose—"

Hozzana leaned forward confidentially and poked his cigar at me. "The only thing you're lacking is some star-power behind your bullshit. Endorsement by the rich and famous, that's what moves units these days. And that's precisely what we offer. Now, why don't you tell me a little bit about your last book?"

"It's, um, kind of gonzo speculation—"

"Bingo! Right away you've helped me narrow down the list of possible blurbers."

"But I had some notion that I'd be able to select the personality whom I wanted to appear on the jacket."

"No way, kid! All our celebrities have patented consistent images that have to be guarded and nurtured. That's the whole product they're selling. If we let the authors pick and choose, it'd be chaos! What if we had the same star endorsing multiple books with radically different viewpoints? Charlton Heston boosting Jerry Pournelle *and* Lew Shiner! Fugheddiboutit! Or what about the case where the totally wrong guy appears on a book—say, Arnold Schwarzenegger's moniker sprawling across the latest Joyce Carol Oates? The consumer wouldn't know what the hell the celebrity stood for anymore! No, there's a science to this racket, and that's what you're buying from me, my expertise. Each star has a certain profile that we carefully match to the author."

"But I pictured Whoopi or Rosie—"

"Not in this lifetime, pal! Absolutely not! In your field, Whoopi only does Octavia Butler and Samuel Delany and Owl Goingback. Rosie handles Connie Willis and Jonathan Lethem. Now, for your kind of Rudy-Rucker-style craziness—have I pegged you right or not?—we want maybe Johnny Depp or Sean Penn, Sandra Bernhard or Janeane Garofalo. Maybe somebody like Jack Nicholson if we're pitching it to an older audience."

"Wow, Jack Nicholson—"

"Whoa, boy—I didn't promise Jack, I said somebody like Jack. How's Dennis Hopper sound to you?"

"Dennis Hopper? Is he even mentally stable enough to write a whole sentence?"

Hozzana burst out laughing like merry old King Cole. "You thought the stars would actually read your book and write their own blurbs? Man, it's a miracle you haven't been eaten alive by this business before now! There's no way these Λ-list people have time for that kind of nonsense. They just lease their names to us. We have an extensive staff here who compose the actual celebriblurbs. They're the schmucks who do the actual reading—sometimes, if the deadline isn't too tight."

"Gee, I don't know, Mr. Hozzana, this seems awfully false and unethical—"

"What's unethical about it? The celebrities have entrusted their names to me, and I apply them in a manner that safeguards them and you. Celebrity endorsements have always been like this. You think Lorne Greene ate Alpo?"

"If you're going to make everything up, could I have some input into the blurbs then?"

"Sorry, kid, no way. If you were capable of pitching your own books effectively, you'd be rubbing shoulders with King, Grisham and Crichton by now. Like I told you, this is a science. Hey, don't look so down at the mouth. The most I can let you do is pick out a few generic blurbs that we can use as a starting point. Take a gander at these."

Hozzana passed me a sheet of paper, and I read the first few entries:

"So shocking it made me spit out what I was chewing!"—Anthony Hopkins.

"More different styles here than in my whole back catalog."—Madonna.

"I read it all greedily in one sitting and it really moved me."—Terry Jones.

"This is the kind of space opera that makes *Star Wars* look like *Battlestar Galactica*!"—Mark Hamill.

"Kept my hard-drive spinning!"—Bill Gates.

"I pictured Mira Sorvino as the lead all the time I was reading!"—Uma Thurman.

"I pictured Uma Thurman as the lead all the time I was reading!"—Mira Sorvino.

"Number One on my list of 'Top Ten Reasons to Shut Off the TV'!"—David Letterman.

"As chilling as the words 'NYPD! Freeze!'"—Rudy Giuliani.

"A novel that's sexier than Viagra!"—Bob Dole.

I handed the list back to Hozanna.

"Well, kid, what'll it be?"

"None of these, Mr. Hozanna. I'm afraid I've changed my mind. In fact, I'm thinking of getting out of fiction writing altogether."

Hozanna shrugged unconcernedly. "Your call, kid. Mind if I ask what you're gonna do instead?"

"I just got an inspiration for a best-selling book of lists: *Bedside Reading of the Rich and Famous*. I'll compile it from your published blurbs for free under the fair-use laws."

"Slick, kid, slick. Well, when you need a blurb for your new book of blurbs, you know who to come to!"

THE FACTCHECKER ONLY RINGS ONCE

"The Red Planet is really butterscotch. After an exhaustive review of 17,050 images from 1997's Mars Pathfinder mission, astronomers are no longer seeing red in the planet next door. 'The red planet is not red but indeed yellowish brown,' scientists concluded in a report yesterday . . . ."
>   —Seth Borenstein, syndicated news article.

When the doorbell chimed I saved my pitifully brief story to disk and stood wearily up. Six straight hours in front of the computer, and I had managed to write only a measly thousand words. I, who had once been nearly as prolific as Lester Dent, reduced to a crummy four manuscript pages per day. But that's just how things went for the average science-fiction writer in this new era under COSTIVE, and I tried once again to reconcile myself to the changed situation.

Still, I couldn't resist glaring hatefully at the stacks of creativity-inhibiting reference books around my work station before I turned to answer the insistent ringing.

The fellow at the door was your typical attaché-toting bureaucrat: as physically unimpressive as an unweaned kitten, yet radiating a glow of self-satisfied power.

"Nelson Nibbler. I'm here on behalf of COSTIVE."

Nibbler flashed his ID, and I flinched involuntarily at the logo I had come to detest: an optical microscope focused on the open pages of a book, above the legend CONSORTIUM OF STORY TELLERS INSISTING ON VERISIMILAR EXACTITUDE.

"I suppose I have to invite you in."

Nibbler smirked. "According to the latest bylaws of SFWA, to which organization you currently belong—yes, you do."

"Come in then. But I can't spare you much time. I'm trying to finish a short story for a new Marty Greenberg anthology, *Thrilling Tales of Quantum Chromodynamics.*"

Nibbler stepped boldly inside, and I conducted him to the most uncomfortable chair in the house. "I won't take much of your time. I just need to go over some revisions for one of your stories."

"Which one?"

"It's the one Jack Dann and Gardner Dozois selected for their new reprint volume, *Patents!* I believe you titled it 'Vandals of the Hyperspace Barrens.'"

"Yes, that's one of mine. But I wrote that story ten years ago, before COSTIVE ever existed. I understood that old stories were exempt from COSTIVE regulations."

"You haven't been keeping up with the decisions of your own writer's union, I'm afraid. Reprints are no longer grandfathered. They need to be brought retroactively up to COSTIVE standards."

I tried to quell my temper. "You're telling me that not only do I have to inhibit the style, themes and speculations in all my new fiction, but that I have to go back and revise any older work of mine that's up for reprinting?"

"Precisely."

"Does this apply to everyone?"

"Of course. Haven't you seen the new edition of Stan Robinson's *Butterscotch Mars?*"

I hung my head in defeat. Nibbler tried to console me. "It's just what the readers demand nowadays. They've grown used to scientific accuracy in their stories since COSTIVE was formed. And think of the students! How could your stories be used in classrooms if they weren't completely accurate? Aren't you happy about all those increased royalties from textbook sales?"

I exploded. "It's not worth the emotional and creative pain! These regulations of yours have given even Hal Clement a nervous breakdown! They made Robert Forward move to Russia! Greg Bear now has a heroin habit, and Stephen Baxter is writing for *Coronation Street*! Greg Benford lives like a hermit inside the Nuclear Waste Repository! But the worst of it is what you guys did to Bruce Sterling!"

Nibbler grew defensive. "We were not responsible for Mr. Sterling running amok. Simply scheduling him for a mandatory six-week re-education camp on the technicalities of piloting ultralight aircraft was no justification for him climbing that Texas clock tower with his rifle."

"You folks practically murdered poor Bruce!"

"Come, come now, we're not that bad. We only have the best interests of the field at heart. Let's step through the revisions of your own story one by one, and you'll see how easy it is." Nibbler took a xerox of my old story out of his briefcase and smoothed it out on his lap. "Let's consider the title first. We propose changing it to 'Some Tentative Speculations Regarding Sub-Planckian Travel Involving Metric Strains.'"

I stared incredulously at my tormentor. "Now that has real zing."

Nibbler red-pencilled a checkmark next to the title. "I'm glad you like it. That's my salient contribution. The other committee members gave me a round of applause for that one."

"Mister Nibbler, tell me, please: exactly what is your own academic background?"

"I have six advanced degrees in subjects ranging from cosmology to paleontology. But I'm just a junior member of COSTIVE. May I continue?"

"Sure."

"In the first paragraph, you describe your heroine as possessing 'a waterfall of hair black as the Coalsack Nebula.' Now, you should know perfectly well that the nebula in question actually radiates at a large number of wavelengths including the visible. The simile is scientifically inexact. We propose this correction: 'no less than 28 centimeters of hair possessing the reflective qualities of refined graphite plus or minus an order of magnitude.' What do you think?"

"It's charming. Any woman would fall into your arms with sweet talk like that. Go for it."

Completely oblivious to my irony, Nibbler smiled and continued. "On page three, you first describe hyperspace as 'an uncanny otherworld, a violent conglomeration of sense-twisting hallucinatory whorls and streamers, a maelstrom of nauseating otherness.' Can you cite any studies from peer-reviewed scientific journals supporting this description?"

"Of course not! I made it all up for the sake of the story! The drama, man, the drama of it!"

"As we thought. In that case, we're going to have to amend that passage to 'a hypothetical landscape whose qualitative essentials have yet to be determined.'"

I slumped in my chair. "Vivid, very vivid. I can almost see the film version now."

"Ah, if only Hollywood still existed! What a role we could have played in straightening out their mistakes! Now, let's take a look at these equations we'd like you to insert—"

My temper had reached its limits. "Equations! I'll show you equations! Do you know 'eff equals em ay'?"

"Of course—"

I hauled Nibbler up by his shirt. "Well, here's the force of my foot on the mass of your ass, sending you accelerating out of here!"

After slamming the door on Nibbler, I went back to my computer and erased the current story. Then I started a new one with the title "Sweet, Wonderful Surrender," involving a woman named Brittany, the beautiful young heiress of a cosmetics empire, and the complications of her romantic life.

And I gave her a waterfall of hair as red as good old Mars.

THIS IS MY GUN, THIS IS MY PEN, SIR!

"Can one be taught to be a book editor or publisher in a few summer weeks?"

—Martin Arnold,
"Creating Editors and Publishers,"
The New York Times, July 1, 1999.

The raw recruits filed nervously off the bus that had carried them from New York's Port Authority to the secluded camp somewhere in the New Jersey Pine Barrens. A motley group of informally dressed males and females, young and old, they each carried the only items they had been allowed and instructed to bring: a Barnes and Noble canvas bookbag held a copy of *Strunk and White*, an unabridged dictionary, a calculator, a wireless Palm Pilot with stock-market access capability, a box of red-ink pens, a spare pair of reading glasses, a pack of antacid tablets, and an ergonomic chair cushion.

The empty bus drove off. Clustering like spooked cattle, the recruits looked around the unpeopled grounds for guidance. But the mute barracks and other camp buildings some distance away offered no instructions on how to proceed.

"Maybe this is a test of our initiative," said one recruit.

"No way," said another. "I've heard some vague but scary stories from graduates. Our every minute here will be strictly planned and scheduled. There's no free time or self-direction at all."

"Makes sense," said a third. "After all, they've only got a few weeks to shape us into top-of-the-line editors."

"Well, all I know is that for the money they're charging us, we should have a better reception—jug wine and brie at the very least."

A door slammed, and all heads turned toward the sound. A lone figure had emerged from one of the barracks and now strode with macho determination toward them. As the elegantly suited small man drew closer, whispers began to circulate among the recruits.

"Is that—?" "No, it couldn't be." "Yes, I swear it's him."

The man reached a conversational distance and stopped. He superciliously sized up the recruits for a long minute, then spoke in a quiet voice.

"Ladies and gentlemen, allow me to introduce myself. My name is Michael Korda."

The huddled men and women visibly relaxed, which was precisely the reaction Korda had been counting on, for he now thrust his face forward aggressively and bellowed.

"BUT YOU MAGGOTS CAN CALL ME GOD! AND GOD'S ONE GOAL FOR THE NEXT THREE WEEKS IS TO TURN YOU PUSILLANIMOUS PUS-BUCKETS INTO EDITORS AT LEAST COMPETENT ENOUGH TO SHINE MAXWELL PERKINS'S SHOES! WHEN I SAY 'REVISE,' YOU'RE GONNA SAY, 'HOW MANY CHAPTERS, SIR!' HAVE I MADE MYSELF CLEAR?"

Several people had fainted. All were trembling. One fellow dared to answer with a meek, "Yuh—yes, sir."

"I CAN'T HEAR YOU, WORM!"

"Yes, sir!"

Korda fell back into a normal stance. Clasping his hands behind his back, he strode up and down surveying his plebes. When he next spoke, his voice was once again quiet and reserved, exhibiting the patrician tones that had smoothed many a profitable publishing deal and soothed many a queasy author.

"I'm glad we have an understanding. Please realize that I bear you no personal animosity. Your histories and characters mean nothing to me, except insofar as they relate to your nascent editorial skills. I don't care whether you've graduated from an Ivy League school or a community college. Tennessee Williams once told me, 'A sweet pot of red beans and rice trumps a lousy plate of lobster fra diavolo every time, sugar-honey.' You're all the same raw material in my hands. And since I have very little time in which to mold your impressionable minds, I've found that terror works best. Consequently, your stay here will be punctuated with frequent unpredictable shocks—akin to the hostile buyouts you'll soon be experiencing in the workplace—all calculated to drive my lessons home."

The brave recruit who had previously responded now dared to ask a question. "Sir, are you the only instructor at the camp?"

"By no means. We'll have a number of visiting lecturers coming in who will assist me in honing your talents. These men and women range the gamut from editors to publishers to distributors to booksellers, from critics and reviewers to literary agents and Hollywood moguls. Each of these experienced experts will share their immense wisdom and knowledge with you—

"—AND YOU'LL SUCK IT ALL DOWN LIKE PIGLETS AT THEIR MAMA'S TEATS AND MAKE IT PART OF YOUR VERY CELLS!"

Once the leaves on the trees had ceased quivering and the sound of shattering window glass had diminished, Korda continued.

"Let me particularize just a few of the visiting editors who have graciously consented to enlighten you.

"We'll hear from Bill Bruford of *The New Yorker*, who'll instruct us how to manufacture superstar writers out of wet-behind-the-ears, squeaky-voiced, creative-writing graduate students.

"Lecturing us on the niceties of claiming posthumous credit for reconfiguring the stories of deceased authors will be Gordon Lish, who will never let you forget his tenure at *Esquire*.

"Alice Turner of *Playboy* will explicate the usefulness of cognitive dissonance, concentrating on the juxtaposition of pubic hair to Norman Mailer-magnitude pontifications.

"Tina Brown of *Talk* will advise us about the benefits and pitfalls of Hollywood synergy.

"The legendary Edward Ferman has very kindly agreed to interrupt his retirement to help us understand how his legal adoption of the current editor of *F&SF* has insured the continuation of the Ferman publishing dynasty.

"And Helen Gurley Brown has likewise broken her well-deserved leisure to help us all achieve washboard abs."

Korda paused, then fixed the potential editors with the same adamantine gaze that had once made his opponent James Jones capitulate in an arm-wrestling bout at Elaine's that had already stretched on for half an hour. Knees wobbled as they awaited his next words.

"But on a day-to-day basis, I'm the only instructor you'll see regularly. And by regularly I mean IN YOUR FREAKING FACE TWENTY-FOUR-SEVEN! When you awake at four A.M. for your mock subway commute, I'll be the annoying fellow straphanger who spills coffee on your irreplaceable manuscript. When you pair off and sit down for a pretend three-hour lunch with your most important author, I'll be the lousy waiter who can't get your orders right. When you're eagerly awaiting the dummy sales figures on what you expect will be a bestseller, I'll be the intern who adds or subtracts an extra zero from the numbers. In short, for the next few weeks I'm going to be both your worst, most hated enemy, and your best, most cherished friend. When I'm done with you, you will have gone through the same baptism by fire that once took an editorial lifetime.

"Now, the first order of business is to get you neophytes into our fully staffed spa and salon for a stylish haircut, followed by a facial, a manicure and a pedicure. After that, you'll each be measured for a tailored power suit. An editor always has to look his or her best. AND RIGHT NOW YOU SLOBS LOOK LIKE A BUNCH OF PUBLICISTS OR SALES REPS! After that, you'll each receive half a dozen 600-page manuscripts which I expect to be line-edited before breakfast."

The recruits made a tentative step or two toward the barracks before being brought up short by Korda's stentorian assault.

"DID I SAY 'DISMISSED' YET, SLIME? NOW, HOLD UP ONE OF YOUR RED MARKERS HIGH, GRAB YOUR CROTCHES, AND REPEAT AFTER ME—!"

HAIL TO THE HACK

"When Charles Brockden Brown, the first professional American author, sent a copy of his *Wieland* to Thomas Jefferson in 1798, he must, beneath his modest disclaimers, have had some sense of his and the President's kinship as revolutionaries . . . . But if Jefferson ever found the time to read Brown's novel, he left no record . . . "

—Leslie Fiedler,
Love and Death in the American Novel

I smiled broadly for the reporter's tiny wireless webcam pasted like a bindi to her forehead. My last answer had been exceptionally well-phrased, and both of us knew my clever words would go down well with her literate online audience at the venerable *Salon/Onion/Washington Post*. Suddenly the Oval Office seemed a warm and cozy parlor, despite all its ostentatious trappings of mid-twenty-first-century status, from genetically modified Secret Service bodyguards to the laserline link to the Lunar Republic.

"So," the young woman continued, "you ascribe the remarkable rise to power of your party mainly to the exhaustion of all other factions, and to the public's disgust with their many scandals and unappealing candidates. 'The blindly unimaginative misleading the marginalized and blindsided' I believe was your phrase of a moment ago."

"Exactly so. Leaders without vision and visionaries without leaders. A regular mess—until we came along. But there was also the not insignificant matter of our enticingly revolutionary platform."

The young woman grinned. "Ah, yes, that famous exhortation. 'Don't leave the lying to the amateurs! Elect the most qualified fictionalizers around!'"

"We adopted that policy from a best-selling book by one of our members who had actually dabbled in politics in the twentieth century. As one of his characters noted: 'They'll vote for me because I'm the best liar, because I do it honestly, with a certain finesse. They know that lies and truth are very close, and that something beautiful rests in between.'"

"And this genius was—?"

"Mark Helprin."

The woman winked, but I didn't misinterpret the gesture as indicating she was offering me a lewinsky. She was only using her wetware to establish a hyperlink to Helprin's name. "So having adopted this revelation as your party's platform, you effectively stepped into a vacuum and took control."

I templed my fingers together thoughtfully. "Not a vacuum, but a chaos. Try to recall the aftermath of the election of 2012. I know you were probably only a child then, but surely some of the national confusion must have registered even on your generation. President Ventura rendered an ineffectual quadriplegic by a Head Drop during his Inaugural Smackdown. Vice-President Rodham holding off the New York State Attorney-General and his charges of Catskill real-estate fraud with one hand, while with the other she tried to dismiss the paparazzi photos of her and Martha Stewart skinny-dipping together off Nantucket. And of course the complete collapse of that economic powerhouse Hasbro-Microsoft-Starbucks under the triple assaults of plastic-eating bacteria, cheap qubit computers in a test-tube and terrorist-unleashed coffeeplant-killer viruses. Why, it took Seattle a month to stop all the riots and fires! And once Speaker of the House Beatty ascended to the Presidency, the moral decline was complete."

"But I still don't see how all this allowed your untested party to sweep the 2016 elections. Coming from nowhere to capture the Presidency itself and a majority in both houses—it was just unprecedented!"

"Agreed. But you have to remember that the voting public was truly desperate for uncompromised leaders. Everyone else had already had their chance at running the country, and blown it. Lawyers, businessmen, generals, entertainers, teachers, gangsters— The only organized and capable group that hadn't had its shot at elective office yet was us."

"The Science Fiction Writers of America."

The majestic words resonated mellifluously in the Oval Office, and I paused to let them sink deeply into the unseen audience's ears.

"Yes, the SFWA. I'm surprised you even recall the origin of the acronym. Nowadays, it's such a well-known political trademark that most people don't have much awareness of its original meaning, anymore than folks once thought 'Grand Old Party' when they heard GOP. But your derivation is accurate. The roots of our party lie in a writer's union."

"It must have been some union."

"Indeed. By 2012, practically every best-selling book and movie in the nation was science fiction or fantasy of some sort. Members of SFWA accounted for the direct production of approximately twenty-five percent of the GNP, and had almost single-handedly eliminated the trade deficit. If you added spinoffs and subsidies, our contribution approached thirty percent. Only the popstars and pornstars rivaled our dominance, and we had cleverly established close alliances with them."

"With an eye toward future political maneuvers, perhaps?"

I gave her the same smile that had once caused Oprah to label me the sweetest writer she had ever spotlighted. "It's hard to say now what we had in mind—although we did devote a lot of our energies to internal elections even then. But we were still getting used to national power. We weren't always a major player, you realize. Once upon a time, we were an insignificant ninety-pound weakling of an organization. But the turning point came with two crucial decisions. The first was rather arcane: the decision to reinstate the Dramatic Nebula. I don't expect you to comprehend all the minute historical details of this award, but basically that move tightened our ties to Hollywood, considerably broadening our membership, and hence our clout."

"And what was the second decision?"

"Making J. K. Rowling our permanent Wizard-in-Chief."

The reporter reached religiously up to fondle the pendant of Saint Potter that hung from a chain around her neck, and whispered a short anti-Muggle mantra. "Of course. Immediately you would have enlisted half the nation in your camp, a whole generation. What a stroke of genius!"

I modestly bowed my head. "Thank you. I was Membership Secretary at the time."

"By 2016, then, SFWA felt ready to lead the country."

"Not completely. But we had no choice, due to the chaos I've described. Hastily, we mounted candidates in as many national elections as we could. We couldn't run Rowling for President, of course, as she was a foreigner, but she campaigned like a trooper for us. Still, no one was more surprised than we when we were swept into office by the landslide results you described earlier."

"And it was smooth sailing from that point onward."

"By no means. We've always had internal dissension, even if we've maintained a smooth facade for the good of the country. The tussles between the autocratic and libertarian elements of SFWA were rivaled only by those between the fantasy gals and the Hard SF boys. If you've ever wondered why we have both a Ministry of Surveillance and a Free Dope bureaucracy, now you know."

"Ah, I see! That also explains why the Mars Terraforming program has a Unicorn Repopulation component."

I shrugged. "No matter what changes superficially, compromise lies at the heart of politics."

"Well, you can't fault success. The United States of America has never been stronger or more dominant. Our mode of government by writers has practically swamped the globe. I understand that even that last holdout, France, is finally turning over the reins to their Academy."

"Yes, it looks rather as if the Utopia we long speculated about is finally here. But that reminds me of a pressing chore. I'm afraid we'll have to terminate our interview now."

The reporter followed my lead and arose. "Time to negotiate a treaty or address the UN perhaps?"

"Not at all. I've got the last volume of a trilogy due this week, and my publisher has already told me he's going to demand my advance back if I don't deliver!"

TWO SAMPLE CHAPTERS, AN OUT-
LINE, AND A SAWED-OFF SHOTGUN

"Acclaimed screenwriter and novelist Richard Price is planning a new novel based on a real-life crime—the slaying of New
York City high school teacher Jonathan Levin . . . . Price's last
book, 1998's *Freedomland* was inspired by the Susan Smith
double-murder case in South Carolina."
—From a notice in *Entertainment Weekly* magazine.

The lights of the sound-proofed police interrogation room blazed
down mercilessly on the seated suspect. The focus of the hard
stares of several detectives, the well-groomed, middle-aged
Caucasian perp nonetheless maintained a calm and confident
demeanor consonant with his expensive suit.

One of the detectives, plainly the senior member verging on
retirement, wearily rubbed his stubble-shadowed chin, took a sip
of cold coffee, then addressed the suspect. "Okay, let's go over this
one more time from the top. Your name is Ruprecht Mordred and
you're a publisher, right?"

"Correct. Majority stockholder in Mordred Limited, PLC. We
incorporate several well-known imprints. Beastly Books,

Precious Press, Enormous Advance Publishing, Bridget Jones AdviceLine, Harry Redwall Children's—"

A second detective, almost as well-dressed as Mordred, interrupted. "Okay, we get the picture. You publish a lot of goddamn books. But we're more interested right now in how you commission these books, how they originate."

"Why, just as I told you earlier—the standard, time-honored way. An author or his agent approaches us with a detailed proposal, either verbal or written, and after appropriate editorial consideration and debate, if we see fit we make an offer. Negotiations then occur, leading to a contract signing."

The third detective resembled a battered prizefighter, long-healed broken nose and assorted facial scars. He thrust this alarming face close to Mordred's now. "Come off it, you lousy unit-mover! That ain't the way we heard it. We know all about your dirty little Real Life Plot Engineering Department."

The dapper detective added, "You concealed its expenses pretty thoroughly, Mr. Mordred. But once we tumbled to it, our crack NYPD Bookkeeping Squad found its activity in your ledgers pretty easily."

Now Mordred began to sweat. "How—I mean, I don't know what you're referring to."

"That crummy lie wouldn't fly in a vanity press publicity packet, Mordred. Besides, we've rounded up several of your authors and already gotten full confessions from them."

"Damn those scribbling skunks! Don't they realize I can sue them now under the non-disclosure portion of their contracts?"

"When you're facing twenty-to-life in a federal pen, Mr. Mordred, a civil suit from a pretty-boy publisher looks pretty tame. Some of your best-selling authors are going down for a nice long haul, regardless of coming clean. At the very least, they've all violated the Son-of-Sam laws against profiting from a crime. And as for you—well, you'll be lucky if you don't find yourself enjoying a three-martini, expense-account last meal soon, before you're bound in leather to a limited-edition gurney for a lethal remaindering. Your only hope for any small leniency from the courts is to make a clean breast of everything."

"Yeah, spill your inky guts, dustjacket boy!"

"All right, all right, I'll make my confession, but under one condition."

"Private cell? Expanded visiting privileges? Designer uniform?"

"None of those. I want first North American Serial rights and all options on my own story. A standard publishing agreement. No release of my confession to the newspapers until Mordred Limited has published an instant book."

The detectives stepped aside and consulted in whispers, even employing a cell-phone, before returning to confront Mordred. The senior said, "We can grant that. The governor has agreed to sign. Now, give with the details."

Mordred adjusted his wrinkled lapels and disarrayed styled hair and settled down for a long pitch. "Well, the whole project started after we realized with a shock that all the good crimes, scandals, controversies, natural disasters and historic landmarks had been used up. Sometime around 2010, we awoke to the fact that the entertainment industry had finally outpaced reality. We had stripmined our mother lode of subject matter, converting our precious natural resources into miniseries, docudramas, feature films, and novels faster than they could proliferate. So we at Mordred Limited decided the only thing to do was to create suitable, ah, incidents for our content-producers to refashion into entertainment."

The ugly detective spat out, "You rotten shelf-stuffer! So you started arranging colorful murders!"

"Well, yes, that was our first step. We wanted to proceed simply at first. Tales of exotic killings had always sold well for us, so it seemed a natural step."

"Let me get this straight," the oldest cop said. "You'd hire paid killers from the Mob—"

"Not always. Sometimes we were able to foment murders among the civilians themselves, with the proper inducements or pressures. But in such cases, the aftermath often did not conform to our needs, despite helpful advance input from our consulting authors. We needed the tighter scripting only professional hitmen could supply—hitmen working in conjunction with marketing experts, of course."

"In any case, once the crime had been committed, you assigned one of your writers to fictionalize it."

"Yes, we had a wide choice of specialists. Some writers concentrated on family murders, others on romantic murders or business killings. High school mass shootings required the panoramic skills of a Dickens."

Expressions of disgust escaped the detectives' lips, but their leader pressed on. "You didn't stop there, though."

"No, not after our initial sales figures started coming in. We realized that we could revive the numbers on our lagging espionage novels with a few real life spy scandals."

"So you betrayed dozens of CIA operatives to unfriendly countries."

"Now, now, don't make me sound like a traitor, gentlemen. We uncovered quite a few Israeli and French moles in the State Department as well."

"And it snowballed from there. Terrorist bombings, hijackings, avalanches, cruise-ship sinkings, bank robberies, sexual shenanigans among the rich and famous, even artificial tornadoes— The list of nasty stuff you engineered in order to sell your crummy hardcovers and paperbacks just goes on and on! I'm surprised you didn't try to start a limited nuclear war!"

"We did, but the Pakistanis backed out at the last minute."

"Isn't there anything in your life you have to be proud of, you filthy page-turner?"

Mordred considered a moment. "There *was* the Mars Landing. Most people regard that as a positive achievement, I believe. Our investments and schemings on that one paid off in several best-selling trilogies for our Aegis Books division."

"Okay, Mars was a plus," admitted the senior detective, before adding, "I suppose Hitler liked kittens too. That's enough for today. Take him away, boys."

Flanked by the crude and elegant detectives, Mordred was led toward the door. The senior detective seemed to be struggling with an urge to blurt something out. At the last possible moment, he succumbed.

"And boys—throw the book at him!"

JUST ME AND MY PROTOPLASMIC
EGO EXTENSION

There were quite a few unfamiliar faces at that year's Nebulas Banquet, enough to make me faintly uneasy. I thought I knew everyone in the field by sight—writers, artists, agents, editors, publishers and even their relatives—and now here I was in a room dotted with strangers.

Most of the unknowns seemed to be excessively attentive and earnest young men and women sitting at the tables otherwise occupied by best-selling authors and their claques. These newcomers hung excessively on every word and gesture of the stars. Were these lucky fans who had somehow been granted tickets? Lawyers? Bodyguards? Throughout the evening, my curiosity grew until I couldn't contain it. Eventually, I decided to approach Dirk Camberwell.

The rubicund Camberwell had that very night won a Nebula for the latest installment in his space opera series based on the paintings of Thomas Cole, *Expulsion from Eden*. Naturally, he was in a good mood, and wouldn't, I hoped, mind my importunate question.

"Congratulations, Dirk. Who's your new friend?"

Dirk dropped a beefy arm on the shoulder of the shy bearded fellow standing next to him. "Why, this is my PROTEGE."

I heard the capital letters, but foolishly persisted. "Does he have a name?"

"Dirk Camberwell, of course."

That surreal reply was too much for me, and I made some lame excuses and then my exit from the whole affair.

It wasn't until a month later that I stumbled onto a clue regarding the mystery of Dirk's PROTEGE.

My own name resembles that of a certain top-selling fantasy author, and one day I received some mail addressed to him. It was a glowing but cautiously worded solicitation to acquire a PROTEGE, from a firm called simply, PROTEGES, Ltd..

I headed straight for the headquarters of this enigmatic agency.

On the strength of the letter, I was conducted into the office of the president, one Gunther Tuppleganger, a confident-looking, well-dressed, cosmopolitan fellow. He greeted me heartily by the name of my fellow SFWAn, but I quickly confessed to the imposture.

Tuppleganger snatched the letter out of my feeble clutches. "Give that here! You aren't supposed to know about this offer! You simply don't make enough money to afford it!"

"Mr. Tuppleganger, I'm here solely out of curiosity. I don't care to undermine your business at all. I just need to understand what it's all about!"

"Well, I'm not certain—"

"Whatever you're doing, it can't remain a secret much longer. Dozens of authors are walking around in public with these human lapdogs you're providing. Sooner or later, someone else is bound to inquire. You're going to have to go public eventually."

Tuppleganger acquiesced to my logic. "All right. Sit down and I'll explain. But I'll have to make it brief. I have appointments with potential clients straight through till dinner."

I arranged myself comfortably, and leaned forward to hear the genesis and rationale for this strange business.

"I'm an entrepreneur, one who's always looking for new commercial ventures. The idea for PROTEGES, Ltd., came to me in stages. I was watching a rerun of *Seinfeld* one day, the episode where Kramer gets an intern. I began to think then about the personal assistants that many well-off writers have—"

"You mean like that Marsha DiFilippo woman who works for Stephen King?"

"Yes. Please don't interrupt again, as my time is very valuable. I speculated that perhaps I could run an agency to train and lease such assistants, a combination of obedience school, boot camp and brothel. But further investigation led me to realize that any percentage I earned from the slave-wages paid to such menials would not provide me with sufficient compensation for my efforts.

"My schemes stagnated until one recent seminal confluence of events. While perusing *Locus*, I learned that the late Marion Zimmer Bradley had been personally grooming Mercedes Lackey to carry on Bradley's *Darkover* series. At nearly the same moment I saw a picture of Stephen Baxter side by side with Arthur Clarke, looking like father and son, and learned that Baxter was writing a novel based on instructions from his elder. That's when the epiphany hit me.

"I would provide PROTEGES to famous writers, designated heirs whose sole reason for existence would be to internalize the writing styles of their models and carry on after their deaths."

"I know you told me not to interrupt, Mr. Tuppleganger, but I have to ask one question: why the capital letters?"

"PROTEGE is an acronym, for PROToplasmic EGo Extension."

"But you've just tarted up a good old word that already means just what you need it to mean."

"I realize that. But this is a marketing strategy! The acronym gives us brandname cachet!"

"Oh, sorry. I should have guessed—"

"I found a ready source of PROTEGES in the helplessly unemployed and hopelessly unpublished graduates of college-level creative writing programs. The vast majority of those who emerge from these expensive university workshops are young adults with wonderful technical talents but absolutely no vision of their own. Oh, sure, once in a while, by a rare fluke, you get a Rick Moody, but what are the odds on that? By and large, these superfluous scams generally function as the shoddiest of diploma mills. And by the time the students are finished with their MFAs, they're quite used to modeling themselves on their famous teachers. Effecting the transference to selected science fiction and fantasy authors involves only a few simple behavioral modification techniques."

"What are the exact terms of the contract between the author and his, um, PROTEGE?"

"The author takes the PROTEGE into his or her household, where the aspirant shadows every waking moment of the author, molding style and intellect along the lines of the original. When the original dies, the PROTEGE assumes his or her legal identity and estate—we make suitable payments to the contentious blood relatives if any—and the substitute continues to turn out perfect imitations of the best-selling work demanded by the millions of habituated readers. I believe you can see the attractions for all concerned. Readymade wealth and prestige for the PROTEGE, and literary immortality for the original author."

"And your take?"

"Fifteen percent of the lifetime earnings of both author and PROTEGE."

I whistled. "Nice piece of change."

"And if the PROTEGE adopts a PROTÉGÉ—"

"Say no more. Well, you've thoroughly satisfied my curiosity, Mr. Tuppleganger, and I'll be leaving now. Thank you."

We shook hands and Tuppleganger conducted me to the exit. "I hope someday you'll do well enough to take advantage of our services."

"Thanks. But I already have a tissue sample frozen for when human cloning's perfected."

I left Tuppleganger frowning deeply.

Scaring people with rumors of technological obsolescence—us low-rent SF writers can still manage *some* things on our own.

I'LL TRADE YOU TWO NOBELS, A MACAR-THUR GRANT AND A PULITZER FOR ONE OF THOSE STARRY PAPERWEIGHTS

Doctor Gravity knocked surreptitiously on the door of the secret hideout of The Nine Well-Known. Looking back furtively over his shoulder as if for pursuers, he nervously awaited a response. A small sliding panel inset at eye-level whooshed open, and someone inside stared out, then spoke.

"The Knight lies sleeping—"

"—at the old mill ford."

"Enter."

The luxurious interior of the hideout reflected the deep pockets of the Nine Well-Known: an oriental rug costing the equivalent of two years' of Michael Korda's salary; a mahogany conference table big as Morgan Entrekin's whole office; crystal chandeliers as weighty as the heritage of *The New Yorker*; and nine ergonomic chairs more high-tech than Amazon.com's backorder system.

Doctor Gravity nodded in a curt but friendly fashion to his peer acting as doorman, and the Chicago Mensch nodded back with the dignity befitting the senior member—senior in both years and stature. Seated around the table, the other members of this ultra-exclusive cabal acknowledged Doctor Gravity in their own ways.

The Footnote Kid bestowed a drugged sneer.

The Puritan looked up briefly from annotating for review the collected works of an obscure seventeenth-century Albanian poet and smiled shyly.

White Noise cocked his forefinger and thumb and fired an imaginary gun.

The Handmaiden pursed her lips censoriously.

Gothic Lady squinted through her big eyeglasses as if she had never seen Doctor Gravity before.

Dame Sherlock offered a tight regal wave of her manicured hand.

And Shikasta the Golden caught his gaze over the rim of her cocktail glass.

"Sorry I'm late, guys," apologized Doctor Gravity. "Had to dodge the photographers and rabid fans as per usual."

Kid Footnote drawled, "I still don't dig this anti-media trip of yours, Doc. You should play them for all they're worth, like I do."

White Noise intervened on behalf of Doctor Gravity. "Shut up, Kid, and quit offering advice to your betters. You stole all your moves off Doctor Gravity in the first place, so of course you felt obligated to change at least one of your career gimmicks."

Kid Footnote shrugged blithely. "Whatever."

The two standing members quickly took their seats, and then the Chicago Mensch, presiding at the head of the table, called the meeting to order.

"My fellow authors, it's that time of the year again, and I must sadly report that despite all of us having outstanding new work published recently, not one of us has succeeded in our perennial goal." The Chicago Mensch held up a piece of paper. "Here's the current final Nebula ballot, fresh from our mole in SFWA, and our names are nowhere to be seen." He slapped the paper dismissively. "What's *wrong* with us, people? Are we losing our fire, our spirit, our chutzpah? We all want this award more than we ever coveted any other prize. It's the only real validation of our novels, despite our titanic mainstream successes. We all admit the other prizes are just meant to impress academics and elite publishing executives. Yet year after year we fail even to come close to winning a Nebula! What are we going to do about this?"

The Puritan put aside his notes, then cleared his throat and said, "I hate to point fingers, Mensch, but you've probably done less than anyone in this room to get on the Nebula ballot. You seem to think the award will just fall into your lap out of respect for your longevity. I mean, the rest of us have all at least written some real science fiction. But the most you've ever done is title one of your books *Mr Sammler's Planet*. That was a good fake-out move—until anyone actually read the book. But since then, what?"

"Yeah," the Footnote Kid said. "I busted my hump to write the biggest novel around, knowing how much the Nebula voters go for epics."

"And I composed a whole interminable series," said Shikasta the Golden, "since I figured trilogies are popular."

Gothic Lady preened. "I'm the only one who ever gets into an actual prozine. *Fantasy and Science Fiction*, of course. And I've boosted Lovecraft so much lately that I've started to see shuggoths."

"The Handmaiden and I took the high road of writing dystopias," said Dame Sherlock. "They're ever so more award-worthy."

"I've probably been writing SF longer than any of you," said the Puritan. "I have an entry in Clute's *Encyclopedia* of course, as do most of us, where my very first novel from 1959, *The Poorhouse Fair*, is cited as science fiction."

White Noise jumped in with his own defense: "Doctor Gravity and I have the postmodern angle pinned down tighter than Oswald covering JFK. A lot of those SF writers are into slipstream these days, you know."

Doctor Gravity spoke humbly for himself. "I realize I'm probably the least prolific of you all. But I *did* convince Jonathan Lethem to write that essay for the *Village Voice* a couple of years ago, explaining how I had been cheated of my Nebula and how the whole SF field missed the boat by not honoring our kind of science fiction. You have to admit that was the most hopeful action we've seen in years."

The Chicago Mensch sought to redeem himself in the eyes of his peers. "I really thought we had an award in the bag that year. But Lethem just didn't do it for us. Is there any way we can sabotage his career as revenge?"

"Too late for that," said the Footnote Kid. "Even *Esquire* has dumped me for him."

"Well, what are we going to do next? It's too late this year, but we've always got 2001."

White Noise spoke first. "I've already contracted for an *X-Files* tie-in book."

The Footnote Kid responded, "I'm sharecropping a novel in the revived *Wild Cards* series."

"Despite my advanced years, which nearly match our chairman's, I guess I could start up a new trilogy," said Shikasta the Golden with a sigh.

"I've got that Godzilla novel of mine almost finished," Doctor Gravity said. "That should resonate with the voters."

Receiving a nod from Gothic Lady, the Puritan divulged their joint secret. "GL and I have collaborated on a big space opera.

Michiko Kakutani has already promised to call us 'the next Niven and Pournelle.'"

Dame Sherlock said, "I suppose I might negotiate to write an authorized *Foundation* novel. We know oodles about empires in my country."

The Handmaiden sniffed dismissively and said, "If the Republicans win the presidential election, I'll have plenty of inspiration for another dystopia."

Eight of the Nine Well-Known looked to their leader, who squirmed nervously before saying, "Well, you all know I'm about to become a new father, so my thoughts have naturally been verging cautiously toward writing something about—about—about mutant children!"

"Excellent!" "Way to go, Mensch!" "*Second City of the Damned*!" "The new Stapledon!" "The new van Vogt!"

The Chicago Mensch signaled his peers to silence. "Thank you, thank you for your confidence, friends. In my new role as SF writer, allow me to make my first prediction for us. Next year in New Atlantis!"

With all due apologies to Saul Bellow, Thomas Pynchon, David Foster Wallace, John Updike, Don DeLillo, Margaret Atwood, Joyce Carol Oates, P. D. James and Doris Lessing.

THE MAGAZINE CHUMS VERSUS THE
BARON OF NUMEDIA

by

C. J. Cutlyffe Heintz-Ketzep

Author of "The Magazine Chums Meet the Distributor of Doom," "The Magazine Chums and the Case of the Disappearing Readers," "The Magazine Chums and the Great Paper Shortage," "The Magazine Chums Apply for an Arts Council Grant," &c, &c

Chapter 1
The Spinning of the Web

Into the cozy dim-lit reading room of the discreet gentlemen's club on Street and Smith Street, a room whose walnut-paneled walls had oft echoed to both the excited battle cries of the Magazine Chums and their contented post-adventure snores, a panting figure burst. Rushing past an elderly manservant—Phillips, the club's quiet and tactful majordomo—and nearly causing the aged butler to drop a tray of Sapphire Gin and Quinine Water cocktails, the immoderately gasping visitor came to a stop at a herd of high-backed leather chairs clustered around a broad table like rhinos at a waterhole on the Rider Haggard estates. The polished tabletop was nearly obscured by dozens of plump magazines featuring gaily colored covers: *Railroad Stories, The Happy Magazine, Black Mask, Weird Tales, St. Nicholas, Blue Book, O,* and many others.

Pausing but a second to catch his breath, the flushed and stocky runner soon burst into speech. "Lord Pringle, Lord Pringle! I have alarming news! We must assemble all the Chums!"

The sober, handsome chap thus wildly addressed looked up calmly from his study. Deliberately folding the Parisian newspaper he had been perusing so as to mark the exact point in that day's *feuilleton* where he had left off reading, Lord Pringle favored the messenger with a look of intense authority mixed with jollity and keen-wittedness.

"Come now, young Ashley," Lord Pringle admonished in a bantering tone, "no news of whatever degree of urgency can justify bad manners. Apologize first to old Phillips, then grab one of those delicious drinks he's compiled, sit yourself down, refresh your throat, and then finally recount your tale in good form."

Young Ashley did as he had been bade by the leader of the Magazine Chums—a group of which Ashley himself was not the lowliest member—and when his breathing had finally reestablished an even modulation and the hectic color had partially drained from his cheeks, he commenced to report on certain late-breaking developments in the very sphere of interests which the Magazine Chums inhabited.

"Despite my numerous professional deadlines, I permitted myself to take a small break this morning," Ashley reluctantly confessed, "in between annotating the entire works of Max Brand and re-reading the last twenty years of the *Strand*, and prior to working up a bibliography of Ayn Rand. Picking up a stray copy

of that cheap trade journal, *Publishers' Weekly*, which I had inadvertently walked away with during my last trip to the library, I
carelessly flicked through its tawdry pages. Imagine my horror
when I came across *this*!"

With dramatic timing, Ashley whipped the magazine in question out of his coat pocket and displayed the offending article to
Lord Pringle. Pringle took the magazine calmly, with a small
smile, and began to read. But his easy demeanor gradually dwin-
dled, until he too evinced some of Ashley's obvious horror. When
he had finished perusing the dread text, Lord Pringle stood deci-
sively and said, "Ashley, your instincts were sound. The Chums
must be assembled in their entirety to deal with this new menace.
You summon those who employ one of Mr. Alexander Graham
Bell's contraptions in their residences, while I dispatch
Morse-o-grams to the others!"

By early evening, all the Magazine Chums who could be
reached and who could arrange swift transportation to the club
sat in congregation around the supper table, as Phillips served
squab and bangers, with bumpers of bubbly. A stalwart group of
men (and a select scattering of brave damsels), the Magazine
Chums boasted a wide range of intelligent and sympathetic faces.
Besides Ashley and Pringle, these noble souls were present:

Sir Francis Robinson, who in Khartoum had once endured
through six hours of hot auction action despite having been
wounded at the outset with a rusty staple.

Little Dicky Lupoff, the suave-voiced darling of those with
Marconi-receivers.

Dame Lucy Sussex, heir to a large Australian sheep-dip
fortune.

Devil-may-care solo aviatrix Elly Datlow, rumored to have
romanced many of the crowned heads of Europe, including the
infamous Count Guccione.

Hirsute Gordy van Gelder, whose mature wit and piercing gaze failed to betray his odd origins: an orphan, he had been raised by stuffed Esquimaux in a diorama at the Museum of Natural History.

Lady Ruth Berman, whose formal gardens at Castle Harmsworth replicated every flower mentioned in both the Shakespearean and Spenserian canons.

Quiet Victor Berch, who had once killed an armed assailant using only his pocket watch.

Wry Johnny Clute, joshingly addressed by his friends as "Mister Sesquipedalian."

Richie Bleiler, who had emerged from the literal shadow cast by his famous father only after he had finally convinced his progenitor to fold up the bumbershoot the old man eccentrically kept open indoors and out, through fair weather and foul.

In addition to those assembled here this fateful night, the Magazine Chums numbered further scores, all of them Titans in their own right, without a trace of brummagem or bloviation in their wise and forthright speech. Those unable to attend this gathering were scattered far and wide across the globe, in such exotic locales as the United States of America (Texas, Pennsylvania, Rhode Island), the Canadian Provinces, and Lapland, pursuing the researches that had made them rich and famous.

When the last sip of postprandial claret had been savored, Lord Pringle stood and silently regarded his troops. Then he began his solemn oration.

"Ladies and gentlemen, despite our multifarious interests we are united on one front. And that front can be summarized in a single glorious word: magazines! Reviews or journals, pulps or slicks, annuals or weeklies, these frail, colorful, exotic vessels of enlightenment are the star around which we all orbit—some of us closer to the primary than others, but all reliant on the stellar warmth and light. From their humble beginnings among the papyri of Egypt"—here Lord Pringle nodded to Berch—"which ancient tradition our own Victor has discovered to include such early titles as *Thrilling Crocodile Tales* and *Astounding Stories of Metempsychosis*, down to the highly developed organs we enjoy today, magazines have drawn us all joyfully together. Our pleasure and wonderment at the myriad manifestations of the periodical printed word have filled untold hours of our lives. In some sense, we have all dedicated our very beings to the continuation and improvement of magazines.

"And now I must tell you that the actual existence and future of magazines as we know them is at dire risk!"

From the Magazine Chums issued a collective gasp of startlement. Lord Pringle capitalized on their undivided attention by displaying the revelatory article. "Brother Ashley has discovered that an evil technocratic genius intends to render all our beloved magazines obsolete within a few years. You see him depicted here, a bloated plutocrat who bills himself as the Baron of Numedia. Employing hordes of ill-washed and unmannerly underlings whom he calls 'software and hardware engineers,' he has unleashed on the unsuspecting globe a creature dubbed 'the worldwide web.' He claims that this Frankenstein's monster of his will soon devour all current magazines, rendering their printed forms exiguous."

Lord Pringle paused, and surveyed the puzzled expressions worn by his comrades. Reluctant to confess their ignorance of the exact nature of this new menace, they were saved by young Ashley's polite cough.

"I've been boning up all afternoon on this new phenomenon, in my spare moments while I was handling the affairs of several dozen literary estates of which I am the humble executor. The 'web' referred to by the notorious Baron is not a physical one, but rather a conceptually subtle lattice of interconnected home televisors and remote Babbage devices known as 'servitors,' which latter machines both hold 'content' and distribute it to the individual 'users,' in both pictorial and alphabetical forms. What the Baron proposes is that all conventionally printed and disseminated magazines shall now 'migrate' to his 'web,' existing only as intangible coded swarms of atomies until displayed on a personal televisor."

Silence reigned as the shocked Chums sought to grasp the full implications of this horrid news. After some minutes, they all burst out in a flurry of questions.

"What of back issues?" "Users be dashed! What will become of good old-fashioned readers?" "No inks! How can there be no inks?" "Can one 'fold down' the corner of a page? I think not!" "Will we still have editors?" "Who will pay good money for such an insubstantial abomination?"

Lord Pringle raised his arms in a quelling gesture. "Decorum, Brothers and Sisters, decorum!" His plea succeeded in restoring quiet to the room, but the sense of shock lingered. Lord Pringle knew he must rally the broken spirits of his followers, and summoned every iota of rhetoric persuasion he possessed.

"I confess I do not have the answers to your questions. Discovering all the implications of this menacing Moloch must be one of our first priorities. But even without all the facts, I can affirm at the outset that we have never faced a greater challenge than—if I may coin a fantastical term—these 'daedalus-zines.' They have the potential to toss our familiar periodicals onto the dustbin of history. Already Brother Ashley has collated some disturbing statistics regarding the otherwise-unexplained falling circulation of such stalwarts as *McClure's* and *Scribner's*.

"How can we meet this crisis? Only by striving to produce the best d—d magazines possible! We handmaidens to the Muse of periodicals must gird our loins for war! All of us who are editors, publishers and writers—whom the Baron would dare to re-label 'content providers'!—must strive for new heights of creativity! We must rethink all our assumptions, jolt ourselves out of any stale ruts, and aspire to empyrean standards! No longer can we plow the same old familiar ground. We must reconstitute ourselves and our products for a new century! Only thus can we insure the survival of magazines as we know and love them!"

A chorus of loud huzzahs—interspersed with shouts of "Down with the degenerate d-zines!"—greeted Lord Pringle's speech. He allowed himself to bask for a moment in the warmth of his comrades' approbation, the thrilling sense of their dedication. But he knew that in reality they faced a dreadful uphill battle, one that would tax every fiber of their beings, with no guarantee of ultimate victory.

Next installment: "The Baron's Secret Weapon: Free Erotica!"

WOOLPULLERS, INC.

"One thing to know about Kent Haruf, author of the novel *Plainsong*, is that he wrote the first draft of the book with a wool stocking cap pulled down over his eyes . . . . [H]is rather eccentric method was, he said, an effort to reach the emotional heart of his story unconstrained by the feeling that someone—an invisible critic—was watching over his shoulder and scrutinizing every word he chose."

—*The New York Times*, December 1, 1999.

The writing game had gotten so bad for me, I'd even given my Invisible Critic a name. Edmund Wilson. He hovered constantly at my back, big as Harvey the Rabbit but much less pleasant company. Okay, so the nickname for my hallucination wasn't that original or clever. But that lack just reflected the depths of the neurotic pass I had reached. I simply couldn't get the words down on paper anymore, with any degree of creativity. Edmund Wilson had me stifled.

I knew I was on the road to perdition. Eventually I'd end up like so many other failed fiction writers, churning out salacious memoirs or vapid content for some e-zine. But then, at the nadir of my despair, I spotted an ad in the back pages of *The New York Review of Books* that promised a cure.

Invisible Critic cramping your style?
For Invincible Confidence, visit
Woolpullers, Inc.

My front door didn't touch the chair-worn seat of my trousers on the way out.

Woolpullers, Inc., occupied a modest office suite in one of the under-rented highrises downtown. A polite but unforthcoming receptionist invited me to supply lots of highly personal information about myself, which she entered into her terminal. But she refused to reveal the nature of the firm's anti-writer's-block treatment.

"Mr. MacArthur will explain everything to you."

I should mention that this otherwise-fashionable woman wore a cranberry-colored knitted stocking cap emblazoned with the firm's name and logo, the latter being a recursive image of a stocking cap. I spent a lot of time trying to avoid looking at this incongruous item of apparel—which made her resemble a rave kid who'd lost her pacifier—before I was summoned into Mr. MacArthur's office.

The neatly suited MacArthur also wore a crimson cap, which, combined with his hearty manner, modest potbelly and trim white beard, rendered him rather Santa-like. I was certain the effect was intentional, even cynically so, but felt myself relaxing nonetheless.

"Welcome, welcome, Paul! If I may be so bold as to call you by your first name, I hope you'll do the same and call me Grant."

"Hi, uh, Grant," I responded weakly, allowing myself to be conducted to a seat alongside a large desk. MacArthur dropped down into his own chair, then swiveled his computer monitor to face me. I regarded a screenful of confusing graphs, histograms and pie charts hopefully, but was soon put in my miserable place.

"Bad news, son. Based on the information you just provided us and according to our patented predictive WriterSoul (TM) software, you'll go from constipated to catatonic in less than six weeks. That is, unless you enroll in our treatment plan immediately."

MacArthur pivoted the screen away with a sad flourish, then composed his features into a receptive blank. I hesitated a moment, but eventually asked the expected question.

"Um, exactly what does your treatment consist of, Grant?"

MacArthur leaned forward and beamed. "Deception, Paul. Pure deception."

My puzzled expression was the only permission he needed to launch into his salestalk.

"You're naturally aware, Paul, that the entire practice of fiction involves deception. But I bet you've only thought about it from the audience's point of view. The famous 'willing suspension of disbelief' on the part of the reader, which convinces him for the duration of the reading experience that he is apprehending real, meaningful events. But what we at Woolpullers, Inc., have chosen to concentrate on is the self-deception that the author himself undergoes.

"You see, every author of fiction must convince himself first of all of the validity of his characters, the integrity of his narrative, the indisputable rightness of the story he is about to compose. Otherwise, lacking this belief, the writer is unable to go on. Everything falls apart, and out of the debris rises the Invisible Critic, whose stern authoritarian voice pooh-poohs all possible sentences on the basis that fiction writing is a meaningless, childish game."

I looked nervously over my shoulder to see how Edmund Wilson was taking this. Just like Mr. Coffee Nerves in the old ads whenever the smart housewife brought out decaffeinated Postum, he was beginning to go a little green around the gills.

"So you propose making me really believe again in the existential heft of my own work. Makes sense. But how do you go about such a confidence-building course?"

MacArthur leaned back in his chair, now that I was hooked, and folded his hands across his charming little tummy. "Drugs. Heavy-duty drugs that open you to the helpful remedial posthypnotic suggestions of our staff psychologists. Nothing illegal, mind you. Just the latest generation of psychotropic helpers out of the Prozac family."

"I could get a prescription for those from my HMO."

"True. But even the Screenwriters Guild HMO cannot take the next step that makes our services unique. We put all our writers into longterm artificial environments which encourage the necessary fantasies that supplement the drug regimen and paradoxically bolster your sense of your fiction's reality."

"For example?"

MacArthur pulled out a sheaf of glossy brochures. "Here's a popular one: *Faux Yaddo*. A simulated artist's colony where all the other residents are actors paid to praise your work in progress."

I scoped out the discreetly printed price at the bottom of the leaflet. "That's beyond my means, I'm afraid."

"Well, here's a simpler construct, the *Thomas Wolfe* package. We set you up in a Depression-era Brooklyn apartment with a signed book contract from Scribner's. All the furniture is scaled down to make you feel as somatically big as Wolfe, so you can write standing up and using the top of the fridge as a desk, just like him. Most writers end up producing ten thousand words a day."

"I hate the city. What else do you have?"

Growing a little testy, MacArthur shuffled through the stack of leaflets before finally selecting one and setting it down triumphantly before me.

"I sense you're just the kind of misanthropic fellow who would appreciate this. It's called *Last Man on Earth*."

Everything clicked. "It's perfect! With no fear of my work ever being read by *anyone*, I could write anything!"

MacArthur smiled knowingly. "We have a deal with the Russians to use a portion of the depopulated Chechen Republic as a stageset. And in your case, besides planting strategic stashes of writing supplies, foodstuffs and medicines, we'll make sure there are dozens of pairs of eyeglasses with the proper prescription lenses scattered about, just to avoid the dreaded *Twilight Zone* phenomenon."

"Where do I sign?"

"Don't you need to ask your Invisible Critic's permission first?"

I looked behind me. A wailing, grimacing Edmund Wilson was fading out faster than an airport bestseller. Immensely relieved, I seized the opportunity and signed the contract MacArthur proffered.

"Congratulations. You'll have to come in a day early for us to apply the fake radiation sores. In the meantime, wear this with pride."

He handed me a red stocking cap. I snugged it on and pulled it down happily over my eyes.

ADVENTURES IN MISHMOSH LAND

BY

A. PATCHWORK GIRL, CUSTOMIZER

"The Frommer's guide to France may be made up of chapters and maps, but most readers know it as an indivisible and coherent whole: a book.

"This fall, that book and a few hundred others will take a new form on the Internet. They will be sold in component parts—chapters, maps and even paragraphs—that can be mixed and matched. Readers will be invited to create customized books by picking pieces of content *a la carte* from an array of already published guides . . . ."

—"Books by the Chapter or
Verse Arrive on the Internet This Fall," by Lisa Guernsey,
The New York Times, July 18, 2000.

The landing party from the *Enterprise*, consisting of Captain Kirk, Scotty, Bones and Spock, beamed down onto the surface of the strange new unexplored world. As soon as they had fully materialized, Kirk flipped open his communicator and hailed his ship in orbit above.

"Lieutenant Uhura, notify Starfleet Command that we've arrived—"

"—on Arrakis, you know, Paul, water is at a premium. That's why we must render down even offworlder corpses for their liquid content. To do otherwise would be to risk—"

—the foul wrath of Sauron. "You have failed me for the last time! How did you let those hobbits escape? By sheer ineptitude!"

The Orc leader dared to snarl back defiantly. "They had help! Elvish intervention from that accursed—"

—Lazarus Long, who smiled now with his trademark centuries-old boyish charm. "Shucks, ma'am, t'weren't nothing 't all. It's just that I was born with—"

A ten-inch-long serpent crawled out of the Healer's pouch. But before the Dreamsnake could escape across the sands—

—of Tatooine. R2D2 whistled a sequence that indicated the little droid was ready to relay a message. Coherent light formed—

—the hologram of Hari Seldon, materializing exactly at the appointed hour. The long-ago-programmed ghost of the venerable savant began to speak. "Members of the Foundation, psychohistory faces its greatest challenge with the appearance of—"

—Rama, an artificial world unto itself, arrowing out of nowhere on its chartless course through our solar system and beyond, heading for—

—Ringworld, whose orbit had been disturbed so that it would soon brush up against—

—Confluence, where an endless river debouched onto—

—Riverworld, where Mark Twain looked up into the sky and spotted—

—Orbitsville, which had recently seen the arrival of—

—the Black Star! "Come on, lads! We can still save the day! I've charged up the accumulators on—"

—the Skylark of Space! Shields coruscating, the mighty spacecraft plunged straight toward—

—the Emerald City of Oz. Here, Dorothy felt, she would at last find the answers to her many questions:

Who can replace a man?

Can you feel anything when I do this?

Who made Stevie Crye?

Do androids dream of—

—the body electric! Grandma, O dear and wondrous electric dream! When storm lightnings rove the sky of—

—Jupiter, where the re-engineered human and his transmogrified canine companion blissfully and telepathically communicated, firm in their agreement that they would never return to—

—Neveryon, where Gorgik fondled his slave collar, vowing—

—that the criminal who had shot down his mother and father in cold blood on the streets of Gotham would someday know the wrath of the Caped—

—High Crusade! Aboard the supernatural iron vessel, the knights hunkered in a frightened mass, while their horses—

—spoke to Gulliver—

—Jones of Mars—

—the dying planet whose empty canals and towering cities beckoned John Carter and his bride—

—the Female Man—

—the Demolished Man—

—who folded himself, on an endless trip—

—across the universe—

—across a sea of stars—

—beyond the blue event horizon—

—beyond the fields we know—

—to the end of eternity—

—destination: void.

ASSOCIATIONAL ROUNDUP

If advance galleys are any indication, this year is shaping up to be the start of a mass exodus from SF by some of the field's veteran writers. As publishers' fiction lines collapse in the wake of the stock market meltdown, smart authors are moving into non-fiction, where big sales and high profits have historically endured even during recessions.

Here are some of the highlights of the upcoming year.

MAY

The Unsurrendered Fembot, by Richard Calder, Taschen, $25.95, 215 pages.

A combination beauty makeover book, marriage manual and French Symbolist rant, Calder's instructive treatise seems aimed at a Generation Y audience of young women who find all the old role models unfulfilling and just not edgy enough. Advocating such disturbing styles as "Leprous Waif," "Neurasthenic Harlot," "Traitorous Jezebel" and "Laura Bush on Absinthe," Calder advises his wannabe-ultravixen readers to inflict pain, uncertainty, and sexual madness on the opposite gender—and that's just during the courtship! With some of the most shocking photos ever captured by the lens of Helmut Newton, this volume should hit the bestseller ranks right out of the gate.

The Big Book of High-Tech Texas Bar-B-Q, by Bruce Sterling, Chronicle, $35.00, 178 pages.

Ribo-ribs. Iced Tea with Nutriceuticals. Lab-baked Beans. Mad Cow Chili. Butterfly-Killing Cornbread. If the names of these dishes are causing your mouth to water already, even as you grow a little queasy, you'll find a hundred more between these pages that will provoke a similar mix of anticipation and unease. Turning his razor-sharp analytic mind to the impact of bioengineering on the state cuisine of Texas, Sterling does not preach the expected gloom-and-doom message, but instead tries to make the most of the new Frankenfoods. His chapter on what to do with a pig after you've harvested its transgenic organs for human reimplantation is a classic of cookbook writing that even Julia Child would envy!

JUNE

A History of Science Fiction and Fantasy in *The New Yorker*, Ursula K. Le Guin, Harcourt, $14.95, 26 pages.

Featuring an introduction by John Updike, this is the inside story from one of the few genre authors ever to crack the pages of the mainstream's most elite publication. Le Guin charts all the highlights of the literature of the fantastic as found over the course of many decades in this classy, money-losing magazine. After separate chapters on Shirley Jackson, Sylvia Townsend Warner, Ursula K. Le Guin and Stanislaw Lem, the author exhausts her topic and retires to her atelier to commune with the goddess.

Faith-Based Fictions: A Conversation, by Orson Scott Card, Andrew Greeley and Barry Malzberg, Shambhala, $32.95, 666 pages.

Gathered together at the religiously neutral territory of a Las Vegas casino, these three authors held a wide-ranging conversation on many fascinating topics over the course of eight hours, twelve rounds of drinks, six trips to the buffet, five to the mens' room, and eight requests from the manager to please keep it down. Faithfully transcribed and edited by a committee of priests, rabbis and the Angel Moroni, their talk ranges over such subjects as best catering schemes for a bar mitzvah, the Pope as action hero, and unobtrusive methods of inserting genealogical infodumps into historical fictions. Sure to cause controversy: the chapter discussing which male editors are circumsized!

JULY

Women Write Fantasy, Men Write Science Fiction, by Nancy Kress and Charles Sheffield, Writer's Digest, $25.00, 189 pages.

In alternating chapters, this husband-and-wife team stake out diametrically opposed positions on which gender does each kind of fiction best. (Kress has to recant everything she's ever written since her first three novels, but does so gracefully and convincingly.) Sheffield's chapters tend to rely heavily on equations, big dumb arguments and invocations to a "sense of wonder," while Kress appeals to feminine intuition and "daintiness," metaphorically weeping and stamping her feet on the page until she gets her way. But eventually thesis meets antithesis in a charming synthesis of brains and beauty. Never since Lucy wrapped Ricky around her little finger has such good-natured hilarity reigned!

AUGUST

I Was a Teenaged Pornographer!, by Robert Silverberg, Grove, $26.00, 514 pages.

Scheduled to be written over the course of a single week shortly before publication, this candid memoir will finally spill the beans on Silverberg's fabled stint during the 1950s writing the softcore smut of the period. Learn what famous names in the New York SF community provided him with sexual escapades and techniques he could use in his quickie novels. (Discovering the secret behind "The Asimov Maneuver" alone should be worth the price!) Find out what effect all this priapic fiction had on Silverberg's own sex life. (His affairs with Sophia Loren, Brigitte Bardot and Mamie Eisenhower come to light.) And study the appendix of over a thousand euphemisms and salacious synonyms for body parts ("milk warmers"; "rod of Moses"; "velvet vestibule"). This book also comes with a free DVD of a B&W stag film based without authorization on one of Silverberg's paperback originals, *Brooklyn Stickball Tramp* ("She'd squeeze anybody's spaldeens!").

SEPTEMBER

Boy Magnate, by Gordon Van Gelder, St. Martin's, $24.95, 305 pages.

How did he do it? How did a lowly lad who started his career just a few years ago as the assistant to the proofreader at Archie Comics become one of the most respected and influential figures in the world of magazine publishing? The whole field has been abuzz with such questions ever since Ed Ferman sailed away on a swan boat to Hy Brasil, leaving his empire to the young unshaven heir. Now in his own words, the mystery wrapped in a riddle concealed in an enigma that is Van Gelder comes clean. A combination of business-management text and Horatio Alger story, Van Gelder's autobiography reveals all the quirks of fate and brilliant strategies that have propelled this shy, unassuming, twenty-first-century Bennett Cerf to his current catbird seat atop a worldwide empire.

Great Mafia Science, by Ben Bova, Casa Editrice Nord, 75,000 Lira, 160 pages.

Blending his dual interests in both the cool, rational world of scientists and the bloody, vicious underworld of gangsters, Bova presents a history of the best Mafia-funded research of the past century. Did you know that the quick-setting concretes that have revolutionized the building trades were first designed specifically for mob disposal of corpses? Or that depleted-uranium ammunition now used so effectively by the U.S. Armed Forces in such theaters as the Balkans was originally created so that the Medellin cartel could take down Colombian tanks? In this compulsively readable volume (the reader is literally compelled to finish it, as he or she must leave a family member hostage until the final page is turned), you'll learn how Richard Feynman arranged funding for the Manhattan Project from Lucky Luciano and how Albert Einstein's affair with Lana Turner sparked the Stompanato murder. Sure to be a hit with the *Sopranos* crowd!

OCTOBER

How to Pick Up Guys, by Samuel Delany, Black Ice Books, $12.00, 98 pages. Can't summon up a semiotic quip fast enough in your favorite leather bar? Finding it hard to make friends even when the fleet's in port? Worried where to go for fun now that Times Square has been cleaned up? Get all the help and advice you need from kindly, dirty-minded "Professor Dhalgren" in this handy pocket guide to the mating game, and you need never feel "Bellona-ly" again!

Corn Likker, Drag Racin' and Coon Huntin', by Andy Duncan and Michael Bishop, Longstreet, 210 pages, $45.00.

A celebration of the authors' Southern roots, this lavishly illustrated book (photos by Sally Mann) evokes a little-heralded world of double-wide trailers, NASCAR groupies, barefoot pregnant teens, Moon Pies, basement meth labs, junkyards full of snarling dogs and marijuana-filled "hollers." Duncan and Bishop recount many amusing tales and anecdotes from their America, some personal, such as the time they sold one hundred pounds of frozen mudbugs from a polluted "crick" to a snobby New York restaurant. Put on your gimme cap, mix yourself a mint julep, and enjoy "southern culture on the skids."

DECEMBER

Andre Norton's Smackdown!, by Andre Norton, New York Times, $32.99, 115 pages.

Who would ever have suspected from her fiction that this little old lady liked to rumble!?! But by the evidence of this riotous, raunchy, rocking exploration of the WWF milieu, she surely does! The sparse text presents Norton's wild-eyed enthusiasm for the whole WWF scene, as she kisses and disses every wrestler from Chyna to Ivory, from Stone Cold to Sexual Chocolate. But as rollicking as the prose is, the pictures here are even wilder, as we witness Norton entering the ring to take on all comers, under the *nom du canvas* of "High Halleck." (For one infamous match, Norton paired up in a tag team with Anne "Dragonrider" McCaffrey, and wiped the floor with Sable and Miss Kitty.) A chair to the head, a fist to the kidneys, a boot to the spleen! Witch World was never like this!

PRESS ONE FOR LITERATURE

"The May meeting of the Bedford-Shire Book Group was a bit out of the ordinary . . . [T]he phone rang [and] on the line was Donna Woolfolk Cross, the author of the group's reading selection. For the next hour and a half, via speakerphone, Ms. Cross led a discussion about her historical novel *Pope Joan* . . . . [S]ince *Pope Joan* came out in paperback nearly four years ago, she has placed calls to more than 350 book groups, sometimes devoting four or five evenings a week to the practice . . . . [On her website] Ms. Cross offers to call any group that chooses the book . . . ."

—Pamela LiCalzi O'Connell,
"Authors Go Directly to Reader With Marketing,"
The New York Times, May 28, 2001.

Of course the phone rang just when the whole blessed family was sitting down to dinner. I had worked for hours that day making the family's favorite meal: fried chicken according to Aunt Minnie's classic recipe, pineapple jello salad from a feature in *Woman's World*, fresh green beans with almond slices (that garnish was my own idea), and, for dessert, peach cobbler. And now the whole beautiful banquet was going to go cold (or in the case of the jello salad, get warm), due to some stupid telemarketer.

Sam and the kids looked at me expectantly. Not one of the four seemed willing or able to get up from the table and answer the ringing phone. So I sighed, wiped my hands on my apron and said, "Oh, all right, I'll get it!"

"Cut 'em off quick," Sam said. "I can hardly wait to dig in!"

"Me too!" chimed Greg, the oldest. The twins, Lisa and Amy, weighed in with a wailed "We're starving!".

Naturally, I was a little curt with my hello. But the perky female voice on the other end of the line didn't seem to notice or mind my irritation.

"Hello! Am I speaking to Wanda Jo Brasch?"

"Yes. How can I help you?"

"This is Nora Roberts, the author, calling."

I could hardly believe my ears. "Is this some kind of joke? Madge, is that you?"

"I'm not your friend, Madge, Wanda Jo. May I call you by your first name? I'd like you to call me Nora."

"Well, that's all right, I guess—Nora." Sam and the kids were making shoveling motions with their empty forks to indicate I should wind this up. But I couldn't just end this interesting interruption so abruptly, without letting this woman tell me why she was calling. What if I really *was* talking to the one and only Nora Roberts?

"Wanda Jo, a little bird tells me that you're currently reading one of my books. Is that correct?"

"Why, uh, yes, it is. However did you know?"

"Oh, just a simple combination of access to your purchase records at Border's and some friendly neighborhood snooping by a reputable nationwide agency. May I ask how you're enjoying it?"

"Oh, it's great. Maybe not as good as your last one, but easily as enjoyable as the one before that."

"Wanda Jo, I appreciate your frankness. Such candor is precisely the reason I'm calling. I need feedback like yours to help make my next book as good as possible. And I want to insure that you enjoy this current one as much as its hopefully minor flaws will permit. Do you have an hour or so free now so we can have a cozy chat about the novel?"

Greg was clutching his stomach and miming cramps. Sam had buried his head in his folded arms upon the table. The twins were turning red as they held their breath.

"Um, Nora, this is not such a great time. Could you call back later tonight?"

"Certainly, Wanda Jo. I understand intimately the unspoken depths and heights of family dynamics. That's why the last five of my novels have all perched on the bestseller lists for an average of ten weeks apiece. We'll talk later. Goodbye, and thanks for your time."

I hung up, feeling rather dazed. Luckily, not one of my "starving" family members even inquired about the nature of the call, which was fine, since I didn't feel I could really explain.

Just as the basket of chicken was being passed around, the phone rang again.

Sam bolted to his feet. "I'll get this one! We're not going to have another gabfest with strangers stalling our dinner!"

Sam practically yanked the phone off the wall and yelled, "Yes, who is this!" But he immediately calmed down. "Well, of course I do, I just bought a copy. Man, you know I do! Right now?" He glanced toward me and his glowering offspring, then said, "Jeez, I can't right at this minute, Kenny. You'll call back? Great!"

Returning to his seat, Sam was practically glowing. "Can you all guess who that was? Kenny Rogers! He knew somehow that I had picked up his autobiography yesterday at the airport bookstore, and he wanted to fill me in on some of the saucy stuff that his lawyers made him leave out!"

Greg said, "Cool, you got a call from some boring old hillbilly. Can we eat now, please?"

"Greg, you watch how you talk to your father. Apologize right now."

"Oh, man . . . . *Sooorr*-ee!"

Our plates were half filled when the phone rang yet again. As if to make up for his smart mouth and maybe to deal more quickly with these annoying calls than his elders could, Greg jumped up to answer.

"Wassup? No way! Yeah, Mick, it rocked! An hour? Can't do it, big guy. Later for sure, though. Chill."

Now it was Greg's turn to strut. "You know anyone else at Ogilvy High who gets calls from big name pro wrestlers? That was Mick 'Mankind' Foley, asking me what I thought of his last book. I figure I'll tell him to put more pictures of half-naked chicks in."

Well, boys will be boys.

We managed actually to savor a few bites before the phone rang again. I caught it this time.

"Girls, it's for you."

Lisa and Amy held the receiver between them so they could both hear. Immediately they let loose that dual squeal of theirs that once actually shattered Uncle Henry's commemorative Gallo wine decanter. "Oh, that is *so* fabulous! Sure, we're wearing your clothes right now! And your book! Of course we've got your book! Oh, darn, we're in the middle of dinner. You really don't mind? Okay, bye!"

The two girls practically threw themselves on me, almost making me spill some Crystal Light. "Mom, Mom, that was Mary-Kate and Ashley Olsen! We talked to the *Olsen Twins*! Everyone at school is going to be like *so* super-jealous!"

"Well now, girls, the Olsen Twins might very well be calling other people up tonight too. We can't be the only lucky ones in town. In fact, I bet authors all across this great nation of ours are phoning households everywhere even as we speak, just to see if their readers are happy. That's what makes them such special people, worthy of our respect and admiration. Now, sit down and tuck in."

We ate in silence for a while. All of us, I guess, were contemplating what they'd say when they got their return calls tonight from Nora, Kenny, "Mankind" and the Olsens. A niggling little worry occurred to me then. But Greg, God bless him, managed after fifteen years of marriage to read my mind for once, and voiced my concern first.

"We are *just* going to have to get another *line* in this house."

KISS OF THE SPIDER CRITIC

One Sunday, while reading the *Washington Post Book World*, I realized that for months now one particular byline had been missing from its pages: that of famous critic Cleverly Taint.

Upon realizing this, I began to cast backward through my recent memories of reading other literary journals. In no case could I recall newish reviews or essays by Taint. *The New York Review of Books*; the *Times Literary Supplement*; *New Republic*; the *Nation*; the *New York Times Book Review*; *Atlantic*; *Harpers*— All of Taint's usual venues had been barren of his idiosyncratic prose. No tapering off, no explanation: just a sudden drought.

This made me sad. I liked Taint's writing. He was acerbic and witty, erudite and perceptive. And he had been kind to me. A review he had authored of one of my early books had been instrumental in landing me my first agent. Although we had never met, I felt a link to him and his critical career.

I put down the *Post* and made a resolution. I would track down Taint and learn the cause of his silence. Perhaps he was sick or broke or otherwise down on his luck. There might be some way I could help him.

So the very next day I began phoning and e-mailing people in the business. Within a few hours, I had Taint's contact information. I dashed off a brief message online, explaining that I was a fan of his work, had noted the disappearance of his writing, and would be happy to meet with him to talk about the subject, on a strictly personal and confidential level.

The very next hour brought an electronic reply: *Good to hear from you. Let's have a drink. But nothing can possibly help my career now.*

A fellow New Yorker, Taint nominated a bar that proved to be midway between our apartments, and a time just hours away. Needless to say I was there well in advance, even more intrigued than I had been, thanks to the dour, hopeless tone of his message.

A dim vinyl booth in back held the critic, familiar to me from his many appearances on various PBS and cable-channel literary chat shows. Of course, off the screen and in his current condition, Taint looked more disreputable and slovenly than the usually dapper *homme de lettres* known to the viewing public. And, having beaten me here, he had already started drinking.

I slipped into the booth, we shook hands, and I ordered a beer. After some inconsequential chitchat about mutual friends, enemies and acquaintances, I broached the crucial topic.

"Why the vast silence, Cleverly? Is it possible you've abandoned literature? Has your passion for explicating fiction guttered out?"

The red eyes of the litterateur grew misty. "Not at all. I still love the damn stuff."

"It must be censorship then. You've been blacklisted. But what could you have possibly done to get on the bad side of so many editors simultaneously?"

Taint glugged his martini and gestured to the waitress for another. "Are you kidding? I have editors calling me daily, begging me for anything—a blurb, a capsule review, even a 'books received' notice. But I dare not submit anything. Nor dare I explain why. And of course, that blanket refusal is indeed finally beginning to piss them off. Soon I *will* be blacklisted."

"I don't understand then. Those are the only possible explanations— No, wait, is it writer's block?"

Taint laughed and held up his hands. "Could these fluent fingers ever fail to dance across the keyboard? No, I'm not blocked. I am positively overflowing with opinions and apercus, harsh flensings and bountiful encomiums. But I cannot commit any of them to print, for fear of the repercussions."

"Oh, come now, I don't buy that. You've always called them as you've seen them, never fearful or beholden to anyone. Besides, you're at the peak of your profession. Who could possibly harm you? Except yourself, of course, which is what I see you doing now."

"How about a witch?"

I was flabbergasted. "A witch?"

"Yes. One of those New Age Wiccans. Perhaps you recall my review some months ago of a certain 'novel'—if one can dishonor the beloved term—by one Luna Samhain. *Nothing Says Lovin' Like Something from the Coven.*"

"That stinker? You positively eviscerated it. And with what damning effect! One week it was on all the bestseller lists, and the next week it was on remainder tables across the nation."

Taint smiled wanly. "My final triumph. Would that I had never heard of that woman and her book!"

"Are you telling me she—she cursed you?"

"Yes. I received her malevolent letter shortly after the review ran. It arrived by messenger bat at midnight. In it she described what she had done to me. Every word of her curse was subsequently proven true. And what a curse! Simple blindness or paralysis would have been merciful. I could still dictate my reviews from inside an iron lung, like that Frenchman and his autobiography."

By now I was nearly dying with curiosity. "Tell me—what did she do to you?"

"Only this. Every book I inveigh against will succeed, and every book I praise will fail. Without exception."

I let out an involuntary gust of breath, as if I had been punched. "But, but—that's fiendish!"

Taint nodded sadly. "Isn't it though? I learned the full impact of it with the very next review of mine that followed the bestowal of the curse. Does the title *Titanium Skirts* mean anything to you?"

"Of course. The debut book of short stories by Esther Pribyl. Everyone predicted great things for it. After all, Pribyl had that unique point of view and publicity hook, being both a NASCAR driver and a top fashion model. But the book stiffed."

"Right after my extolling of it."

"But surely that's mere coincidence."

"Is it? Then how do you explain the success of, gack, *Howling Blood*, as soon as I sought to bury it?"

"That horror novel by the ten-year-old ex-fundamentalist preacher kid? Well, you know the tastes of the public . . . ."

"Oh, don't try to convince me everything is just random synchronicity. I went through all these chains of reasoning myself at first, reluctant to believe in anything so foolish as a curse. But the misfirings continued to pile up. Then I began to experiment. I'd wait until the critical consensus was in on a book, and it was well on its way either up or down the charts. Then I'd weigh in. And the book would inevitably reverse its direction! There was no mistaking the cause and effect relationship."

Taint's doleful expression and grim certainty forced me to accept his conclusions. "But this is awful! If you render your true opinion, you bestow upon a book the exact opposite fate it deserves!"

"Correct. And what if I try to get around the curse by lavishing kisses on the stinkers and hurling brickbats at the exemplary books? Sure, the individual authors will benefit or suffer appropriately. But what about my reputation? I'll be seen as an idiot! All the virtue and respect I've accumulated will be as naught! My peers will call me a hack, a tout, a vulgarian, a Philistine! My name will rank with Rex Reed's and Walter Kirn's as a laughingstock!"

I thought furiously for fifteen minutes, but came up with no solution other than: "Couldn't you apologize to Samhain? Promise to praise all her books from here on, if she removes the curse?"

Taint erupted. "Never! That would leave me in exactly the same spot I'm in now! My good name allied on the side of crap. No, a brooding silence is my only recourse."

I pushed away from the table and slid out of the booth. "Well, Cleverly, I'm very sorry. If I have any more helpful ideas, I'll be sure to get in touch with you again."

I left him drowning his sorrows in liquor, fully expecting never to hear from the poor doomed bastard again.

Great was my surprise when Taint called me only three weeks later. His voice was filled with glee.

"I thought you'd like to know I've gotten a new job! I'm out of books now, and into television."

I confessed to bafflement. "Doing what?"

"I'm a producer with one of the networks. I called in a few chits—you remember when I gave a smashing review to that novel by the soap-opera actor, calling it a 'postmodern shattering of the intermedia barriers of self-reflexiveness'—and now I'm one of the people in charge of developing new shows. I'll be making scads more money than I ever could as a lowly critic."

"I assume the curse has been lifted then."

"Not at all!"

"But won't your endorsement as producer continue to damn the shows you admire and boost the ones you hate?"

"Exactly! But that's *just* what I need to happen. You see, every time I manage to get a literate, witty, experimental show on the air, just the kind I admire, it will earn immense praise from the critics but garner only low ratings typical of its kind and eventually fail. However, my star will shine brightly in the press as a daring executive willing to take risks for 'quality programming.' Here's one pitch I've already made. 'High Art with Jonathan Franzen.' One hundred percent talking heads on a set that looks like every tenured English professor's living room."

I murmured approvingly.

"Now on the other hand, any commercial dreck I promote yet detest will of course soar in the ratings, earning my network millions, and making me the golden boy. I've got one such project greenlighted already. It stars Meryl Streep as a transgendered single parent, and it's called 'Ex-Why-Question Mark'."

"Did she go from female to male or vice versa?"

"That's the beauty part! You never know! Sometimes she dresses butch, sometimes she's all Ru Paul. Her sex life is totally open-ended. Lots of hunky and babelicious guest stars, including Ellen Degeneres. The watercooler buzz will be enormous!"

I failed to repress a groan.

"No, don't look at it by your outmoded standards. This is a win-win situation!"

I tried objectively to see a flaw in Taint's reasoning, but failed. "You don't suppose that other television producers share your curse, do you?"

"There's no supposition about it! I've already been initiated into their secret society! Would you like to join our screenwriters' auxiliary? We have staff witches who can make the necessary adjustments in your talents."

I thought about tossing off lefthandedly potboilers that hit the bestseller lists, and slaving over brilliant masterpieces that met endless rejection.

"No thanks, it's too much like what I'm already used to."

ULTRASENATOR VERSUS THE
LOBBYISTS FROM BEYOND!

"Democrats already have indicated that they're prepared to filibuster, if necessary, any legislation that includes the [Alaskan wildlife] refuge issue. 'It's kryptonite and will kill the energy bill,' predicts Sen. Ron Wyden, D-Ore."

—"Arctic drilling foes include 7 GOP senators,"
Associated Press.

FROM *THE CONGRESSIONAL RECORD* FOR
NOVEMBER 12, 20—

SPEAKER OF THE HOUSE: —and HR6183, the Omnibus Golden Age Superhero Pension Bill, has passed unanimously. Now, on to previously scheduled debate. The Representative from Atlantis has the floor.

UNIDENTIFIED VOICE: Which Atlantis? The Submariner's or Aquaman's?

SPEAKER: Um—well, let's hear from the Honorable Prince Namor first.

SUBMARINER: Thank you, Speaker. May I begin my remarks

by complimenting you on your new costume?

SPEAKER: Do you really like it? I was a little worried about the lines of the mask. Are they too severe?

SUBMARINER: No, no, the mask not only conceals your secret identity quite well, but it harmonizes nicely with your new stylized chest symbol, Speaker Green Lantern.

ADAM STRANGE: Can we move directly to the issues at hand? I only have two hours left on Earth before the Zeta Beam takes me back to Rann.

SPEAKER: Out of order, Representative Strange! You know perfectly well that discussion of costumes takes precedence over all other business! Prince Namor, please proceed.

SUBMARINER: Thank you, Mister Speaker. I wish to use my time here today before I must return to my watery home district to address a persistent problem. Namely, the continual intrusion of my fellow Congressmen into the sovereign affairs of my district. Just last week, for instance, a certain resident alien from Krypton took it upon himself to repair a quake-triggered underwater fissure that threatened to open up and swallow my kingdom. I'm sure the taxpayers of his district—who rely on him for speedy service—don't appreciate his meddling in other Congressional precincts any more than I do.

SUPERMAN: Just one minute. I admit intervening in Namor's realm. But my actions were strictly necessary. I detected the tectonic activity with both my telescopic vision and super-hearing, and immediately flew at super-speed to the underwater scene and sealed the plates together with my heat vision, thus saving Prince Namor's scaly ass.

SUBMARINER: We Atlanteans are perfectly capable of rescuing ourselves!

SUPERMAN: Yeah, right, like you could melt entire geological structures together!

SUBMARINER: We have possession of captured Skrull technology—

SUPERMAN: Oh, here we go again! "The Kree-Skrull War, the Kree-Skrull War." I curse the day Tom Brokaw ever labeled you guys "the greatest generation." Now, "Crisis on Infinite Earths!" *There* was an armageddon for you!

SPEAKER: Gentlemen, gentlemen, please! We need to get input from other members of our body on this pressing issue. Ah—yes, the Specter.

SPECTER: You will all burn in the inextinguishable fires of the afterlife for your sins of hubris.

DOCTOR STRANGE: By Dread Dormammu, I concur.

GHOST RIDER AND DEADMAN: Bet your sweet soul!

SPEAKER: Um, yes, of course. Just the kind of useful perspective we have come to expect from our more, ah, mystical members. Can we please have some more decidedly *practical* insights into this problem? Yes, I see the Bat Signal flashing on the ceiling.

BATMAN: Supe and I have worked together for sixty years now. Can't we once and for all institute a similar kind of reciprocal arrangement among all the elected members of our august body? You know—I can kick butt and take polls and meet with constituents in your burg, and you can do the same in Gotham?

SPEAKER: An admirable suggestion, Caped Crusader! I hereby appoint a committee to draft just such a treaty. Representatives Martian Manhunter, Mister Fantastic, Dr. Fate, Red Sonja, Scarlet Witch, Sandman, and Howard the Duck.

HOWARD THE DUCK: Aw, cripes, not another stinkin' lame-ass committee! This puts my tail-feathers in a twist!

SPEAKER: Such assignments are non-transferable except in the case of the nominated Representative having an android or robot duplicate, as you well know, Representative Duck, so complaints are useless. Now, let's move on to various budgetary issues.

HULK: Hulk hate budgetary issues! Hulk smash Congress if budget not tabled for today!

SHE-HULK: That goes double for me!

DARKSEID: I too am disinclined to deal with such trivial pecuniary matters when such important affairs as my quest for the Anti-Life Equation remain unresolved.

SPEAKER: Er, perhaps now is not the ideal time to deal with the budget.

PHANTOM GIRL: Speaker, I'd like to bring up the issue of trademark infringement.

INVISIBLE GIRL: Not this again! I've had it with your griping about my invisibility being a ripoff of your talents! You know I can't pass through solid matter like you! Doesn't that satisfy you? And you originated five hundred years in the future anyhow! We're not even contemporaries!

CAPTAIN MARVEL: I concur with Invisible Girl. This is a delicate and sensitive area, best left undisturbed. You don't see Superman and I fighting over such things any longer, do you?

SWAMP THING: I forgave Man-Thing a long time ago.

THE THING: Hey, youse guys're worse'n the Yancy Street crowd! Give Sue a chance to speak her piece, or it'll be clobberin' time in the Capitol!

HUMAN TORCH: You go, Sis!

SPEAKER: Order, order! Do I have to get Galactus or the Watcher in here? That's much better. Now, Representative Hourman is indicating that it's almost time to adjourn for lunch, so let me outline our agenda for the afternoon session. We'll be hearing from Representative Captain America on the proposed national anti-missile shield. Representative Conan will be reporting on negotiations with Cimmeria regarding sword exports. Representative Flash has a paper to present on Amtrak—I believe he paced the Metroliner from Washington to

Boston and timed it at a record slowness recently. Representative Spiderman has been examining the nation's infrastructure—the undersides of bridges and such. Representative Silver Surfer has just returned from a junket to Australia, where he made a thorough examination of wave conditions there in comparison to Hawaii's, with an eye toward boosting America's share of the tourist trade. Representative Blue Beetle wants to address the issue of non-biodegradable pesticides. We'll hear a speech from our esteemed colleague from next door, Senator Doctor Doom. And Representative Wonder Woman has a few words to say about reviving the ERA. So, until you hear the call "Congressmen, assemble!", please enjoy your various pills, elixirs, tonics, magic potions, and radioactive baths. I understand the Dirksen Cafeteria today has a special on cosmic rays.

MY LIFE—AND WELCOME TO
FIFTEEN PERCENT OF IT

"Many [literary] agents have always been career planners as well
as deal makers . . . . Robert Gottlieb, head of the newly formed
Trident Media Group, said he believed that 'agents need to spend
much more time doing something more than selling manuscripts . . . .'"

> —"Making Books" column, by Martin Arnold,
> The New York Times, October 26, 2000.

My agent actually came to my house to see me.

Again.

This visit made the third time today he had shown up unan-
nounced. I wondered how he expected me to get any actual
writing done, with all these helpful interruptions.

Herman Bundersnatch, when I first met him over twelve years
ago, was a suave, trim fellow, a snappy dresser who looked
perpetually ready to stride onstage with any of his clients lucky
enough to win some award, from the Oscar to the Edgar, the
Nobel to the Nebula. But this new regimen imposed on him by the
literary agency he worked for (Pitchfork Media Grope) had

rendered him a burnt-out husk of his old self. His clothes looked slept-in, spotted with various special sauces from the fast foods he was forced to subsist on during his mad dashings about town. His tie askew, his face unshaven, his hair a haystack, he could have been some down-on-his-luck, jobless middle-management type, instead of the quondam deal-making wizard once known from Hollywood to Frankfurt.

The first two times Herman had appeared on my doorstep today, he had borne fresh croissants, and then my mail from the local post office. On this noontime visit he carried my newly plastic-wrapped drycleaning, and a bag of take-out Szechuan food. The expression on his worn face commingled servility, irritation and desperation in equal measures.

"Here's your lunch and clean clothes. The charges will show up as line-items on your royalty statement as usual. Can I use your phone?"

I accepted the items from Herman, and stepped aside. "Sure, come on in."

Herman shuffled after me into my kitchen, spotted my old-fashioned wall phone, uncradled the handset and began dialing.

Hungry from a morning's work on my new novel—*Burning Shadows*, the story of a future, energy-starved world which turned to photovoltaic vampire-immolations as a new power-source—I took the cardboard containers of Chinese food out of the sack. "No cell phone anymore?" I asked.

"Liebfraumilch took them away. Economy measure. He figured that since we were always with our clients, we could just use their phones. Any long-distance calls I place will show up as credits on your royalty statement, by the way."

"Fine, whatever." I began forking out golden morsels of General Tsao's Chicken onto a plate when Herman got his connection.

"Hello, Anne? I'm afraid I'll have to put off walking Tiddles until four-thirty. Why? Because I have to be at Dale Pitchblend's house at four to vacuum his pool for a party tonight. No, I can't come at two! I need to drive Julie Swope's little brat to soccer. No, no, three-thirty's out. Vestry Flick needs his gutters cleaned, and I've been putting him off for weeks. Well, hell, if Tiddles can't hold his business an extra half-hour, then you'd better put him in some doggie diapers! He already wears diapers? There's no real problem then, is there, Anne? Goodbye."

Herman hung up the phone, then leaned against the wall and began to weep. I finished chewing and swallowing a delicious mouthful of garlic eggplant, then conducted my agent to a chair, brought him some kleenex and a glass of water, and patted his back until he regained his composure.

"Thank you. Thank you very much. You were always a brick, kid, never made too many demands. I'm sorry I had to break down in front of you."

I sat down opposite the weary and despairing man. "Does the agency let you actually make any deals anymore, Herman?"

"No, not really. Liebfraumilch reserves all the glory stuff for himself and a few ass-kissers. The rest of us have to run around all day keeping the clients happy and productive, tending to all their mundane chores. I'm so sick of it! Home Depot, Midas Mufflers, Roto-Rooter—I've dealt with more tradespeople than Jeeves! Do you know that the checkout clerks in all the local groceries know me by name? Toys 'R' Us gives me their kindergarten teacher's discount. And there's a whole tray reserved with my name on it at every Dunkin Donuts in this crummy burg!"

"It's a tough row to hoe, Herman. But once Pitchfork adopted the policy of smoothing out their clients' lives, you should have seen the non-reversion clause on the wall."

"I thought we were only going to direct their professional

careers! I had no idea we'd be getting into the nitty-gritty of their personal lives. It's so mortifying! Oh, I don't mind the straightforward, impersonal chores. But the romantic entanglements and family relationships—those are hell! You don't know how many 'Dear John' and 'Dear Jane' letters I've drafted and delivered, how many birds-and-bees lectures I've given to adolescents, how many white lies I've told to elderly aunts."

I continued to enjoy my lunch as Herman unburdened himself.

"Oh, god, I can't remember the last time I actually held a manuscript or placed a phonecall to an editor! To think I selfishly once complained about such things!" He bestowed an imploring gaze on me. "Do you think—that is—could I just read a little of what you've written today?"

I finished my fortune cookie, then dabbed at my lips. "I don't believe I can allow that, Herman. If word ever got back to Liebfraumilch, it could count as a breach of my contract with Pitchfork."

He sagged in his seat. "How about letting me talk to an editor then? Does anyone owe you money? How about that van Gelder guy?"

I gathered all the take-out containers up and dumped them in a bulging trashbag. "No, I'm square with all of them."

Herman got wearily to his feet. "Well, thanks for listening to me anyhow. Keep me in mind for any little oldstyle business dealings in the future. Maybe I could try to promote some foreign sales—? Non-European, of course. No? All right, I'll be going then. Candela N. Thewin will be expecting me soon to mow her lawn."

As Herman moved toward the rear door, I twist-tied the trash bag and held it out expectantly. He spotted it, sighed, took it from me, then disappeared with it out the back door.

I was really going to have to remember to give him a decent tip this Christmas.

GAMES WRITERS PLAY

"Those who like to exercise their minds with crossword puzzles can now do so doubly. Bantam Books is publishing a series of murder mysteries by Parnell Hall in which a female crossword constructor is a main character, with some of the clues in crossword."

—Martin Arnold, "Making Books,"
The New York Times, February 8, 2001.

I approached the door of Ludic Literary Productions with some trepidation. I didn't really want to be here, but I had no choice in the matter. My last book—a mystery novel titled *The Burglar in the Pergola*, and issued without any gaming support—had tanked. My publisher, Hasbro-Knopf-Sega, had insisted that my next book be released with complete "interactivity," or it wouldn't be printed at all. I forebore from asking how much more "interactive" I could get than the traditional, ages-old process of having another human being interpret the words I had written, and instead headed straight for the offices of this middleman-packager, Chester "Checkers" Ludic.

Once seated in Ludic's inner office, I sought to compose myself, vowing to listen objectively and non-emotionally to Ludic's salespitch. The man himself possessed an appearance that was reassuring enough. A rolypoly, tuft-haired, sharp-nosed chap, clad in a plaid vest and checkered pants, he resembled no one so much as Superman's silliest Golden Age foe, the Toyman.

"Welcome, welcome, it's so good to see you, Mr. Di Fallopian. I've already brought myself up to speed on your novels, and feel that your talents will synergize nicely with many of our programs here. Let me begin by saying that I see you as a boardgame."

"A boardgame?"

Ludic held up a placatory hand. "Oh, I know, it's a bit old-fashioned. But so are your books. And the boardgame is eternal. Every generation discovers it anew. Do I have to quote the latest sales figures on standard Monopoly and its many fine regional variations to make my point?"

"I—I guess not. Please continue."

"I've already taken the liberty of having our design department construct a few prototypes for your inspection. Now of course at this stage, we've labeled them with pre-branded names. But your game-novel will of course bear its own title."

Ludic reached down a construction from the shelf behind him and unfolded it across his broad desk.

"This is the Risk version of your novel. Exciting geopolitical thrills, combined with your page-turning thriller! Each player begins the game with a set number of random pages from your book, distributed across his various countries in place of armies. With each roll of the dice, each 'battle,' pages change hands. And every time any player conquers a country, he assumes the remaining pages associated with that nation. The ultimate winner of the game finishes with a substantial portion of your novel in hand, pages which he may then use in future games. Multiple playings, of course, are required to complete the novel."

Ludic sat back with a self-satisfied air. I could hardly choose my first question out of all the many troubling ones that arose. But finally I asked, "And when do these jolly gameplayers find the time actually to read my book?"

"Now, now, Mr. Di Fallopian, don't assume the worst. Why, the purchaser *could* read your novel immediately upon opening the box, if he or she wanted. It's all included, of course, beneath the shrink-wrap, on laminated sheets for easy cleaning. People do tend to snack heavily during these play experiences. But of course, no one will immediately jump to the straight text. People nowadays want a challenging play experience to precede their literary one. They'll get to your text in due time, I assure you."

I had my doubts about that, but could only say, "What's the next option?"

Ludic put away the first game and displayed another. "Here's the Clue version of your prose. Perhaps a tad too predictable for a mystery novel, but the public likes reassuring formats. The cast of perpetrators mirrors your own cast of characters, just as the gameboard mimics your setting. I'd advise you to keep your locales simple, or the lithographing costs can shoot through the roof. In any case, every round of the game brings us up to another plot-point in your book. Our test audience, by the way, reveals that they prefer at least a dozen murders to achieve satisfactory play."

"No, no, this just won't do!"

"Well, here's the Monopoly version. Your novel is printed on the Community Chest cards—"

"No!"

"In the Life format, each career milestone completes a chapter of your—"

"No!"

"Battleshi—"

"Argh!"

"Operation—"

I carefully cradled my head in my hands and began to weep. Ludic came around his desk to comfort me.

"Sorry—"

I jolted upright. "Don't mention another goddamn game!"

"Checkers" hastened back around to the refuge of his desk and waited until I had ceased seething before speaking.

"Mr. Di Fallopian, apparently you regard boardgames as too lowbrow and frivolous a vehicle for your exalted prose. You seem to demand something daring and dramatic. Therefore, I am not even going to try to interest you in many of our other fine programs, such as the Carousel, where riders on festive wooden ponies snatch pages of your novel instead of brass rings as they whirl gaily around. Or the Flag Football experience, where pages are plucked from the butts of the rival team. Instead, I am going to do something I very rarely do."

Ludic opened a desk drawer and took out a revolver. He examined the chambers, spun the barrel, then placed it on the desk before me.

"Mr. Di Fallopian—allow me to present your book as Russian Roulette!"

EXCERPT FROM DECAD

Hello, readers. Mark Kelly here, with a brief explanation of what you are about to read.

Shortly after the appearance on *Locus Online* of Nick Gevers's controversial essay, "The Best SF and Fantasy Writers: A Contemporary Top Ten," Nick was very pleasantly surprised to be approached by a publisher with a proposal. Could Nick, upon relatively short notice, assemble an anthology featuring original stories by the writers he had selected? If so, this landmark book—to be titled simply *Decad*—would be rushed to market for the Fall 2002 season, to capitalize on the furore created by the article. Moreover, it would receive massive publicity from the publisher—a mainstream firm of impressive commercial clout, who do not want their identity divulged at the moment—as well as being issued in a spoken-word edition (with the entire cast of *Lord of the Rings* being mentioned as potential voicers!).

How could Nick refuse? Here was proof that Science Fiction had finally come of age, and was receiving long-overdue attention from the powers that be. His only concern: whether or not the ten busy writers could come up with a new story apiece in time—

But here I'll let Nick take over in this brief bit from his much longer introduction, closing with my personal thanks to both

Nick and his publisher for a chance to excerpt this milestone anthology in the venue that inspired it!

Introduction to *Decad*
"When We Were Ten"
by
Nick Gevers

Thank god for the Internet!

This one refrain ran through my head time and time again during the frantic process of trying to cajole stories from the ten illustrious authors involved, edit and revise them, and coordinate their delivery to the publisher, along with this introduction. Just a few years ago, such an instant book as this would have been deemed impossible. Yet today, thanks to the miracle of technology—a technology we in the SF field helped to birth with our visionary dreams—*voila*!

And of course, without the Internet, how could a simple, top-of-the-head, scribbled-on-a-shirtsleeve-cuff list like mine ever have inspired such controversy, or attracted the attentions of any publisher at all, much less such a famous house as ******?

Of course, without the hard work and eager response of all of the writers involved, this majestic Phoenix would not have flown. It's impossible to offer enough thanks to all who contributed, but let me just offer props to Lucius Shepard for "extraordinary measures" (no problem with Fed-Ex's silly "rules" about what can and can't be shipped on this end, Lucius!), and to Gene Wolfe for that whack upside my head with his cane (that lump just won't go down!).

You hold in your hands a unique volume, a snapshot if you will of the best and the brightest our field has to offer at this particular moment in time. But if sales merit, this book will not stand alone for long, since we are considering compiling up to nine more books, extending the list to include all those fine writers who unfortunately did not make the Top Ten.

Who will be the one-hundredth best writer in the field?

If you're like me, you can hardly wait to find out!

The Heart's Drear Tonnage

by

Lucius Shepard

Like an insane lover, the kudzu has wreathed itself around the telephone pole in gross draperies of viridian plushness, climbing high to grapple the catenaried wires in a choking embrace. Standing at the base of this obscene tryst, Floyd Minouskine tilts back his hard hat and looks upward. The harsh Mississippi sunlight slashes like rusty blades across his eyes, digging jagged barbs into his brain, and Minouskine regrets the excess of oxycontin he snorted the day before. But a lineman's life is a hard one, hard as the climbing spikes that rattle at Minouskine's waist (as if the revived Christ were forced to perpetually carry the very nails once hammered into his flesh), and only the promise of more drugs tonight carries any solace or salvation, however temporary.

But standing here all day will not suffice, and, whistling an old Glen Campbell tune, Minouskine begins his fateful ascent . . . .

Mother Capybara

by

Michael Swanwick

It seemed impossible to say now, at this late date, just when the world's biggest rodent had become a rodent as big as the world. But indeed, at some point in the continuum of probabilities and likelihoods which might strain even the imagination of a professional lapidary whimsicalist, this metaphorical conceit had indeed been actualized.

Now, of course, long habitation of Mother Capybara had rendered our situation merely mundane. Like any incredibility relentlessly recomplicated, even this affront failed any longer to razzle-dazzle us.

Living around the Third Teat as we did, our small settlement had quickly become a focus of commerce, as the caravans of hairshirt weavers and toothknife dealers continually flowed in and out to exchange their humble wares for cartons of our fine milk: plain, strawberry and chocolate, and you don't even want to know where the latter two flavors came from . . . .

Pissing in the Snow
by
Andy Duncan

Wa'al, honeychile, set yo'self right down here by Mawmaw's knee and I'll tell you up a story rich as fatback about the time the Devil's own Self came to our poor little town of Sportsbra, Tennessee. It all began during the big snow of 1999. Ya see, we ain't never had sech a snow here in the Deep South like that before, just gallopin' piles 'n' piles of Yankee white flakes. Turned out 'twas all a promotion for the local radio station, what had brung down some snow-makin' machinery from Aspen, where them Hollywood types like to hang out. But the Devil, ya see, didn't know that, since he didn't happen to listen to that pertickler MOR station, being more of a heavy-metal dude hisself, and so he showed up fumin' and fussin' on the very doorstep of Shoat's Roadhouse, concerned that all us sinners was a-gonna get some relief from the natural-born, skull-boilin' Tennessee heat that addles our brains and makes us'all talk like this . . . .

The Stochastically Godelized Fashionista
by
Charles Stross

Amped-up mitochondria and a Super-Squishy(TM) amygdala obviated REM's nightly grapples, so the photo shoot had now gone on for seventy-two continuous hours.

Under the massed lenses of floating telemediated cameras, Frenzy Xerox earned her outrageous salary, roughly equivalent to the entire pre-Croggle GNP of Uzbekistan, before that ex-Soviet, never-fully-capitalized satrapy had been assimilated into the Greater Rotarian Co-Prosperity Tetrahedron. Posturing her languorous hyperattenuated limbs in various iconic asanas of formalized First World indifference to the poverty and lack of really nice shoes found in the struggling urbiomes scattered across the globe (now really only half a globe, after the invasion by the Gadarene Swine and their giant slicing machines), Frenzy conveyed a supreme unconcernedness, a mindless exaltation of her own augmented flesh, in service now to the necessary voyeurism that sustained the remnants of humanity.

But beneath her supermodel cool, Frenzy's Oxford-trained brain (running Palm Pilot's latest operating system atop a Unix-Bayer wetware foundation with inbuilt aspirin trickle) was busy factoring ten simultaneous sets of Null-SAT equations, in search of the one solution that would allow her to perfect her Valence Destabilizer and strike back against the Swine—or, barring that, at least score tickets to the sold-out concert by Lourdes Ciccone that night . . . .

Seventy-two Stories
by
Ted Chiang

When the man whom later generations would crown as the supreme creator across all of humanity's long history was born, he was endowed by his destiny and karma with the capacity to produce precisely seventy-two stories. No more, no less. Just one for every year of his productive adult life. (For he lived to the advanced old age of 102.)

At first, when the man realized he had within him sufficient sustenance and resources to produce but a single story each year of his career, he rebelled, and cursed the fates. What injustice! What indignity! Every story earned him riches, acclaim and awards. Yet he was limited to only one per annum. What heights could he not scale, if he could but increase his productivity? To say nothing of writing a novel!

And among his readers, too, sadness reigned. How they longed for additional treasures from their beloved author.

But after some while, both writer and fans reconciled themselves to this situation.

And then came the year with two stories . . . .

The Fairy Prince's Bad Day
by
Ian R. MacLeod

Price Waterhouse ambled through the foggy marsh surrounding his cottage in the Shuttlecock region of England, hard by the village of Sumphole. Lugubrious nightingales serenaded him from hoary branches, while the weepy-eyed sun strove in vain to disperse the mists that wreathed Waterhouse and his world, isolating him from all of his fellows.

If only his life had eventuated differently, he would still retain his post of Minister of Knitting under the post-Blair government of Lord Archer. But the scandal, the media swarm, Waterhouse's appearance in a bikini as Page Three Girl— These were tragic incidents which no amount of moping could overcome.

And his career as public servant had begun so well. His handling of the relief effort for the sufferers of the Dropsy Plague in the Sudan had earned him public accolades equal to the later brickbats. And all those cardigans had looked so stylish on the emaciated tribesmen.

Waterhouse paused by a hummock—or was it a hillock?—and recalled his mother's voice, reading to him an Andrew Lang story about a Fairy Prince who had been exiled from the Fairy Court, for failing to adhere to Fairy Protocols. Weeping, Waterhouse stumbled onward, until his foot encountered an ill-placed root . . . .

A Loquacious Exegesis of the Chronicles of Humblegrim
by
Jeff VanderMeer

As a historian, Pember Crumblebuns flourished an exactitude of punctilio which contributed in no small manner to his being frequently misunderstood. Perhaps in the forty-third century prior to Crumblebuns's reign as Chief Misnomerist of the amberine, gristful city of Humblegrim, when such savants as Dingus Hackberry and Veale Piecrimper filled with their impenetrable tomes the scholarly libraries of the sprawling, specter-haunted city of Humblegrim, hard by the Armorall Ocean, bisected by the Magwheel River, in sight of the Turtlewax

Mountains ("Vistas for all predilections!" boasted the tourist brochures of the city)—perhaps in this dim former age men of similar fusty peccavity had existed. But in his own day, Crumblebuns was irreproachable for his contrarian incertitude.

One day, during the Festival of the Weary Lexicographer, Crumblebuns sat in his otiose study with its view of the Plaza of Tag Sales, contemplating a tattered manuscript fetched for him at no small cost from the ruins of the Temple of Kreplach. Writ in the cursive font of the Lesser Walmart's Touters, the scrap of text seemed to be praising the virtues of certain small appliances no longer manufactured in this decadent age. Now, if only Crumblebuns could decipher this one key cryptic word, "xbox" . . . .

The Old Woman's Lament

by

Ursula K. Le Guin

In an undistinguished village named Wispelway on the island of Gravelstone lived an old woman whom her fellow villagers knew only as Nurse Selfless. Versed in simples, yarbs and psychomimetic mushrooms, Nurse Selfless, when she was not abroad gathering her botanicals, could oft be seen trundling her trundle and other bundles from house to house, dispensing her healing potions and elixirs to ailing townsfolk, at reasonable rates. A plump chicken, several yards of the finest Rackjobber silk, the pot of coins buried in the backyard, the young wife's first-born—these were the minor fees exacted by the beneficent Nurse, and she was much beloved, especially by those seeking to commune with the Mother Mushroom.

One day, whilst strolling the strand in search of cockles and mussels and the wrack of the ships lured onto the reefs by her witchfires, Nurse Selfless came upon a sight that made her pause and gasp. A man lay upon the sands, his clothes in tatters, unmoving, with arms outflung like one who grasps after a coin that has fallen down a sewer grating.

Hastening to the motionless yet still breathing form, Nurse Simple quickly turned the pockets of his trews inside out. The man regained awareness enough to mumble some small plea. But finding naught in his pockets, Nurse Selfless swore vividly, gave him a small pettish kick, and moved on . . . .

Cosmic Pizza
by
Paul Di Filippo

Milton Marmoset was late for work. And now he would catch hell for sure. The last time Milton had failed to clock in on time for his shift as sausage-slicer at Pepperdine's Pizzaria, his boss, Preston Pepperdine, had threatened to put him on the delivery route out to Tumbletown as punishment. Six drivers had been lost in just the last week on the Tumbletown route. And not to casual violence or armed robbery, either. No, the idling cars and empty uniforms of each driver had been found intact and untouched outside the very same house, 1296 Alien Masquerade Lane. The police were baffled, since 1296 Alien Masquerade Lane was the residence of an innocent old African-American widow named Mrs. N. Saysha Belle Broodmother. Milton himself suspected that the drivers had simply gone crazy from Pepperdine's insistence that they recite the Pepperdine Pizzaria jingle when delivering each pie. Upon losing their wits, they had subsequently run naked through the streets, heading for Bora Bora or some other idyllic refuge from the crass commercialism of modern life.

Pushing open the door of his place of employment, Milton confronted the glaring visage of his boss, and knew he would soon get a chance to learn firsthand what had happened to his coworkers. Gritting his teeth, Milton began mentally rehearsing the requisite company jingle: "Pepperdine pies pervade the skies/Galactic monsters have gotten wise/They've crossed the lightyears to our humble globe/To make our drivers roughly disrobe/In search of the secret only Milton could guess/It's his funky sweat that gives the sausages zest . . . "

Oobleck for the Obelist

by

Gene Wolfe

So it chanced on that morning that when I first thrust my private member out the window to make water upon the grass, I turned my eyes to the skies and saw the green rain begin. A meteorological phenomenon hitherto unknown to us who in recent generations had settled this strange world, a world of megrims and clandestini, hurkles and gnurrs, lawyer-birds and septugenarians. Alarmed, yet queerly serene, as I was under most circumstances, I hastily entrousered my serpentium and turned to my recumbent wife upon our narrow cot.

But my wife no longer lay there. In her place was a bird, a dark bird, with glossy plumage and oracular mien. Then the bird transformed into a mer-creature, an aqueous siren of the deeps. Then the oceanic bride changed into a ghost, a portentously talkative ghost of one of the natives we human colonists had slaughtered—if indeed such enigmatic yet highly symbolical lifeforms had ever existed or if we weren't the natives ourselves.

My wife suddenly reappeared, and I realized that she had been simply turning the pages of a book, and I, all catafluxed and addlegostered, had mistaken the images on those selfsame pages for actual personages and creatures. Yet who was to say whether image or flesh presented a more eternal presence in the eyes of the One who ruled over us, the great Pornocrates?

Setting down her book upon the coverlet, my wife said to me, "And who shall make breakfast this morning of the green rain?"

And I answered her thus, "Let us employ this coin I have carried purposelessly but unswervingly for years ever since we left the Place of Vague Description, and flip for it . . . ."

NEBULA AWARDS VOTING CANCELLED

Paris, France (AP)— Appearing to hastily assembled reporters at his chateau in the exclusive artists' district of his adopted European city, the president of the Science Fiction and Fantasy Writers of America, Norman Spinrad, announced today that the voting for the 2001 Nebula Awards had been abruptly cancelled.

"The whole damn farce is over," said the visibly furious author and chief executive, clad in a maroon velvet smoking jacket and irritably stroking the large gold medal from the French Academy of Literature hanging from a purple sash upon his chest. "Despite my best attempts to oversee a clean contest based solely upon the literary merits of the ballot selections, the membership of this goddamn organization of greedy sharecroppers, heartless franchisers and media whores has seen fit to disrupt the whole process by their insane campaigning. This year the constant undercurrent of voter seduction encountered in past elections has reached such an absurd fever pitch that the integrity of the Nebula Awards has been irreversibly compromised. I have no recourse other than to shut the entire process down, until such point when all the nominees agree to cease the immoral and unethical tactics they have childishly indulged in during the past few months."

In response to questions about when, if ever, the Nebula

Awards would be revived, Spinrad offered only the cryptic, "Maybe the same time Richard Calder wins the Booker Prize," before turning sharply on his heel and retreating to his cork-lined study and felt-topped escritoire.

The beginning of this unprecedented calamity for the professional writers' organization arose innocuously enough. During the 2001 Worldcon, two educational speakers were engaged to address a closed gathering of SFWA members. The speakers were two famous political campaign managers, James Carville and Roger Ailes, and their onstage dialogue was innocently advertised as "Staging Elections for Fun and Profit."

But accounts pieced together recently from attendees reveal a much harsher and more dangerous performance. The testy banter between Carville and Ailes soon descended into vituperations and accusations. Each man accused the other of having waged internecine political war on the behalf of past candidates, utilizing a grab-bag of dirty tricks, all of which were gleefully recounted by one man against the other in great detail. Furious note-taking by the audience insured that not one nasty stratagem went unrecorded, up till the point when the acrimonious presentation devolved into an onstage wrestling match.

Not long after this Labor Day debacle, the tenor of the Nebula campaigning—at this point still in the stage of nominating works to the preliminary ballot—took a decided turn for the worse. But initially, in the wake of the chaos and tumult pursuant to the events of September 11th, this dramatic shift went under-reported by the media.

The first incident in October was a mass spamming of the SFWA electronic mailing list. The message, routed anonymously through an identity-stripping server, consisted solely of a digital photo depicting the topless author Catherine Asaro seated upon Bill Clinton's lap. Plainly the work of a Photoshop prankster, the photo nonetheless resulted in several outraged members—both feminists and rightwingers—withdrawing their recommendations for Asaro's *The Quantum Rose*. This misfortune was offset, however, by an equal number of new recommendations, accompanied by proposals of marriage and offers of modeling jobs.

The next indication that the conventional jockeying for votes—usually restricted to online forums, whisper campaigns and weekend conventions—had been ramped up to heretofore unprecedented levels occurred at a Barnes and Noble store in Weedpatch, Alabama, where author Andy Duncan was conducting a signing. After Duncan was ensconced inside, an unidentified man stationed himself by the door and was witnessed handing out xeroxed copies of Duncan's story, "The Pottawatomie Giant," another Nebula frontrunner. Upon closer inspection, the story proved to be not Duncan's prose but rather some particularly outrageous "slash fiction" involving an erotic encounter between Lex Luthor and Clark Kent in their *Smallville* incarnations. The story quickly ended up on the internet under Duncan's byline, and the ensuing controversy threatened his place on the ballot.

By now the SF world was abuzz with discussion and rumors concerning the dirty tricks. Authors were alert for sabotage—and perhaps also busy planning countermeasures of their own—but no one anticipated the nature of the next strike.

Headlines across the country in November told of a dramatic upstate New York bank robbery by one "George 'Hysteria Machine' Zebrowski." Identified as an expatriate Polish associate of the Brooklyn-based Russian Mafia, who also dabbled in "pulp fiction," Zebrowski led police a wild chase for a week, stealing cars, holding hostages and generally spooking the residents of four states before being caught. Of course, once in custody the criminal was definitively proven not to have any connection with the author of "Wound the Wind." But intense damage had already been done to Zebrowski's sterling track record.

This pivotal event triggered a massive outburst of reputation-damaging pranks in December and January, as if all the new instigators felt they must strike first before they were themselves attacked. Soon a flood of Carvillian hijinx swamped the staid science fiction arena.

Across New England, James Patrick Kelly found his every scheduled reading of "Undone" broken up by protestors accusing him of destroying protected wetlands and endangered species during the construction of his humongous New Hampshire McMansion.

Geoffrey Landis, on the ballot for his *Mars Crossing*, discovered a scientific paper promoting cold fusion posted under his name in several cyber-journals.

Jack Williamson, author of "The Ultimate Earth," was startled to learn through the *Drudge Report* that his longevity was a result of porcine xenografts and regular baths in the blood of virgins.

The disclosure that James Morrow was actually a Vatican employee seeking to give atheists a bad name caused the ranking of his "Auspicious Eggs" to plummet.

Connie Willis was forced to curtail her efforts promoting her novel *Passage* in order to deal with the assertion in the *Weekly World News* that her daughter was fathered by UFO aliens.

The picture of Jack "The Diamond Pit" Dann enjoying sexual congress with a kangaroo caused every copy of every parental cyber-censor to crash simultaneously around the globe.

The revelation in the pages of a counterfeit issue of *The New York Review of Science Fiction* that Kelly Link was really a transgendered Craig Strete cast a dismissive light on her story "Louise's Ghost," which was automatically assumed to be plagiarized.

Spurious endorsements from "John Clute" and "Gary Wolfe"—"The best novel since Time began." and "Makes every other novel this year look like a pile of vomit."—nearly sank Tim Powers's *Declare*, when recanted by the genuine critics.

Not every plot succeeded in hurting its intended victim, however. Many backfired against their masterminds. One such was the attempt to tar Lucius Shepard.

A teenaged Guatemalan boy of mixed ancestry turned up on Shepard's doorstep, claiming to be a byblow of Shepard's past sojourns among the Miskito Indians. Obviously the perpetrator of this plot expected to ensnarl Shepard in a long and expensive legal battle, complete with DNA tests. But instead Shepard welcomed the impostor in with open arms, saying, "Hell, for all I know your story's true. I was pretty messed up in those days." He proudly adopted the boy and sent him off to college, causing the stock of his "Radiant Green Star" to soar.

By February the whole SF world was reeling from this extension of common Beltway political tactics to their cloistered domain. Stories and novels ping-ponged on and off the preliminary Nebula ballot, as reputations were shattered and painstakingly rebuilt on a daily, even hourly basis. Exhausted and wary, the membership of SFWA tentatively enjoyed a few weeks of calm. But then came the final blow, which caused President Spinrad to suspend the whole awards process.

A masterful break-in at the offices of *Locus* went undetected until it was too late. The hacker who logged on that night to the magazine's computers managed to substitute his files for the entire issue just about to go to the printers. Afterwards, intercepting the alarming proof copies and substituting ones that matched Publisher Charles Brown's expectations, the conspirators insured that their bogus issue would be distributed without editorial intervention.

"*Locus*gate" had all the impact its perpetrators intended. When the subverted edition reached the hands of subscribers, chaos erupted.

Deaths of beloved SF icons were falsely announced. Numerous publishers were ostensibly bankrupt. Editors were committing suicide and murder to cover up embezzlement. Patricia McKillip had enrolled in a Zen community and withdrawn *The Tower at Stony Wood* from Nebula contention. Mike Resnick had won election as the new president of the Congo and pulled "The Elephants of Neptune." And George R. R. Martin, as the new CEO of the WB network, withdrew *A Storm of Swords*...

Given the massive disruption and unreliability of all normal channels of news and publicity, President Spinrad deemed it impossible to conduct the Nebula voting with any assurance of accuracy.

It is to be fervently hoped that once the national Presidential election of 2004 begins to heat up—sometime around September 2002—the science fiction authors who have picked up a taste for such shenanigans will find employment with various PACs, and perhaps the Nebula race can return to its quondam gentlemanly ways.

THE UNKINDEST CUTS

Introduction

These manuscript fragments were recently found among the papers of [name of famous dead SF writer].[1] Unfortunately, the papers had been stored in the author's wine cellar, and when the supports on a rack of [name of an expensive vintage] gave way, the subsequent flood of wine ruined almost the entire trove of stories, essays, letters and [name of embarrassing type of fetishistic pornography]. Only the laborious efforts of [name of famous SF critic] have succeeded in recovering even these small portions of one random text. The gaps in the manuscript have been assigned grammatical and contextual labels based on the scholar's best understanding of the author's published work. The editor hopes that readers will be able to enjoy these gap-ridden story fragments, by allowing their imaginations to fill in the blanks.

THE [cosmological noun] THAT [past tense verb] EARTH

by

[name of famous dead SF writer]

[1] This introduction itself has suffered from numerous obscuring editorial coffee stains that necessitate interpolations upon the part of the reader.

Tony [unusual-sounding last name] occupied the junior spot on the staff at [name of classic science fiction writer indicative of author's influences] Observatory. Fresh out of his stressful post-grad stint with the [derogative adjective for female behavior] Professor Angela Wiltdonger, Tony faced in his new job the subtle discrimination leveled by the senior scientists against the unproven newcomer. Tony consoled himself with the thought that over time his professional status would [verb]. Unless, of course, everyone secretly hated him because he was [name of an ethnic stereotype].

In any case, Tony's low rank secured him the absolutely worst viewing times on the big, expensive [name of super-science gadget]: the five minutes just before dawn. Only during these scant hours could he collect data for his researches. Tony's controversial theory about the origin of [name of quantum particle] in the [name of distant nebula] during the [name of past era] and their effect on [name of one type of human behavior] had brought him nothing but [unprintable obscene noun]. Nonetheless, Tony clung [adverb] to his pet theory.

Little did he suspect that today would prove the turning point in his [name of nerdy neurotic compulsion to succeed].

As he pressed his [name of body part] to the [name of very cold portion of super-science gadget], Tony quivered with [name of emotion]. He could barely believe his [adjective involving F-word] senses! There, clear as day, stood revealed a Big Dumb Object composed entirely of [plural name of quantum particle]!

"Mr. [unusual-sounding last name]! Exactly what do you think you're doing?"

Striking him like an unexpected blow, the hated voice of Professor Angela Wiltdonger caused Tony to slip from the observing platform and land clumsily at Wiltdonger's feet, which were shod in the very latest style from [name of classy designer].

Tony picked himself up and brushed [name of yucky science glop] off his pants. "Um, just finishing my observations, Professor Wiltdonger. And you won't believe what I just discovered—"

"I don't give a [name of part of rodent's anatomy] about any of your trivial observations. It's one minute past dawn, and you're supposed to be swabbing out [name of radiation-producing lab equipment]. Get busy!"

Tony bit his [name of body part]. No point getting in an argument with Wiltdonger now. Once he had his discovery firmly documented, it would be a short step to winning [name of one of the few prestigious prizes whose reputation is not marred by SFWA-style infighting] and scientific immortality. Then he'd see what kind of [name of a dish best served cold] he would enjoy!

* * *

. . . the ruins of the [name of classic science fiction writer indicative of author's influences] Observatory. Barely two walls of the structure remained standing beneath the night skies, in the wake of the attack by the [mythologically suggestive plural name], who had poured forth from the Big Dumb Object once it assumed Earth orbit. Who could have believed that just one eventful week separated Tony's dawn-hour discovery from the current [noun descriptive of a seemingly immutable global catastrophe]? And to think that Earth's last hope against the invaders resided now in a desperate collaboration between Tony and Professor Angela Wiltdonger!

Brushing back a lock of her [adjective] hair, Wiltdonger swore, then refocused her attention on the delicate task before her. Manipulating her [name of improvised tool] with trembling fingers whose chipped painted nails revealed the merciless alien eradication of beauty parlors everywhere, the [sympathy-provoking adjective] professor sought to join [name of computer part] with [name of unlikely cross-discipline gadget]. Tony steadied his hand holding the [name of primitive improvised source of illumination] and uttered encouraging noises. Finally, after what seemed like hours, Wiltdonger sat back on her [sexy-sounding adjective] haunches and said, "It's done. This inspiration of yours had better prove golden, kid. Otherwise humanity is destined to serve for all eternity as [slang term among convicts denoting prisoner's "girlfriend"] for our new interstellar overlords."

"I—I think it'll work—Angela . . . ."

This unprecedented use of her given name caused Professor Wiltdonger to look at Tony in a new way. Her [adjective] blue eyes filled with [name of emotion], which was returned in triplicate by her companion. Suddenly they were no longer two rival scientists, but simply a man and a woman alone beneath the stars.

Without any planning on Tony's part, he found that he and Angela were [gerund]. With the shattered bits of the [name of super-science gadget] digging into his [name of body part], Tony began to murmur sweet words into Angela's [name of body part]. In the midst of her passionate reciprocation, she murmured back, "[Sultry exclamation]."

* * *

With the final coruscating flares of the [name of heretofore unknown type of ray] dying down around them, Tony and Angela stood upon a mound of rubble in the ruins of [name of major metropolitan area], clutching each other's [name of body part] and gazing skyward. Fleeing like a pack of [plural name of cowardly kind of beast], the few surviving celestial invaders made a beeline toward their Big Dumb Object.

"We did it, Angela! We did it!"

"[Wry observation indicating basic cynicism tempered by newfound empathy]."

Tony turned to hug his new mate. "Well, it's up to us now to restore civilization."

"Considering that ninety percent of humanity has been wiped out, there's an awful lot of [gerund] to do."

Tony blushed. "I'm up to it, Angela. If you are."

Angela smiled [smarmy adverb]. "We'd better get busy then. Because if I know anything about the way the universe works, there's one thing we can be certain of. The [mythologically suggestive plural name] will be back!"

READIN' AND 'RITIN' AND ROYALTIES

"[David] Halberstam was, eccentrically, also the editor of the Parents' Association newsletter [at the Upper East Side girls' school attended by his daughter] for several years . . . ."
—*New York* magazine, 11-26-01.

I had just finished one of my most hated tasks—filling out the monthly spoiled-milk-wastage report for Superintendent Overholtz—when Mrs. Pribyl burst into my office. I should have known then and there that something highly unusual was up. Mrs. Pribyl is not the kind of assistant given to barging in so precipitously. Even after seventeen and a half years of working together, I had never seen her enter without a timorous knock. And now the flustered look on her flushed face was further confirmation of the untoward circumstances that had compelled her to intrude without warning.

"Principal Vansyckle, it's just awful! We're going to be sued! Philbin Elementary School will have to close its doors forever!"

I hastened to Mrs. Pribyl's side in an attempt to calm her down. "Now, now, it can't be as bad as all that. We've both dealt with angry parents before. Most of them are quick to realize that their grievances are trivial or unfounded. It's natural for every mother and father to think that their child can do no wrong. They generally bull in, all enraged and making wild threats. But once the facts of the case are presented rationally, they soon come around. And I've yet to see a parent who wouldn't respond with smiles to a cup of hot cocoa and a plate of your famous snickerdoodles."

"But that's just the trouble," wailed the inconsolable Mrs. Pribyl. "This isn't a parent, it's, it's—an agent!"

"An agent? Do you mean some kind of salesman, like an insurance agent or a real estate agent?"

"No! Ten times worse than that! This horrid fellow is a *literary* agent!"

A literary agent? Whatever could bring such an unheard-of creature to our backwater school? For a moment, I allowed myself to indulge in a fantasy. Was it possible that this agent had caught wind of my memoir in progress, even though the project amounted to only a manila folder full of notes, tucked away in the file cabinet containing every permission slip ever signed during my tenure? True, I had mentioned the title to a few select acquaintances, since I was certain that gem alone would guarantee a bestseller. *Cherrybombs in the Lavatories of Outmoded Pedagogy: Victor Vansyckle's Heuristic Maxims.* But certainly if some freelance book-huckster was going to approach me as a potential client, they wouldn't have issued threats and accusations of the sort that had so upset Mrs. Pribyl.

Well, guessing would accomplish nothing. I'd just have to confront the stranger.

"Mrs. Pribyl, show this gentleman in. And why not treat yourself to a small break in the Teachers' Lounge? Pour yourself a little something from the 'medicine cabinet.' You have my explicit permission."

Sniffling, Mrs. Pribyl departed, and hot on her heels the agent entered.

"Principal Vansyckle? My name is Howard Dowthitt." Neatly dressed in an expensive suit, his smooth-shaven face composed in a neutral expression, Mr. Dowthitt hardly seemed such a monster as to have caused Mrs. Pribyl's breakdown. But his next words belied his looks. "I'm afraid that your school system owes my client approximately one hundred thousand dollars in royalties. Failing to secure full and immediate payment of this sum, we will be forced to initiate a lawsuit for millions in damages."

I sat down heavily, my brain all awhirl. But then decades spent negotiating with striking teachers, schoolyard bullies, town council members and aggrieved parents came to the fore, and I began to try to take command of this implausible situation.

"First off, Mr. Dowthitt, just who is your client?"

"Peter Shallcross."

"Ah, the father of Pashmina Shallcross, one of our fourth-graders."

"Not simply the father of one of your students, but also the editor of the *Philbin PTA Newsletter*. You do not deny this, do you?"

"No, of course not. Mr. Shallcross has done yeoman duty on the newsletter. Why, the Halloween issue alone was a masterpiece of news and entertainment."

"I'm glad to hear you evaluate my client's contributions so highly. You'll no doubt be in accordance then with this accounting of his billable hours."

Dowthitt lifted up his briefcase, opened it and withdrew a piece of paper, which he handed to me. Scanning it quickly, I saw that it was an invoice detailing the hours Peter Shallcross had put into the PTA newsletter, and assessing each hour at some astronomical sum.

I tried to hand the paper back to the agent, but he motioned for me to keep it.

"But, but," I stammered, "we never intended to hire your client for a paying position. This was strictly a volunteer effort on his part."

"Perhaps, perhaps. But any arrangement you entered into with my client occurred before his recent success. He's just sold his first book, a technothriller titled *The Lordosis Position*, for several million dollars. Instantly, his past writings appreciate in value considerably. Hence our legally justifiable attempt to recover the monies owed him."

Now my dander began to get ruffled. "This—this is unconscionable blackmail! Picking on a little public school like this! Have you no shame, sir?"

Dowthitt buffed his manicured nails and appeared bored and untroubled. "Mr. Vansyckle, no one is picking on you and your school in particular. You are simply part of a nationwide effort to secure just and fair compensation for our hard-working authors who are also parents of school-age children. For too long now, our clients have been at the mercy of educators such as yourself, who plead poverty to secure their valuable professional services. Norman Mailer, Kurt Vonnegut, George Plimpton, John Cheever—it's too late to help them now, their parenting years are long behind them, and certain statutes of limitations apply. But young contemporary writers with children—that's different. Lord knows how many millions of dollars worth of prose has been extorted from them, just to exalt your little fiefdoms. Why, the work Thomas Pynchon has done on his son's school lunch menus alone is worth millions! Well, let me just tell you this, Mister So-called Educator: the days of such coerced servitude are now over, and justice will at last be done."

"Justice? Where's the justice here? You just told me Mr. Shallcross earned more than our school's entire budget for the past five years, and yet he still wants to bleed us for more?"

Now came the first break in Dowthitt's composure. "Ah, well—Mr. Shallcross has not expressly ordered us to go after these debts. But a certain small sub-clause in his contract with us gives us authorization to do so."

A ray of hope entered my heart. "Then this is all a devious plot by literary agents to get an extra fifteen percent of money they're not even really owed! I'm calling Mr. Shallcross right now. We'll see what he thinks of this. And I don't imagine he'll be too happy once little Pashmina's peers hear how her daddy bankrupted the school and ended such beloved extracurricular activities as the marching band and the numismatics club. Juvenile taunts can be most cutting, and no parent likes to see his or her daughter socially ostracized."

Dowthitt intercepted my hand on its way to the phone, and I was gratified to see a line of sweat on his brow.

"Wait just a minute, Mr. Vansyckle. There's no need to act so precipitously. I'm sure we can come to some sort of negotiated settlement on this matter."

The subsequent discussion took hours, but by the end we were both happy.

The PTA would indeed have to sponsor a few extra bake sales, liquor-basket raffles and car washes over the next year. But the Philbin newsletter was guaranteed at least one new Joyce Carol Oates story during that period, or two poems by Stanley Kunitz, whichever we had room for after running all of the kindergarten-ers' drawings.

A VADE MECUM FOR THE THIRD MILLENNIUM:

A REVIEW OF THE NEW SFWA HANDBOOK

The Official Handbook of the Science Fiction and Fantasy Writers of America, Fourth Edition, compiled by the Officers and Membership of SFWA, published by Talk/Miramax Books, illustrated with over 100 color photos, cover art by Jeff Koons, 256 pages, $29.95 for non-members, $35.00 for members.

At last, under the guiding and chastising hand of President Norman Spinrad, we working science fiction and fantasy writers (and also the hobbyists among us who published three short-shorts in *Dragon* magazine fifteen years ago and nothing since) now have a truly world-class Bible of professionalism to guide us through each and every stage of our careers. For the first time in its history, SFWA courageously acknowledges the bracing realities of our business, dispensing with the facade of mild-mannered nerdiness that has for so long hidden the sharklike savagery of the SF publishing scene, where only the bold and shameless survive and flourish. Gone are all the naive and simplistic essays on manuscript preparation and world-building, proofreading and constructing believable aliens. In their place are forthright strategies and tips for dealing with everyone from big-box retailers to high-powered agents, from whining fans to obstreperous editors, from alimony-crazed spouses to syco-phantic academics.

The new handbook is divided into four main parts: "Income from Books"; "Income from Periodicals and Anthologies"; "Income from Conventions"; and "Income from Other Media". Additionally, several appendices cover such vital subjects as:

* "Plastic Surgery: Getting that Perfect Author Photo"
* "Creative Income-Tax Exemptions: How Jamaica Inspired Your Mars Novel"
* "Insuring Posterity's Adoration: If You Can't Get Harold Bloom on Your Side, Who's Next Best?"
* "Sabotaging the Careers of Your Rivals"
* "Campaigning for Awards: Lessons from Tammany Hall to Watergate"
* "Monica Lewinsky on Mentorship"
* "Brushes with the Law: There's No Such Thing as Bad Publicity"
* "Clarion Call: Spinning a Six-Week Workshop into a Six-Figure Deal"
* "Hitch Your Wagon to a Star: Selecting the Most Prestigious Public Charity to Endorse"

Let's take a brief survey of the magnificent resources afforded us by each quarter of this revolutionary guide to all that's utili-tarian in the dealings of the self-interested author.

"Income from Books" manages to turn the current model of authorship and sales on its head, revealing how easy it is to generate huge profits from the least amount of work. Vision? Talent? Those are things of the past! The new model is Enron refined, without any messy public disclosures, and the with-it writer will soon be forming creative financial "partnerships" with himself, his dead relatives and his pets. Taking a page from historian Stephen Ambrose (and what could be more fitting?), several big-name writers show us how to recycle proven tropes and concepts from past blockbusters into repackaged hits. (Tie-in and sharecrop authors need not read this already familiar material.) When the employment of starving graduate students as ghostwriters is factored in, churning out that series of military SF novels starring a plucky female lieutenant or the mega-volume saga of an orphaned waif who holds the key to defeating the Dark Lord looks as easy as having sex in a Delany novel.

One tactic, the "Mariah Carey Option," applies only to writers already well established. Deliberately turning in one stinker after another in fulfillment of a multi-book contract can result in huge buyout payments for no work whatsoever! But what about moving on from the apparent disaster of being dumped by your publisher? That's what pseudonyms were invented for!

Perhaps the most intriguing advice in this section concerns breaking out into the mainstream (with all its glories and rewards) by cleverly camouflaging your SF or Fantasy. Choosing the correct chi-chi university to attend (they're all ranked, from Brown to Bennington!); training oneself to instinctively say "magical realism" instead of "fantasy" and "transgressive postmodern surrealism" instead of "science fiction"; picking the most glamorous agent (or marrying her, *a la* Thomas Pynchon!); emphasizing autobiographical elements in your fiction (sexual dysfunction a plus!)— With the guidance given here, you'll soon be leaving Mary Doria Russell and Karen Joy Fowler in the dust!

Given the diminished importance of short fiction and magazines in today's SF world, "Income from Periodicals and Anthologies" boasts less heft than the other divisions of the *Handbook*.

But still, there's no underestimating the career boost still conferred by the appearance of an eye-catching story in *Asimov's* or the latest flagship theme anthology, and in these pages you'll learn all the secret tricks to grab editorial attention. Greeting cards on their birthdays (cash is one present that's never exchanged!); gift certificates for local masseuses or gourmet grocery stores stapled to your title page; the blatant Tuckerizing of mutual friends . . . There's hardly a stone left unturned by the five experienced authors of this section, who have a combined record of three thousand Nebula nominations in the novella category alone!

Who among us hasn't enjoyed the camaraderie of a well-run convention from time to time, the schmoozing and boozing, the high-minded intellectual stimulation of the typical genteel panel discussion? Some of us even seem to live solely for such weekend affairs! But how many of us realize that an actual subsistence-level existence can be garnered from the never-ending circuit of conventions? The famed mathematician Paul Erdös never had a fixed abode or income in his entire professional lifetime, sponging off a series of fellow math savants who gratefully hosted him in their homes in rotation so that he could continue his work without the trivial preoccupations of daily life. This Erdös model is formalized here for the SF writer so inclined. Names and addresses of gullible fans are provided, and a circuit of conventions, from Worldcon down to Biloxi's WWF/SF Contusion, is arranged so that the peripatetic author need never change his sheets again. And for those of us homebodies who are not quite ready for such a migrant existence, we find plenty of tips on extorting cash payments from con-committees by last-minute refusals to perform, and similar labor union moves.

When "other media" is invoked, the mind of the savvy writer naturally turns to film and television options, and there's plenty of practical wisdom here on these pot-of-gold payoffs. Writing your novel as if you were reverse-engineering it from an already finished film of itself; capitalizing on hot trends (can you say "dinosaur" or "matrix"?); coining a weird name for yourself (Z. Twilight Chameleon) and producing and directing your own derivative screenplays; babbling on about "five-year story arcs"— You'll find a lot of helpful hand-holding in this last major division of the *Handbook*. But Hollywood and the Sci-Fi Channel are just the tip of the iceberg! Think Maya Angelou writing verse for Hallmark cards! Think Stephen King endorsing a *Road Rage* videogame version of his near-fatal accident! Think Robert Jordan singing songs from his *Wheel of Time* series! Think *Lord of the Rings* Underoos! If there's a spinoff left untapped here, it hasn't yet been invented.

As a thoroughly modern, singleminded SF writer who has put aside all quibbles about esthetic matters and dispensed with such outmoded concepts as "sense of wonder," the literary world is your oyster! And the new *SFWA Handbook* is the sharp-edged knife that will slice it open for you! Just be careful not to cut yourself on its sharper edges.

PROSE BY ANY OTHER NAME WOULD SMELL AS SWEET

"Like many little-known authors, Janis Jaquith often wishes that some of the people buying best sellers would pick up her book instead. Now the online retailer Amazon.com is giving her a chance to express those feelings.

"Two weeks ago, Amazon's Web site added a feature that lets users suggest that shoppers buy a different book than the one being perused, and Ms. Jaquith, the self-published author of the memoir *Birdseed Cookies*, has taken full advantage . . . ."

—*The New York Times*, May 5, 2002.

I was dreading going into work today. The Mittelschmerz contract needed a final revision, and my boss, Sandy Fleabane, was riding my tail hard to get it done. So as I endured my commute into Manhattan on the packed LIRR train, I tried to forget my troubles by immersing myself in the latest Keene Dunst book, *Fear of Terror*. It took me a while to get back into the novel. It wasn't quite as good as Dunst's last one, *Deathly Living*, or the one before that, *Suspicion of Mistrust*, or even the one before that, *Life Amidst Death*. But after a while, I found myself lost in

Dunst's technically adept prose, glad to have put aside my worries thanks to a somewhat engaging book.

A few stops before the city, my seatmate got off, and I moved my briefcase into the empty seat, hoping that no incoming passenger would claim it. Having the extra space would have been another small comfort in my harried day. But of course, the way my luck was running, not only did a new passenger, a woman, quickly zero in on the seat, but she was carrying an enormous clunky duffel bag. When I saw she was intent on sitting next to me, I sighed and removed my briefcase from the empty seat. She plopped down with her load, banging my knee in the process. The duffel held something hard-edged, and it hurt.

"Ow!"

"Oh, I'm terribly sorry!"

Although pretty, and dressed conventionally enough, the woman looked a little ditzy, and I didn't want to start a conversation with her. So I simply said, "No problem," very cursorily, then tried to return to my book. But she wasn't letting me off so easily.

"Are you sure you're okay? Perhaps you should go to the lavatory and see if I bruised you. Maybe get some ice from the café car for it?"

Well, my knee *was* throbbing, and I thought it couldn't hurt to have a look. "All right. But I assure you, even if I do develop a little bruise, it's really inconsequential."

She smiled. "Still, I'd feel so much better if you checked."

I laid my book down on my seat and went to the lav. When I returned, I was able to reassure the woman that my knee seemed fine.

"I'm so relieved!" she gushed.

I smiled wanly and tried to shield myself from any further conversation behind my book. But immediately I encountered something that baffled me. The Keene Dunst novel no longer resembled what I had been reading. The text was completely different. Mistrusting my own senses, I looked at the dustjacket, then the pages, then the dustjacket again. The incongruity between package and contents was baffling.

During this inspection, my new seatmate, contrary to her earlier effusiveness, tried to hide behind a copy of *The New York Times Book Review.*

Finally I had an inspiration. I removed the dustjacket and examined the spine of the book. There I read an unexpected legend: *Paper Poppies*, by Barbara de Seville.

"What's this now?" I demanded, turning to the woman. "Have you switched my book with another one?"

She set down her tabloid shield. "Me? Of course not! Why would I do a crazy thing like that?"

I had no way of disproving her claim of innocence. Still, who else could have played such a trick . . . ?

"Well, did you notice anyone messing with my book while I was away from my seat?"

"Yes, now that you mention it, I did. He was a tall Hispanic man with a Zapatista mustache and a limp—"

Just then her cellphone rang. "Hello, Barbara de Seville here, Alternative Author Project—"

"Ah-ha!" I snatched the cellphone out of her hand and cut the connection. "It *was* you then!"

Caught red-handed, Barbara de Seville put up a bold front. "All right, I admit it. I took your horrid piece of bestseller trash and replaced it with a heartfelt, winsome, slice-of-life, coming-of-age memoir. At least that's what *The Chicago Mercantile Intelligencer* said about it. Instead of berating me, you should be thanking me!"

"Thanking you? For stealing my book?"

"Oh, come now, I merely substituted something of equal or greater value. Monetarily, you're no worse off. And as for entertainment value, your experience has been greatly enhanced. Trust me! Can't you see that I'm trying to broaden your tastes and literary experience? Surely you didn't really want to be reading that awful *Dunst* book, did you?"

"Why would I have bought it if I didn't want to read it?"

"Because you've been brainwashed! You and all the other poor deluded readers whose collective purchases constitute the immense sham that is the bestseller list! You've never been exposed to the marvelous alternatives that are out there. Wonderful books composed of the authors' blood, sweat and tears which go begging for readers."

The image of books dripping precious bodily fluids repelled me for a moment, but then I started to consider Barbara's argument. Perhaps I hadn't really invested much thought in acquiring the latest Dunst book. What had once been a real consumer choice based on past enjoyment had become a mere habit leading to boredom and stultification.

As if sensing that I was weakening, Barbara pressed her case. "All I'm doing is engaging in a little guerilla marketing. As a businessman yourself, surely you can understand about positioning your product where consumers can find it. And this is not about just *my* book. I'm striking a blow for all unsung authors everywhere!"

My innate cynicism came to the forefront. "Oh, really? Then why didn't you slip me a copy of someone else's book, and not your own?"

Barbara blushed. "Well, I only get the author discount on multiple copies of my own title . . . I'm not as rich as Keene Dunst, you know! If *Paper Poppies* really takes off, then I'll expand to other authors. I have a friend who's written this exhilarating tale of sisterhood. Belle Kerve, *Sistahs and Mistahs*—"

Barbara's sincerity had won me over, at least partially. "Okay, what if I'm willing to give your book a try? Can I get my Dunst back if I don't like yours?"

"Certainly!"

"All right then. I'll give it a shot."

"Wonderful! Here, let me autograph it! What's your name?"

I told her. As she signed my new book, I took the chance to look her over more closely. Somehow she didn't look so ditzy any more.

"Let me get you a real dustjacket to go with that." Barbara unzipped her duffel, revealing a few dozen copies of her book.

"What are your plans once you're in the city?" I asked.

"Oh, not much. I'm going to hang out at Bryant Park and Washington Square, wherever I'm likely to find people reading. Then I'll pull a few more switches, just like I did on you."

"Isn't that awfully tricky, all by yourself?"

"Oh, yes. You wouldn't believe how many times I've almost been caught. Having a confederate would make things easier, but most of my friends are home writing." Sizing up my new interest, Barbara said, "Want to help?"

I considered the Mittelschmerz contract and Sandy Fleabane for less than a minute.

"Sure. If I can pick even just a few of the bestsellers we sabotage."

WE, THE PUBLICISTS

"Once a book is written, often the most important individual in
an author's life after the editor is the public relations person . . . .
Stuart S. Applebaum, chief spokesman for Random House Inc . . .
describes his job this way: 'In giving life to a book, if the editor is
the midwife, then we the publicists are the neo-natal nurses.
All-purpose caregivers to both the newborn and the
author-parent in those first six weeks.'"

> —Martin Arnold,
> "Pitchers at the Fair,"
> *The New York Times*, May 2, 2002.

When I woke up that morning there was a strange man lying in
bed between me and my wife.

The stranger hadn't been there when Esther and I fell asleep last
evening, shortly after the ten o'clock news. He must have crept
into the house and insinuated himself in the middle of the night
with the grace and guile of a cat.

Surprisingly enough, I did not immediately scream or yell or
flail about or threaten or bolt from under the covers. (The
stranger, thank God, lay atop the duvet, not beneath.) My unnaturally gentle and accepting reaction had more to do with the

stranger's reassuring looks and calm demeanor than with any resort to common sense.

The intruder wore a very expensive suit, remarkably unwrinkled despite his night's recumbent posture. He was a clean-shaven Caucasian, fairly young, sporting an affable grin. He boasted a very nice haircut. From his hands folded across his stomach sparkled a college ring I recognized as belonging to a Princeton grad.

Generously allowing me a few moments to compose my thoughts, the stranger continued to beam at me, his tilted face just a few inches from mine. Then he reached into a coat pocket and pulled out a business card.

Feeling as if I were still dreaming, I took the card. I found my specs, donned them, and read the card.

Hapwood S. Stutterbalm, Chief Publicist
Rumdum House Publishing

Stutterbalm extended his hand for a shake, and I timorously took it. "Mr. McFoozel—may I call you Ken?—it's a pleasure to meet you at last. I can't tell you how much I enjoyed your book in manuscript. It's Rumdum House's very great privilege to publish your authorized biography of Britney Spears, *She's Stoopid to Conquer*, and I'm here now and for the next six weeks to make sure we maximize all the impact and rewards from your hard work and authorial brilliance."

Of course, these were the kind of words every author dreams of hearing from his publisher, and I felt somewhat more kindly disposed to Stutterbalm, despite his unconventional entrance into my life. Still, I was at a loss as to how to treat this nocturnal intrusion.

Esther, always a heavy sleeper, moaned and mumbled, "Ken, shut the clock-radio off . . . ." She pulled the covers up over her head, and I could see that she was going to be absolutely no help in this situation.

"Mr. Stutterbalm—"

"Hapwood, please. Or Hap. Whatever makes it easier for us to work together."

I found it impossible to raise any anger in the face of this disarming desire to accommodate me. "Well, uh, Hap, could we continue this conversation in the kitchen, please?"

"Certainly."

I slipped out of bed, scuffled into my slippers, donned my robe, and headed for the bathroom.

Stutterbalm vaulted agilely out of bed, and seemed ready to follow me into the john. He had a PDA in his hand and seemed to be inditing notes with his stylus.

"Please, er, Hap, could I have some privacy for just a moment?"

"But Ken, it's so important that I monitor all the intimate aspects of your life. There's no telling what small detail might lead to a valuable tie-in for your book. For instance, based on what brand of toothpaste or toilet tissue you use, we might be able to bring onboard a co-sponsor for your book-signing tour. We've already got you booked in forty-five cities, after all, at not inconsiderable expense."

Forty-five cities? I had needed six months to recover from my last tour, a ten-city number for my YA biography of the Russian president, *Rootin' Tootin', Sure-shootin' Putin*. What had I ever gotten myself into by accepting this latest assignment? The last female pop singer I had enjoyed listening to had been Carly Simon. I silently cursed my agent, and swore that I would never do another book on any starlet younger than seventy-two.

Stutterbalm waited patiently, stylus posed, a cocker-spaniel eagerness on his face. Forty-five cities indeed implied a certain level of sales . . . .

"Oh, all right, you can come in. But at least turn your back while I use the toilet."

"Of course, Ken!"

In the kitchen, Stutterbalm insisted on brewing the coffee and fixing me a large breakfast, all with gourmet provisions he had brought with him. When he placed my plate in front of me, I noted that he had made no arrangement for his own breakfast.

"Aren't you going to eat too?"

"Not right now. Truly dedicated publicists generally fast during the six weeks while they're nursing a book along. I'll have a protein shake at noon. Right now we have to utilize every minute to groom and coach you for the rigors ahead. Just let me set up this camera—"

Unpacking a duffel bag he must have previously planted, Stutterbalm erected a video camera on a tripod, as well as some small studio lights. He snapped on the fixtures and I flinched at the wash of harsh radiance. He activated the camera and sat down across from me.

"We'll skip the makeup just this once. Please, Ken, eat up! This will be good practice for conducting interviews over coffee and Danish. Now, I'll play the part of the interviewer, and you just be yourself."

The mock interview lasted half an hour, during which I failed to taste a single forkful that went into my mouth. When we were done, Stutterbalm reviewed my performance in the camera's small screen, clucking his tongue all the while.

"Well, Ken, I'm afraid we have a long road to travel before you're fit to appear on national TV. For one thing, we need to do something about that haircut."

"But, but—I've been wearing my hair like this for years."

"Exactly the problem. Let me make an appointment for you for this afternoon with my stylist." Whipping out his cell phone,

Stutterbalm did just that. "Now, let's try on some new clothes I've taken the liberty of bringing."

As Stutterbalm was expertly hemming the cuffs on my new trousers, Esther drooped into the kitchen. She was taken aback at first by this impromptu fitting, but when I explained that it was all part of the publicity for my new book, she just shrugged and poured herself some coffee.

"Try some of those croissants, Mrs. McFoozel. They're from a little bakery on the Upper West Side."

"Mmmm, delicious!"

How cheaply and quickly Esther had been won over by this PR tyrant! Was I being an ingrate by harboring some small vestiges of resentment at this dictatorial treatment?

Stutterbalm erased chalk marks off my tailored jacket. "There, perfect! Now, let's see your walk, Ken. Pretend you're crossing the stage to receive a Pulitzer."

"For a biography of Britney Spears?"

"It could happen," said Stutterbalm, winking and making a money-rubbing gesture with his fingertips.

I pranced up and down the kitchen for ten minutes, trying vainly to follow Stutterbalm's suggestions about varying my stride. At last I had had enough of this vainglorious strutting, and said so.

"That's fine, Ken, we can work more on the walk later. There're plenty of other tasks to tackle. Let's see your standard signature. No, no, much too time-consuming. You want to shorten it. After all, you might be doing thousands per day."

"Th—thousands?"

"Let's work a little on your personal bio sheet. I've got the one from your last book here. The first thing we've got to change is your birth date. What say we make it, oh, 1972?"

"Do I look thirty years old to you?"

"Oh, don't worry, we've budgeted plastic surgery." Esther looked up from the newspaper hopefully. "Oh, yes, Mrs. McFoozel, for you as well."

"But I—"

"Now, about your hobbies. We've changed them to spearfishing, snowboarding and bungee-jumping. Naturally you'll need to acquire a modicum of proficiency in each of these areas."

"I can't swim! And I never go out in the snow without my galoshes."

"Tut-tut, Ken. Everything will soon be different. There's nothing that can't be accomplished with a little effort and enough money. Don't underestimate my determination or perseverance. You're looking at a fellow who's driven countless producers to madness and beyond."

I collapsed into a chair. "And that's just where you're driving me! I just don't think I'm up to the level of involvement in the publicity machine that you're demanding of me."

Stutterbalm patted me tenderly on the shoulder. "There, there, Ken. We've anticipated that possibility as well. Take a look at these photos."

I studied a sheaf of headshots. "Who are all these smiling idiots?"

"Eager young actors and models looking to bulk up their CV. Any one of them will happily stand in for you throughout this whole process. A simple *Mission Impossible*-style latex mask is all we need to fool your fans. Your signature right here makes it happen—"

The documents appeared with suspicious alacrity. But I nonetheless signed the forms as quickly as I could.

"Very good. Never let it be said that we were unwilling to give you a chance at the limelight, Ken. I'm sorry it had to end this way, but I suspected it might, based on my many years as a 'nurse' to authors. After all, as we publicists traditionally say: an actor masquerading as a writer is always a better bet than a writer masquerading as an actor."

PUBLICATION HISTORY

"Falling Expectations" was first published in *UnEarth*, 1977.

"My Alphabet Starts Where Your Alphabet Ends" was first published in *Nebula Awards 24*, 1990.

"The Great Nebula Sweep" was first published in *Nebula Awards 25*, 1991.

"Your MoneyTM" was first published in *The Magazine of Fantasy and Science Fiction*, 1995.

"It Was the Blessed of Times, It was the Cursed of Times" was first published in *The Magazine of Fantasy and Science Fiction*, 1996.

"Manuscript Found in a Pipedream" was first published in *The Magazine of Fantasy and Science Fiction*, 1996.

"Have Gun, Will Edit" was first published in *The Magazine of Fantasy and Science Fiction*, 1996.

"Nature, Wineberry in Tooth and Claw, with a Hint of Claret" was first published in *The Magazine of Fantasy and Science Fiction*, 1997.

"Narrative Contents May Have Settled During Shipment" was first published in *The Magazine of Fantasy and Science Fiction*, 1997.

"The Only Thing Worse than Yet One More Bad Trilogy" was

first published in *The Magazine of Fantasy and Science Fiction*, 1997.

"You Won't Take Me Alive! (Without At Least Ten Percent of the Box Office Gross)" was first published in *The Magazine of Fantasy and Science Fiction*, 1998.

"Next Big Thing" was first published in *The Magazine of Fantasy and Science Fiction*, 1998.

"Escapist Velocity" was first published in *The Magazine of Fantasy and Science Fiction*, 1998.

"Never Let Them See You Nova" was first published in *Interzone*, 1998.

"Scissors Cut Paper, Paper Covers Schlock" was first published in *The Magazine of Fantasy and Science Fiction*, 1998.

"As Through a Pair of Mirrorshades Darkly" was first published in *The Magazine of Fantasy and Science Fiction*, 1999.

"And I Think to Myself, What a Wonderful World" was first published in *The Magazine of Fantasy and Science Fiction*, 1999.

"The History of Snivelization" was first published in *The Magazine of Fantasy and Science Fiction*, 1999.

"Missed Connections" was first published in *The Magazine of Fantasy and Science Fiction*, 1999.

"In the Air" was first published in *The Magazine of Fantasy and Science Fiction*, 2000.

"When You Wish Upon a Midlist Star" was first published in *The Magazine of Fantasy and Science Fiction*, 2000.

"The Factchecker Only Rings Once" was first published in *The Magazine of Fantasy and Science Fiction*, 2000.

"This Is My Gun, This Is My Pen, Sir!" was first published in *The Magazine of Fantasy and Science Fiction*, 2000.

"Hail to the Hack" was first published in *The Magazine of Fantasy and Science Fiction*, 2000.

"Two Sample Chapters, An Outline, and a Sawed-off Shotgun" was first published in *The Bulletin of the Science Fiction and Fantasy Writers of America*, 2000.

"Just Me and My Protoplasmic Ego Extension" was first published in *The Bulletin of the Science Fiction and Fantasy Writers of America*, 2000.

"I'll Trade You Two Nobels, a Macarthur Grant and a Pulitzer for One of Those Starry Paperweights" was first published in *The Bulletin of the Science Fiction and Fantasy Writers of America*, 2000.

"*The Magazine Chums Versus the Baron of Numedia*, by C. J. Heintz-Ketzep" was first published in *The Magazine of Fantasy and Science Fiction*, 2001.

"Woolpullers, Inc." was first published in *The Magazine of Fantasy and Science Fiction*, 2001.

"*Adventures in Mishmish Land*, by A. Patchwork Girl, Customizer" was first published in *The Magazine of Fantasy and Science Fiction*, 2001.

"Associational Roundup" was first published in *Locus Online*, 2001.

"Press One for Literature" was first published in *The Magazine of Fantasy and Science Fiction*, 2002.

"Kiss of the Spider Critic" was first published in *The Magazine of Fantasy and Science Fiction*, 2002.

"Ultrasenator Versus the Lobbyists from Beyond!" has never previously been published.

"My Life—and Welcome to Fifteen Percent of It" was first published in *The Magazine of Fantasy and Science Fiction*, 2002.

"Games Writers Play" was first published in *The Magazine of Fantasy and Science Fiction*, 2002.

"Excerpt from *Decad*" was first published in *Locus Online*, 2002.

"Nebula Awards Voting Cancelled " was first published in *Locus Online*, 2002.

"The Unkindest Cuts" was first published in *The Magazine of Fantasy and Science Fiction*, 2002.

"Readin' and Ritin' and Royalties" was first published in *The Bulletin of the Science Fiction and Fantasy Writers of America*, 2002.

"A Vade Mecum for the Third Millennium" was first published in *The Bulletin of the Science Fiction and Fantasy Writers of America*, 2002.

"Prose by Any Other Name Would Smell as Sweet" was first published in *The Magazine of Fantasy and Science Fiction*, 2003.

"We, the Publicists" was first published in *The Magazine of Fantasy and Science Fiction*, 2003.